LAST
BUS
TO
EVER
LAND

Also by Sophie Cameron

Out of the Blue

LAST
BUS
TO
EVER
LAND

SOPHIE CAMERON

Roaring Brook Press

New York

To Mam & Dad

AUTUMN

ONE

THIS NEVER WOULD HAVE HAPPENED IF I HADN'T NAMED THE bloody cat Tinker Bell.

He stares at me over Leanne Watson's shoulder as she sprints up Leith Walk, his face squashed against her neck. Fake fingernails dig into his ginger fur; one gold hoop earring falls over his head like a lopsided halo. Leanne glances back, almost tripping over a buggy sliding out of the co-op, and grins.

"Come on, Fairy! Come save Tinker Bell!"

Tink wriggles and yowls, the way he always does when anyone but me tries to pick him up, but Leanne's grip is like a vise. (I should know; she's had me in a headlock more than once.) Michelle McInnes chugs along after her, pulling up her jeans as she runs.

"Yeah . . . Fairy," she wheezes. "Come . . . get . . . him."

My calves ache, and my lungs are starting to burn, but I force myself up the street, cursing my sister for leaving the door open, and Leanne for being the school's top long-distance runner, and Tink for being slow enough to let her catch him in the first place. Heads turn as the girls run past. Someone yells something about calling the SPCA, but nobody tries to stop them. Nobody ever tries to stop them.

"Fly, Fairy, fly!" Leanne shouts. "Go on—you can do it!"

They dodge an elderly couple and a man carrying a crate of fruit into the Chinese supermarket and disappear around the corner. I follow them along an empty street, into a car park bordered by two blocks of dull gray flats. Leanne comes to a halt by a shiny red Mini; Michelle collapses against the boot, her cheeks the same color as the bodywork.

"That's actually no' bad, Brody." Leanne hasn't even broken a sweat. Her ponytail is still neat, her winged eyeliner slick as ever. "Where was that sprint in PE yesterday, eh?"

Tink mewls and kicks against Leanne's denim jacket. I know how he feels. Leanne and Michelle have been giving me grief since I moved to Mackay House five years ago, after they caught me roaming around the yard shouting after a cat named Tinker Bell and decided I would do for target practice. Should have called him Peter, or Smee, or Captain Hook. Nobody would mess with a cat named Hook.

"Come on, Leanne." I can feel my face burning, no doubt turning the spots on my cheeks reddish purple. "Give him back. You're hurting him."

"Leaaaaanne, you're hurting hiiim," she mimics, making my voice two octaves higher and a whole lot whinier. "Ask nicely, Fairy."

Aye, like that'll work. I lunge and make a grab for Tink, but Leanne lifts him out of my reach. I'm on the tall side for a fifteen-year-old boy, but Leanne's a giant: six foot one in trainers, an NBA player in heels. Tink screeches as she dangles him over her head.

"*Naaaaaaants ingonyamaaaaaaa bagithi Baba,*" she sings, like Rafiki presenting Simba on Pride Rock. "Oh, sorry, Peter Pan. Wrong Disney."

Michelle breaks into giggles. "I know! He's got to say, 'I do believe in fairies.' Like in the film, eh? That's the only way you're getting him back, Brody."

Leanne looks at me expectantly. I glance around the car park. There's nobody to help me. No one unloading their shopping. No parents wrestling a toddler into the back seat. Tink squirms from side to side, mewling pitifully. Leanne's grip tightens.

"I do believe in fairies," I blurt out. "There. Gonnae give him back now?"

Michelle shakes her head. "Nah, you've got to say it like you mean it. Louder. Clap your hands an' all."

My cheeks burn. I loved *Peter Pan* when I was wee. Tinker Bell in particular—so much so that I named my cat after her. At five years old, I didn't realize there was anything "unusual" about that. I haven't read the book or seen the film in years, but still . . . that story meant something to me. I don't want my memories of it to fuse with that time I made a tit of myself in a car park off Leith Walk.

But I know Leanne. She won't give up until she's served me my daily dose of humiliation, and I need to get the cat back. So I say it. I say it at normal volume, but she's still not satisfied. I say it slightly louder, then louder again, and again. Soon I'm shouting the words, slapping my hands together so hard the palms sting, until—

"Hey!"

My chant cuts out, and the girls' sniggering with it. Above us, leaning out of a third-floor window, is a boy: a boy of around seventeen, with light brown hair, a cigarette in one hand, and wings. Bright blue wings, tall and sleek as a ship's sails, bursting past the window frame—two strokes of color against the pebble-dash landscape.

For a moment, Leanne and Michelle are completely silent.

Then they explode into laughter.

The boy frowns. For a second, I think he's about to have a go at me for shouting about fairies outside his window at half six on a Wednesday evening, but instead he stubs his cigarette out on the windowsill, gently maneuvers his wings past the frame, and disappears back into the flat.

Leanne is laughing so hard she can hardly breathe; Michelle's bent double, screeching harder than she did the time Rachel Rhodes sat in red paint in Art and it looked like she'd got her period.

6

"Hey, another fairy," she says, spluttering. "Your fairy god-mother, Brody, come to rescue you."

Black Rimmel tears are running down Leanne's cheeks. As she goes to wipe them away, Tink soap-slips out of her grip and shoots away from us, sliding beneath a battered Vauxhall Astra. I start to run after him, but I hear a door being violently flung open behind me. I turn to see the boy with the wings striding across the car park. He looks thunderous.

The girls' laughter peters out. The guy isn't that big. He's tall but skinny—I can see the outline of his ribs beneath his paint-splattered T-shirt—and yet there's something imposing about him, even with the wings on. The tension in his shoulders, maybe, or the way his boots scuff the gravel. He comes to a halt just a few centimeters from Michelle.

"Get out of here." His accent is hard to place: mostly English, with a dash of something else. Spanish, maybe. "Go on. Piss off."

Leanne scoffs. "Nice wings, pal," she says, though her voice has a nervous wobble to it. "This your boyfriend, Brody?"

It's supposed to be a dig, but all I can think is, *I wish.* This boy is beautiful: high cheekbones, dark brown eyes, curly hair that flops down to his eyebrows. A constellation of freckles spans his tanned cheeks and nose, and his pale lips tilt into a sneer as Leanne speaks. He takes another step forward. Michelle blanches.

"I told you to leave," he says, his voice low. "You're going to go now, and you're not going to bother him again. Okay?"

After a long moment, Leanne rolls her eyes. "All right, fine. God, Fairy, learn to take a joke."

She bumps into my shoulder as she moves past me, and Michelle steps on my foot, but they leave. They actually *go*. If I weren't so relieved, I'd be pissed off at how easy this guy has made it seem. I've tried everything to get Leanne and Michelle off my back: ignoring them, arguing with them, begging them to just piss off and leave me alone . . . Nothing works. Well, my friend Megan snapping at them sometimes does the trick. Or my brother, if he's around. Jake's sick of fighting my battles, though.

"For God's sake, Brody, deal with it. They're *girls*," he always says. Like that makes a difference.

As soon as they're out of sight, the embarrassment mutates into rage—Tink could so easily have jumped out of Leanne's arms and straight under the wheel of a car, and I'd have been left to scrape my favorite family member off the road. My eyes are prickling, but I won't cry. I never cry.

As I turn toward the Astra, the guy puts a hand on my shoulder. "I'll get him. Cats like me."

Before I can tell him that Tink hates every living creature on the planet except me, the boy's on his knees and coaxing him out from behind the tire. The poor cat's trembling all over. It'll take an entire block of cheddar cheese (his favorite food) until he even comes close to forgiving me for all this . . . but to my surprise, he sits quietly in the crook of the guy's arm as he's carried across the car park.

"There we go." The boy strokes the spot between Tink's ears before passing him back to me. "What an ordeal."

"Cheers." I shift Tink onto my shoulder, wincing as his claws dig through my school shirt. "You didnae have to do that, you know."

The guy brushes his hair out of his eyes. His hands are smeared with paint and glitter, and his nails are royal blue.

"Just making up for all the dickheads I didn't stand up to when I was younger. Do they often catnap him like that?"

"Nah. Well, no' this far, anyway." My eyes glide over the wings. "Are you . . . are you off to a fancy-dress party or something?"

Up close, I see they're made from simple papier-mâché and covered with dozens—hundreds—of bits of blue. There are dried flowers, foreign stamps, swatches of satin and lace, sweet wrappers, splashes of nail polish, clusters of sequins and sea-battered glass. There's a butterfly pinned above the guy's left ear, and the eye of a peacock feather just below the right, all blending into a glittering swirl of turquoise and sapphire and cobalt.

It's the sort of thing I wouldn't be seen dead wearing.

It's the sort of thing that I'd rather die than admit that I kind of, maybe, like.

The boy tugs at the straps over his arms, making the wings flap together. "Something like that. Though to be honest, wearing this type of stuff . . . It's the only time I feel like I'm not in costume."

Another face appears at the third-floor window: a girl, maybe seventeen or eighteen, wearing a vivid orange headscarf.

"Nico? Kasia needs help making her claws."

"Okay, two secs." The guy—Nico—pauses for a moment, then shouts up to the girl. "Hey, Zahra, could you chuck me down a bit of paper? There's some on Kasia's desk."

The girl's eyebrows twitch into a frown, but she nods and turns away. After a moment, something falls from the window: a small origami lily, folded from pale green paper. The guy runs to catch it, takes a pencil from behind his ear, and writes something on the petals.

"You should come here tomorrow," he says, handing me the flower. "I think you'd like it. Don't worry—you don't have to dress up if you don't want to."

I turn the lily in my hands. Written in thin, slightly wobbly letters are the words *Calton Hill. Thursday, 11:21 p.m.—and not a minute later!*

"Aye, all right," I say, looking up at him. The girl is still watching from the window, a curious expression on her face. "I'll be there."

The boy smiles. His freckles shift upward, like stars realigning.

"Great. See you then, Fairy."

He gives another flap of his wings and winks at me before walking back to the flat. My cheeks flush. *Fairy.* That's the word that has haunted me since third grade, when some genius realized that just adding a *y* to my surname could get my eyes to water and my face to turn scarlet. It's the nickname that has followed me down corridors and into classrooms and on school trips, the nickname that's never been pinned to Jake, even though his name is Fair, too. But though it's not okay when Leanne and Michelle say it, it's different coming from Nico. In his voice, it doesn't sound anything like an insult.

It sounds like an invitation.

TWO

STUFF LIKE THIS NEVER HAPPENS TO ME. MY DAYS ARE USUALLY made from the same few ingredients: school, homework, fighting with Jake and Keira over the computer. There are good things, like drumming or bingeing on Netflix and pizza at Megan's house, but nothing like this. Boys with blue wings don't appear at flat windows. Paper lilies don't come fluttering down from the sky. Walking home, Tink pressed against my chest with one hand and Nico's invitation in the other, Leith Walk seems different in a way I can't put my finger on. Like something in the world has shifted, just a wee bit.

Nothing's changed back at Mackay House. The concrete courtyard is empty—Leanne and Michelle have probably gone in to watch *Hollyoaks*, thank God—and our flat is exactly how I left it. Jake's still doing his homework on our ancient PC, and Keira's in her room listening to music at full blast. Dad's sewing a button onto one of Keira's school shirts while he watches a documentary, probably his ninth or tenth of the day, and Mam's in the kitchen making our supper. Nobody's even noticed I was gone.

"Home sweet home," I mutter to Tink, as he slips out of my arms and onto the carpet with a bump. He turns to me, hisses, then slinks off to sulk under my bed. I flip him the finger as he goes.

"Oh, you're welcome. Next time, I'll no' bother."

My dad's balding head appears over the back of the sofa. "There you are, Brodes. Here, come and see this."

I carefully flatten the petals of the lily invitation, slide it into my back pocket before anyone spots it, then perch on the arm of the sofa. On the TV screen, a tiny puffer fish is gliding over the seabed, creating storm clouds of sand with the movement of its fins. After a moment, the camera pans out to show a pattern in the sand: a perfect circle of delicate ridges, hundreds of times bigger than the fish itself.

Dad grins at me. "Amazing, eh?"

"Aye, it's cool."

It's impressive and all, but I'm too busy thinking about the lily in my pocket to focus on artistic fish. *Calton Hill. Thursday, 11:21 p.m.—and not a minute later!* My parents aren't that strict, but there's no way Mam will let me go out that late on a school night. Especially not to a party on Calton Hill. (If it even is a party. "*Something like that*" could mean anything. Could be a church fete or an accounting conference, for all I know.)

My eyes swim around our living room. After five years, I know every inch of this cramped wee flat: the Bolognese stain shaped like France on the faded tan carpet; our heights marked in pencil on the kitchen door frame; the crack in the bathroom wall when I tripped and smacked my head during a game of tag with Keira. I didn't think I could see it in a new light, but suddenly this room has become an obstacle course. Dad falls asleep on the sofa most nights, and Jake's always on the computer until one or two in the morning. I've got no idea how I'll sneak out of here without them noticing, or without Mam vaulting out of bed to see what I'm up to.

Dad puts down the needle and thread to rewind the scene. He loves documentaries. He's seen every Deeyah Khan film two or three times; David Attenborough is practically the seventh member of our family.

"Smart wee buggers, aren't they," he says as the puffer fish zigzags backward through the water. "All that just tae attract a mate. Heck of a lot more than I did! Eh, Sally? Sal?"

No answer. I glance into the kitchen: Mam's leaning against the counter, looking at her phone and biting a fingernail. Behind her, hot water bubbles over the edge of a pan, sending clouds of steam billowing through the door and into the living room.

"Mam!" I shout. "The water's boiling over."

Her head snaps up. There are coffee stains on her lavender work uniform, and half of her hair has fallen out of her ponytail.

"Crap! Quick, Brody—give me a hand."

She turns the hob off, batting away steam. I slide down from the sofa and set the colander in the sink before she pours the spaghetti in. We had pasta yesterday, too, and the day before that. Usually I'd moan about it, but my stomach's all jittery, and I'm not that hungry. Which is weird. I'm always hungry.

"How was school?" Mam opens a jar of tomato sauce and pours it over the spaghetti. "Did you get to play the drums?"

"Nah. I did reserve the room, but some sixth-year band got there first."

She clicks her tongue, like it's somehow my fault Phil Haynes and his pals can't respect the music-room rota. "Will you get a shot tomorrow, then?"

Before I can answer, Keira swings into the kitchen singing something from *Hamilton*. She holds her hands up—the fingernails of her left one are painted glittery lime green.

"Mam, I need you to do my right hand."

"We're almost ready to eat, Keira. After dinner, okay?"

Keira's voice jumps up ten decibels. "But I'm gonnae go up to Amanda's afterward and I need it to dry by then and—"

Mam throws up her hands. "Fine, fine! Give me a second."

While Jake and I are both tall, dark, and quiet, my twelve-year-old sister is the opposite: a tiny blond whirlwind who does everything at full volume. My parents always give in to her demands. It's just easier than dealing with her sulking. Mam gives my shoulder a squeeze on the way out of the kitchen.

"Could you set the table, please, love?"

Counting out the knives and forks, my mind drifts back to the boy with the blue wings. Nico. My stomach flips. It's not just that he was hot—though I can't lie, that's part of it. It's also the way he walked out wearing those wings, like he didn't give a damn who would see or what they might think. It was the way he looked at me like he got it. Almost—though we'd only met a few minutes before—like he got *me*.

I've got to go to Calton Hill tomorrow. Somehow. I have to.

As I go to shut the cutlery drawer, something catches my eye: Mam's rota for the care home where she works, stuck to the fridge with a magnet my auntie Rhona brought back from her holiday in Tenerife. Her hours for Thursday are written in purple ink: *5 p.m.–1 a.m.*

My heart leaps. Sneaking past Mam would be like dodging a Rottweiler. In comparison, Dad's a lazy old beagle—he might even be asleep before eleven if I'm lucky. I can easily slip out without him noticing, and if I'm back by one o'clock, Mam won't even know I was gone. I can hardly stop the stupid grin from spreading across my face as I go to set the table.

Mam comes out of Keira's room, rubbing at a green smudge on her thumb.

"You're on night shift tomorrow?" I ask, just to make sure.

It's a blatant clue that I'm up to something—I never normally ask when she's working—but only Jake seems to notice. He looks up from the computer, stares at me for a second, then goes back to his homework. Jake's hoping to go to Cambridge next year. Right now he's basically incapable of concentrating on anything other than schoolwork for more than five seconds at a time.

"Unfortunately so," Mam says, pushing her hair out of her face. "Still, can't complain. Some of the others haven't got any shifts at all this week."

She calls everyone for supper, even though we're all in the same room—a holdover from when we lived in a bigger flat—then tosses an almost-empty bag of grated cheddar onto the table. I pick out a few bits to save for Tink. I owe him: If he hadn't gotten himself kidnapped, I never would have met Nico. Tomorrow would be just another Thursday, and not . . . whatever tomorrow is going to be.

Something out of the ordinary.

THREE

I NEED A COSTUME. EVEN IF THE BOY WITH THE BLUE WINGS SAID it wasn't necessary, I want to dress up. Whatever this thing on Calton Hill is, wherever I might end up tonight, I want to feel like I belong. And I get the impression it might be the sort of place where you need to stand out to fit in.

When I get home from school on Thursday, I head straight to the room I share with Jake. I say hi to Tink (he gives me an evil look and goes back to staring out of the window—still in a crappy mood after his trip across Leith) and pull open the wardrobe. Rows of faded T-shirts and school jumpers greet me. Not exactly fancy-dress material. Other than a kilt that Jake's friend lent him for their school ceilidh, there's nothing even halfway fancy.

Still, there must be something I can use for a costume.

Rummaging through a pile of trainers at the bottom of the wardrobe, I find a plastic box full of relics from when we were wee: toy cars, a deflated football, rainy-day drawings. After a bit of digging, I find a papier-mâché skull mask that I made in Art back in junior high. And on Jake's side of the shelves, there's the perfect thing to go with it: a black T-shirt with the torso of a skeleton drawn on. It's very un-Jake—maybe one of his pal's, or something he had for a Halloween party. I lay it out on my bed and place the mask above it. It's not exactly Damien Hirst, but with a bit of color, it might look all right. (Plus, it'll cover up my stupid acne.)

There are only three Biros and two dried-out highlighters in my school bag, so I head to Keira's room to nick some of her fancy pens. She's upstairs at Amanda's, Mam's already gone to work, Jake's at a rugby game or orchestra practice or whatever Oxbridge-friendly activity is on the schedule for today, but Dad's at home. Dad's always at home.

"All right, Brodes. Good day?" He leans through the bathroom door, yellow rubber gloves on his hands, and points to a DVD on the sofa. "Just giving the bath a scrub, and then I was gonnae stick that on. Fancy it?"

I pick up the case: *Jiro Dreams of Sushi*, with a label proclaiming it property of Jake's school library beneath the title. I do usually watch Dad's documentaries with him when Jake and Keira aren't around. Some of them are pretty interesting, especially the ones about cults and conspiracy theories. And sad as it sounds, it's sort of nice having my parents to myself sometimes;

Keira sucks up attention like a Dyson, and Jake has this way of making everything I say or do seem stupid. I think Dad likes having someone to watch with, too. Someone to share his small slice of the world.

I don't have time for Jiro and his sushi right now, though.

"I cannae, Dad. I've got Spanish homework. Just need to borrow a pen off Keira."

An embarrassingly bad accent calls out from behind the bathroom door. *"Muy bien. Excelente. Dos cervezas, por favor."*

I slip into my sister's room and scan the mess for those glitter pens she used to like. There's nothing except a few blunt pencils, but she's got a collection of nail varnishes lined up on her windowsill. Tiny bottles with matching black caps, all pinks and purples and greens.

That feeling starts. It's that same creeping sense of shame I used to get when I was seven or eight, when I'd watch *My Little Pony* or look at Barbies in the Argos catalogue. Like I was doing something I shouldn't.

I wrestle the feeling away and drop a few bottles into my pockets. It's just paint, I tell myself as I hurry back to my room. Just paint in tiny tubs with fancy names. I unscrew a bottle of something called Poison Apple, wrinkling my nose at the smell, and outline the skull's mouth with deep green. I spread clear glitter across the cheeks, paint on Indigo Night eyelashes, then add a Red for Filth rose on the left side of its forehead. I hold it up to show Tink.

"What d'you think? No' bad, right?"

He yawns and starts licking his butt. I try not to take that personally.

I touch up the rose, then add some more flowers and leaves over the skull's chin and cheeks. Part of me wants to go all out and do my nails as well, like Nico. I could paint them green to match the mask's lips, or maybe red. If I hide them under my sleeves, nobody will—

The bedroom door opens. Jake comes in, pausing when he sees me sprawled out on the floor. The nail polishes are scattered across the carpet, guilty as spray-paint cans beneath a wall of graffiti.

His eyebrows rise. "What's all this?"

"It's for Art." I dropped Art after eighth grade but Jake won't remember that. "We're doing Día de las Muertos."

He smirks. That smirk is the reason I prefer to do my homework at school or at Megan's rather than in here, surrounded by all his awards and piles of library books. That smirk makes me feel like I'm thicker than cement.

When Jake was nine, his third-grade teacher referred him to a psychologist for an IQ test. I can't remember the exact score, but it was high enough for the headmistress to call Mam and Dad in for a meeting after school. It wasn't the first time they'd been brought in to talk about Jake—he was constantly in trouble, always interrupting or throwing things or wandering off in the middle of class. But this time, when they walked across

21

the playground to collect us from the swings, something was different: Mam's eyes were all shiny, and Dad kept looking at Jake like he'd just realized his son had a second head he'd never noticed before.

A few months later, Jake sat the entrance exams for some private schools up in town. He was accepted to three of them. Full scholarships.

Everything changed after that. Before, Jake and Keira and I had been three equal weights on a perfectly balanced scale; when he started at his new school, everything tipped in his favor. *Get off the computer, Brody. Jake needs it for his homework. Turn down your music, Keira. Jake's trying to study.* Even now, Mam just about bursts with pride every time he puts on that dumb navy blazer.

Part of me used to hope for the same—that someday I'd get my own *You're a wizard, Harry* moment and turn out to be a genius, too. But nobody ever suggested I might be able to get a scholarship. I asked if I could sit the exams, and they let me, but I didn't pass. I didn't even come close. When I looked the fees up online, I thought I was seeing double—one term was almost as much as Mam's entire salary.

I didn't bring it up again after that.

"Día de *los* Muertos," Jake says now. Of course he does. "Want help doing your nails?"

My cheeks flare. "Piss off, Jake."

He throws his hands into the air, all mock innocence. "God, Brody, I was just asking."

He dumps his bag on his bed and goes straight back to the computer, shutting the door behind him. The mask stares up at me, its friendly grin suddenly more like a leer. It feels like it's mocking me, too.

By quarter to eleven, the nerves are making it hard for me to sit still. No one's going to physically stop me going out—Dad hardly ever goes past the front door, and Jake wouldn't give up precious minutes of study time to come after me—but even so, I'm all fidgety and jittery. It's not like I usually tell my parents my every move or anything. They'd probably be surprised at how many times I've been drunk, and Mam would skin me alive if she knew I'd even thought about smoking weed. But I dunno—this feels different.

"Good God, Brody. Get a grip," I mutter to myself. "You're just going up to town, you loser."

I take a deep breath, tuck the mask inside my hoodie, and step out of my room. Dad's fallen asleep in front of *Question Time*, and Keira finally went to bed fifteen minutes ago. There's just Jake left, hunched over the keyboard, surrounded by sky-scrapers of library books. He's typing so loud, he doesn't even hear me walking past.

Holding my breath, I tiptoe toward the door and slip out-side. I take the stairs three at a time, not caring if my clunky steps wake up Mrs. McAskill in 8B, not thinking about what might happen when ten minutes turns into an hour and I'm still not home. All that matters is making it onto the next bus into town and getting to Calton Hill before 11:21 p.m. I'll deal with the fallout later.

I get to the bus stop just as the number 22 pulls up. I hop on, flash the pass Jake uses to get to school (we look alike enough for me to get away with borrowing it), and then hurry up to the top deck. It's only when I sit down, panting slightly, that a huge, stupid grin breaks across my face. Nico's smile swims in front of my eyes, making my stomach flutter. This is actually happening. I'm actually going to see him again.

There's not much traffic at this time of night, but the bus feels slower than evolution as it crawls up Leith Walk. I get off just before Princes Street, hurry along Waterloo Place, and run up the steps to Calton Hill. I follow the path toward the National Monument, a row of Greek-style columns at the top of the hill, scanning the area for some sign of an event.

There's nothing. No music. No people setting up for a party. A pair of tourists have braved the cold to take photos of the skyline, but there's nobody else around. No sign of a boy with blue wings.

The rain is heavier now; when I take out the invitation to check the time, thick drops soak through the paper and blur Nico's letters. It's still just about legible: *11:21 p.m.*—two minutes to go. Down on Princes Street, the big hand of the Balmoral Hotel's clock edges forward. Maybe he's running late. Maybe they called off the party because of the weather.

Or . . . maybe there never was a party.

A sickly feeling crawls up my throat. That must be it. This

was obviously just some joke. He must have been taking the piss out of me: for chasing after my cat like a moron, for not being able to stand up to two girls. "Shit," I whisper. I'm such an idiot. Of course he wouldn't invite me to come out with him. Why would a guy like him have any interest in hanging out with an awkward, spotty loser like me?

A lump swells in my throat. It's stupid, but . . . it really felt real. The look on his face when he told Leanne and Michelle to piss off. The stuff he said about sticking up to his own tormentors, and the way he grinned when he called me—

"Fairy!"

I turn around and see a group of shadowy figures moving over the hill, one of them wearing wings and waving. And for the first time in years, I'm happy to hear that word.

"You made it!" Nico smiles, a slice of moon in the darkness. "Get ready for the best night of your life."

FOUR

FOR A MOMENT, ALL I CAN DO IS STARE AT HIM. HIS HAIR IS DAPPLED with raindrops, and a faint streak of blue eyeliner glimmers under his lower eyelashes. The wings sprout from his denim jacket, each one protected by a thick black trash bag. Just behind him, two more figures come into view: a werewolf in a NASA T-shirt, and a small, chubby Sailor Moon fiddling with the bow on her costume.

"Sorry we're late," Nico says. "Kasia's tail fell off, and I couldn't find one of my boots, and then we missed the bus."

The werewolf looks me up and down and throws its paws into the air. "Another one of Nico's Lost Boys. Brilliant." Its voice is low and muffled behind the werewolf mask. "Just what we need."

Nico rolls his eyes. "Ignore Kasia. She gets grumpy around

the full moon." The werewolf starts to protest, but Nico laughs and steps to the side so his left wing is blocking her face. "How are you doing? Has your cat recovered from yesterday?"

Before I can answer, Sailor Moon claps her hands. It's the girl who threw down the origami flower yesterday, Zahra, now wearing a long blue skirt, a red bow, and a bright yellow headscarf twisted into the character's blond buns.

"Small talk later, Nico. We've got about thirty seconds to get inside."

She strides past us; the werewolf shakes its head at me then hurries after her. When I turn around to follow them, my jaw drops.

The National Monument has changed. In the gaps between the stone pillars, where just a few seconds ago were slices of smoky sky, there are now colors. Greens, blues, and purples, shimmering and swirling—as if the Northern Lights had been cut into strips and draped like flags from the stone. Pictures emerge from the swirls, blurry faces outlined in thick black strokes; between the two central pillars, the haze solidifies into a deep green. I finally remember to blink, and when I open my eyes, I find myself staring at a row of stained-glass windows and an enormous green door, with a golden knocker shaped like the head of a unicorn at hand height.

It takes a moment to find my voice again.

"What. The hell. Is *that*?"

Nico laughs. "I always forget how weird it seems the first time. Quick, we don't have long."

Though the steps leading to the monument are almost as tall as she is, Zahra climbs onto a stack of bricks at the base and smoothly pulls herself up. Nico vaults onto the lower step, then holds out his hand to help me. I scramble up after him, bumping my knees on the edge of the stone, and follow him to the pillars.

The werewolf twists the unicorn's horn counterclockwise and pushes the door open. My brain is fumbling for sense in what I've just seen. They must have a projector somewhere . . . Someone must have propped up the door while I wasn't looking. Disorientated, I stumble through it, Nico just behind me. The door closes behind us with a loud sucking sound.

"That was close," Zahra says. "We've got to stop cutting it so fine."

"We'd have been all right if Nico hadn't spent ages fiddling with my tail," the werewolf mutters.

Nico snorts. "That sounds so wrong."

They keep bickering, but the words soon fall out of focus. Something about this place feels weird. I look down: the stone base of the monument has been replaced by a long, sloping stretch of grass. Above us, the cloudy gray sky has cleared into a deep navy filled with stars—millions of them. More than I've ever seen before. And as I follow Nico and his friends, I see something that makes my heart stop.

Edinburgh has disappeared.

Instead of streets and cars and blurry neon, I'm looking down at a vast green valley. Three rivers spill down the pine-clad hill-sides and snake across the basin; at the point where they meet is a sprawl of bright golden light, trickling out into little pockets of life dotted across the grass. In the distance, a row of mountains is half-hidden behind low-hanging clouds. I can see more lights behind them, then a slick black that could be the sea. But there's no Leith Walk, no Firth of Forth, no lights of Fife in the distance. The entire city has vanished.

I turn around. The green door is still behind us, but the pillars of the National Monument have gone. So have all the other buildings on Calton Hill. My heart is pounding. There are no trees like this up here, and definitely no rivers. This must be an illusion, some sort of trick—a really bloody impressive one, too.

Before I can ask how they've done it, I realize Nico is introducing his friends. As casually as if we'd just walked into McDonald's and not . . . wherever this place is.

"This is Kasia," he says, tugging on the werewolf's ears, "and you kind of met Zahra yesterday. Guys, this is—it's Brady, right?"

I can still hardly speak. "Um, B-Brody."

"*What?*" Kasia pulls the mask off. Long, wispy blond hair flutters around a pale, narrow face; her eyes are gray-blue and furious. "You didn't even get his *name*? For God's sake, Nico. Is there anyone else you'd like to invite? How about the girl who works in the co-op around the corner? Or maybe that skinhead with the pit bull we saw at the bus stop?"

"Maybe I will. He seemed friendly. Loved the neck tattoos."

Nico pulls the trash bags from his wings; they drop off like co-coon husks, revealing the swirl of blues underneath. "I don't know why you get so pissed off about this, Kash."

"Because it's not supposed to work like this!" she snaps. "You're supposed to let people find this place themselves, not invite every random you come across."

"I've invited three people. *Three*. My friend Privashni, Mark from my art course, and now Brody. It's not like I put a bill-board up on the A9." Nico shoves the trash bags into a museum tote bag, rolling his eyes. "Besides, you don't even know that's true. There are no rules to this place. It's not up to you to decide what's allowed and what's not."

Kasia grits her teeth. She mutters something in Polish and takes off down the hill, tail swinging behind her. Zahra and Nico exchange a look I can't read.

"Sorry about her," Nico says. "Her girlfriend used to visit here and . . . Don't worry about it—she'll come around."

I'm still too busy trying to work out what the hell is going on to be offended. "That thing with the door," I eventually choke out. "How did that work? Where did all the trees come from? And the river? What is this place?"

Zahra smiles. "Don't try to understand it all at once. Just enjoy it for now, okay?"

They keep talking as we walk down toward the valley, but most of it goes over my head; I'm too busy staring around me, trying to work out how the hell all this is possible. Soon, the blur of lights in the distance starts to take shape. There's a small town built where the three rivers meet, a busy market, bonfires burning in the distance. Different sounds rise up from the valley, forming a dim buzz around us. I pick out someone speaking Arabic, a string instrument twanging, a woman singing "Heroes" by David Bowie. Deer are grazing across the hillside, but not the type I've seen up near my gran's in the Highlands—these are smaller, with tan hides and white spots. Huge yellow birds fly overhead, and the river sparkles with schools of neon-blue fish.

I have no idea how they've pulled this off, but it's totally and utterly amazing.

When we reach the bottom of the hill, we cross a stone bridge spanning one of the rivers and arrive in a square lined with red-brick buildings and lit by old-fashioned lampposts. Standing in the middle is a door, just like the one we came in through, only it's red instead of green and has a dragon knocker rather than a unicorn. Dozens of people are milling around: an old man is playing a sitar; two girls kiss under a lamppost; a nun and three guys in rugby shirts are laughing over a game of cards. Most people are in everyday clothes, or some are in traditional dress or uniforms, but quite a few are in costume, too—I spot a guy dressed as a First World War soldier, a pirate, a Marie Antoinette lookalike. Zahra cuts across the square to talk to two girls wearing *salwar kameez*, leaving me alone with Nico.

"So. Let's see your costume." He steps back, hands on his hips, and looks me up and down. "All black—so you're supposed to be . . . the night sky. A panther going to a funeral? A raven eating burned toast!"

"It's supposed to go with this . . ." I unzip my hoodie and pull the mask out. It feels a bit childish compared to his wings and all the other costumes around us.

"Nice! Did you make this?" He takes the mask from me and holds it up to his face, becoming a bird-skeleton hybrid. His nails are the same deep blue as yesterday. Makes me wish I'd painted mine, too. "It's good!"

My cheeks burn. I have to fight the urge to snatch the mask back and hide my face behind it. "Nah, it's crap. No' like these," I say, tapping my knuckle to his wings. "These are awesome."

He crosses one foot over the other and does a twirl. "Thanks. I'm applying for art school next year, so I made them for my portfolio. My dad called them 'facile *Fantasia* nonsense.' But whatever—I like them." His eyes darken for a moment, but then he looks down at me and the expression vanishes. "How's your cat doing, by the way? Has he recovered from his kidnapping the other day?"

"Aye, he's . . . fine."

It feels weird, somehow, talking about Tink in here. I only snuck out about half an hour ago, but right now home and the rest of my life all seems miles away. Besides, it's hard to focus on anything else with all *this* going on around me. As my eyes begin to wander, a goth strolls past with a woman who must be at least ninety, and a man casually rides by on a camel. Nico puts his hand on my back.

"Come on—I'll give you a tour."

He leads me through the square, waving to a few people he

spots along the way, and down an alleyway between two of the buildings. We step out into a cramped, chaotic marketplace, where paper lanterns hang overhead and makeshift wooden huts overflow with food and baubles and trinkets. Nico zigzags through the narrow paths, past stalls selling strange fruits and pastries, snow globes and worry dolls. I hear French, Mandarin, and Russian, plus a dozen other languages. The air smells like chocolate and cinnamon, and the place is throbbing with sound and movement. All around us, people are laughing, haggling—

Dancing. Suddenly, everyone around me is dancing. I look around, blinking, but the market is far behind us. Instead, we're in the middle of a parade, lost in a sea of sequins and feathers and giant, colorful headdresses. Music fills the sky and shakes the ground, but I can't tell where it's coming from; a light rain of confetti is falling out of nowhere. Nico spins through the crowd, arms in the air, wings melting into hazy streaks of blue. I race after him, past people dressed as birds or angels or in intricate golden ball gowns, the skirts blooming outward as they twirl to the music. A guy covered in green feathers spins me under his arm and shouts something in Portuguese, and I—

Almost stumble into the water. We've reached a beach, some-how, though the water had looked like it was miles away. A little farther up the shore, an enormous flaming bonfire is spitting sparks into the darkness. Some people are sitting around it and talking, or skimming stones across the inky black water; others are waving sparklers against the night sky, drawing hearts or spelling out words in alphabets I can't read. Fireworks explode into color above the mountains. As a blast of gold lights up Nico's face, he turns to me and grins.

"You all right, Brody?"

I open my mouth, but I'm too stunned to speak. I follow Nico along the shore, then through a noisy wedding and into a Holi celebration that leaves us covered in orange and pink. Just as I'm starting to feel overwhelmed, the crowd trickles away, and we arrive at a long stretch of moorland. I look behind me, trying to get my bearings. The party is just a blur of color in the distance; the noise is fading away into nothing.

"What . . . was . . ."

My head is spinning. There's a garland of flowers around my neck, and a fizzing sparkler in my hand, and I have no idea how they got there. The whole thing felt like five minutes, but it also seems like we came through the door hours ago. Nico smiles at me.

"Bit chaotic, I know." He flops down onto the grass. A few white-spotted deer look over at us, then go back to grazing. "Don't worry—it's not always like this."

He keeps talking, but I tune it out and force myself to think. This has to be a trick. Some sort of prank, maybe. Dad and I once watched this Derren Brown show where he staged a zombie apocalypse, all to give some lazy twentysomething a kick up the arse and get him to do something with his life. Maybe my mam's behind this. Maybe this is some crazy way of telling me to stop daydreaming and focus on my exams. Maybe they drugged me, and this is all an elaborate film set out in the countryside—something like that. It's the only explanation left that makes sense.

"What's going on, really?" I ask, interrupting Nico. I spin around, looking for hidden cameras. "Are we on TV right now? Are you, like, filming this for YouTube?"

Nico bursts out laughing. "God, how much money do you think I have? There are no cameras—I promise."

"Then what *is* this?" I turn around again, scanning the landscape for a hint of something familiar—the shape of the shore, or the outline of Edinburgh Castle. But there's nothing. This place is a whole different world.

"Seriously, don't try and work it all out right away." Nico gives a tug on his wings, pulling them together. "You're here, Brody. You can spend the whole night stressing about how all this is happening . . . or you could just go with it, and have fun."

My mind is still a dizzy kaleidoscope of sounds and images, but out of it surfaces the memory of meeting Nico yesterday. I think about how I knew, even after a few minutes, that I could trust him. I think about Leanne and Michelle kidnapping Tink like that, and all the times they've taken the piss or pushed me around. I think about Jake rolling his eyes at me, and Keira interrupting me, and the countless times I've had my parents' attention just to have it snatched away again. Nico is different. I don't even know him, but I can tell. He just . . . sees me. Even the *Fairy* nickname feels different in his voice. He takes this word that's always made me want to wriggle out of my skin and transforms it into something good. Something I can be proud of.

The sparkler in my hand is still burning, shedding sparks onto my skin. I take a breath, and I do as Nico says. I sweep the questions aside and decide I'm just gonna enjoy myself. I deserve a break. I deserve an adventure.

So I nod. "Okay."

Nico grins and stands up, sending specks of confetti falling from his hair. Between those and the Holi paint and his bright blue wings, he's a whole spectrum of color.

"In that case," he says, "welcome to Everland."

FIVE

I'M USUALLY PRETTY GOOD WITH DIRECTIONS, BUT WALKING BACK through the valley with Nico, I don't recognize any of the places we come across. We go through a masked ball in the gardens of a huge regal palace, and down a narrow street where people dressed as devils charge past, shrieking and carrying torches. There's a water fight going on in the next square, and a huge gospel choir singing and dancing in the one after that. Nico moves through it all with total ease. No matter where we end up, he looks like he was meant to be there, even with his wings on. Maybe *especially* with the wings on.

"How the hell did you find this place?" I ask him as we make our way through a crowd dancing around a steel band.

"I came across it about two years ago, when I was fifteen. I'd moved here from Spain with my dad and my stepmum about six months before." He edges past a group of girls, forcing one of them to duck under his wings. "Kasia turned up a few weeks later, and Zahra's been coming since last March. We're here every week. Always on a Thursday. Always at eleven twenty-one p.m. We never miss it."

I don't know how long we walk for. It could be minutes or miles; I just can't tell. But the moment I start to feel over-whelmed, the crowd trickles away again, and we arrive at a quiet stretch of grass by the river.

Kasia is stretched out on a blanket reading a thick hardback book, and Zahra is sitting by the water with two other people: a boy in a denim jacket and a girl wearing a school uniform a bit like Jake's, with a violin case in her lap. As we approach them, the boy looks up and waves. He's not bad-looking: light brown skin, thick eyebrows, bleached blond hair, ears that stick out in a way that's sort of cute. The way he smiles at Nico—and the way Nico smiles back—makes my heart sink.

"Everybody, this is Brody. My latest 'Lost Boy,'" he adds, smirking at Kasia as he flops onto the grass.

Over the top of her book, Kasia rolls her eyes. The guy in the denim jacket says something in Spanish to Nico, who throws up his hands and laughs as he replies. I take Spanish at school, but they're speaking way too fast for me to make out much—all I catch is "*niños perdidos*." But unlike Kasia, the guy doesn't seem annoyed that I'm here. He shifts onto his knees and reaches out to shake my hand.

"I'm Dani," he says, switching to English. "Welcome to Everland."

"It's not *officially* called that," Kasia says, still with the same irked edge to her tone. "There are lots of different names for this place. Everland is just one of them."

"Thanks for that, Siri." Nico sits back and grins at me, his right wing nudging Dani's shoulder. "You should have seen his face when we walked in. I'm surprised his jaw didn't actually fall off."

Dani laughs. "And who does this make me think of?" He throws his hands up and puts on a sort-of British accent. *"Where am I?! What is happening? Is this a dream?!"*

Nico pretend-punches his jaw, a big grin spreading over his face. Dani leans in and kisses him lightly on the lips. The disappointment smarts. It's stupid—I'm probably too young for Nico. And even if we were the same age, he'd probably be out of my league. Not wanting to be a third wheel, I sit a bit away from them, beside Zahra and the girl with the violin. She smiles and gives a short nod.

"I'm Miyumi. Nice to meet you." Her voice is light and musical, with a faint Japanese accent. "Are you okay? The first time I came here was so confusing. I pinched myself so hard I bled."

Zahra winces. "I jumped into the river, trying to wake myself up." She picks a pink flower from the grass and grins at me. "Let me guess. Nico took you to, like, a rave, and then a music festival, and then some party so radge it makes Ibiza look like a quaint afternoon tea."

"Um, kind of. There was a steel band . . . and a parade . . . fireworks . . ."

I try to remember the rest, but it all happened so fast . . . it's already a blur.

Miyumi shakes her head fondly. "Nico is always partying. Always in the crazy places," she says. "Not everywhere is the same. In here, a lot of places are very quiet."

Zahra nods toward Kasia, who has gone back to reading her book, *Physics of the Impossible*. "This one spends most of her time in here in the library. Wild, huh?"

Kasia makes a rock 'n' roll sign with her right hand. She glances up from the page, and for the first time, the steely look in her eyes disappears. "It's unbelievable. More books than you could even imagine—like the Library of Alexandria or something. I'll take you there sometime, if you want."

"Um. Aye, okay." A library wouldn't exactly be top of my list of places to visit, but I don't want to put myself back in her bad books. "That'd be . . . cool."

Nico grins. "Great, and then we'll take you to the Lawnmower Museum and an exhibition of paint drying. So much fun."

Kasia gives him the finger; Zahra calls him a philistine. But for all Nico winds them up, it's obvious they're really close friends. Normally, I'd feel a bit awkward trying to slot myself into a group of people who have known each other for ages, but they fold me into their conversations as if I'd been hanging out with them for years. Some of Dani's friends join us for a while, and a girl with a cello who Miyumi knows stops by to talk to her. On the river, dozens of boats float toward the sea: gondolas, schooners, canoes. Two guys in a canal boat play us a tune on ukuleles as they drift past, and a floating theater troupe drops anchor to put on an impromptu play when they see us on the shore.

I want to ask where they're all going and what's beyond the water—but I push the questions out of my head and remember what Nico said about just enjoying myself.

And I really, really am. I feel different in here. The only time I ever feel this relaxed is when I'm hanging out at Megan's, away from Jake, and from Leanne and Michelle and all the other wankers at our school. I'm not worrying about saying the wrong thing or doing something to make anyone take the piss, and I don't feel out of place. It's like when it doesn't click how hungry you are until you start eating, or when you get into bed and realize you're exhausted. Something you've needed for ages, and you didn't even know it.

As a regatta of sailboats races past, Nico sits down beside me. He's disappeared a couple of times tonight: once on his own, and once with Dani. There are now white petals tucked in his hair along with the last few pieces of confetti.

"How are you getting on? You don't still think I'm punking you for YouTube hits, do you?"

I grin. "I'm well impressed if you are. This place . . . It's unbelievable."

"I knew you'd like it. Kasia's convinced you're supposed to find your way into Everland by yourself, but I don't buy it. As soon as I saw you yesterday, I knew you were right for this place. That it was right for you."

He smiles at me. The disappointment of seeing him with Dani hasn't totally disappeared, but it's starting to fade. Out of everyone Nico knows, he's only invited three people here. I'm one of them. That has to count for something.

"Besides, I like sharing it. It's the best thing in my life, this place," Nico says simply. "I'd stay forever if I could."

That's a good point. How long *have* we been in here? I take out my phone to check the time, but the screen has gone blank—must have run out of battery. Still, it's definitely past two o'clock by now. Mam might panic and call the police if she gets back before me. Reluctantly, I get to my feet.

"I'd better head back, now you mention it," I say. "It must be getting late."

"But we still have—" Nico starts, then cuts himself off. He takes a pack of cigarettes from his back pocket. "Okay, I'll be out right after you. Just need to catch up with a few people first."

The others wave goodbye. Dani and Miyumi, at least—Kasia gives me a stiff nod, and Zahra says the same as Nico, that she'll be out in a minute. I start walking back along the water, toward the cluster of light where the three rivers meet. I pass through places that I haven't seen before—a neat garden filled with bright flowers around a star-shaped fountain; a campsite of multicolored tents—but somehow I remember the way back to the bridge, up the hill, and toward the green door. I take one last look at the valley below me, just to make sure it's still there, then pull it open and step outside.

A wave of cold air bites into my skin. It's started raining again. Still dark, though, which is a relief; at least I'll be home before morning.

As I climb down the huge steps, the door behind me swings open. Kasia appears, followed by Nico and Zahra. I blink—they must have been right behind me. How the hell did I miss that?

"Brody, hey!" Nico beams, as if days have passed since we last hung out, and not just a few minutes. He hops down the steps after Kasia. "Settle a debate for us: custard creams or bourbon biscuits?"

"Uh . . ." Behind him, the green door fades and disappears. I look up at Nico, blinking. "Custard creams, obviously. Who likes bourbons?"

He holds his hand up for a high five. "See? You're basically a heathen, Kash."

Kasia scoffs. "You don't even eat biscuits! God, Nico, I could say I liked breathing, and you'd find a way to argue with me."

We head across the hill and back down the steps to Regent Road. Zahra is singing something under her breath, and Nico and Kasia are still bickering about snacks and oxygen. As New Town comes into view, all the questions I'd pushed out of my mind start to reemerge. The river, the trees, the waterfalls. All those people, and all that space. Like, they couldn't have just . . . They must have come from somewhere . . .

The riddles are snowballing in my head, becoming too big for me to grapple with. So instead, I tune into Nico and Kasia's conversation and let my questions melt away. For now.

When we reach the west end of Princes Street, I point out my bus stop.

"This is me," I say. "Can I, eh . . . Can I come back next week?"

Kasia's face goes stony, but the others smile.

"Of course you can," Nico says. "It's your place now, too. Here, I'll give you my number just in case."

My phone's still dead, so Nico produces a pen from his pocket and scribbles the digits on the back of my hand.

"Remember: eleven twenty-one p.m. Don't be late!"

I watch them head down Princes Street: Sailor Moon, a were-wolf, and a boy with blue wings. When they reach the corner, Nico spins on his heel and waves back at me. Two men turn to stare at him, but he doesn't notice. Or if he does, he doesn't care.

The skull mask is still on top of my head. I wait until they're out of sight, then shove it back under my hoodie. Unlike Nico, I would notice. I would care.

My phone wakes up as soon as I step onto the number 22. No missed calls, and weirdly enough the time is saying 11:38 p.m.—the lack of signal in Everland must have messed the clock up. As the bus edges back down Leith Walk, my stomach starts to squirm. Mam is going to kill me. There's not much she can do, really—she could ground me, yeah, but I hardly go out anyway, and I don't get an allowance for her to take away—but still, I don't like stressing her out. She's got enough on her plate without me disappearing.

Not that it'll stop me doing the same next week.

Fifteen minutes later, the bus pulls up down the road from Mackay House. I race through the courtyard and up the steps to number 9B. Jake is still at the desk, leafing through a textbook while the computer screen flickers white. He looks at me and yawns.

"Where have you been?"

"I . . . just needed some air. Got a sore head." I look around—Mam's shoes aren't by the door, and there's no coat hung over the back of her chair. "Where's Mam?"

He blinks at me. His eyes are sickly pink around the irises from staring at the screen too long. "Not home yet. She's not done till one or something."

"Oh. Right."

I stare at him, then glance at the bottom-right corner of the computer screen: 11:57 p.m. Wait . . . *11:57 p.m.?*

Jake gives me a funny look, then goes back to his essay. An idea, an impossible idea, is gnawing at the back of my head. I take off my jacket, store the mask (now a bit damp from the rain) back in the cupboard, then turn on the old radio that sits on Jake's shelf. Tink starts, narrows his eyes at me, then goes back to snoozing at the foot of my bed. My hands shake as I wait for the Take That song to finish playing. Finally, a man's voice overlaps the final bars.

"This is Forth One," the presenter says. "The time is two minutes to midnight."

Two minutes to midnight. My phone could be wrong, my computer could be wrong, but surely this can't be.

Apparently, though we traveled all throughout the valley, though we went to a dozen parties and festivals and celebrations, though I talked to Nico and Zahra and the others for hours . . . I walked into Everland just thirty-seven minutes ago.

SIX

"SOMETHING'S UP WITH YOU."

It's Friday, lunchtime, and I'm sitting in the school courtyard with Megan, watching *RuPaul's Drag Race* on her phone while she picks at a tuna-mayo wrap. We're on season six, one of my favorites, but the entire episode has gone over my head. I've been in a daze all morning; Michelle made a joke about my face having "more craters than the moon" in History, and I hardly even flinched. I can't stop thinking about Everland—about the way that green door appeared out of nowhere, and how the night felt so long, but I got home so fast, and how the hell I'm going to sneak out again next Thursday without getting caught. And Nico.

I can't stop thinking about Nico.

"Hello-o? Brody?" Megan nudges me with her elbow.

I glance up at her, blinking. "Huh?"

"Seriously, where are you today?"

"What do you mean?" I look back at the screen. RuPaul is describing this week's challenge. A new episode must have started. I hadn't even noticed.

"You're so quiet," Megan says. "I mean, you're never exactly the chattiest, but today you're, like, *Silence of the Lambs* quiet."

"There's no' actually that much silence in *Silence of the Lambs*, Meg," I tell her. "Not many lambs, either."

She pulls another crumb from the edge of her wrap. I scoffed my chicken tikka baguette in two minutes flat, but it takes Megan a whole lunch break to get through one sandwich. Her mouth is always talking, and her right hand is constantly scrolling through her phone, which makes eating kind of difficult.

"I bet there's more conversation, though." She rolls the crumb into a tiny ball and flicks it at me. "Maybe I should have lunch with Hannibal Lecter tomorrow. Much better chat than you."

A football smacks off the wall above my head, making me jump. A kid in a red jacket scrambles across the yard to fetch the ball, ignores me, but apologizes to Megan. Megan is almost popular. That's partly because her older brother, Harry, is known for his "legendary" house parties, but mostly because she's really, really pretty: perfect Hollywood teeth, and hair that looks like a Garnier advert. Smart, too—she's in all the top sets. We've been friends since we were nine, when she moved up here from Manchester after her parents' divorce. She could have graduated to the popular kids or the overachievers long ago, but instead she spends her lunchtimes hanging out in the music room or watching videos with me.

"There's nothing up," I say. "I'm just concentrating on the show."

I can feel her studying me as I look back at the screen.

"Yes, there is. You're all . . . faraway." Her eyes darken. "Did Leanne and Michelle say something? Do you need me to deck them? I know you're a pacifist or whatever, but those two are well overdue for a beating."

I grin at her. "Nah, it's fine. I'm just tired. Some drunk guys woke me up playing the trash cans outside our block like bongos—I couldnae get back to sleep for ages."

Megan raises two small fists. "Well, Dwayne Johnson and the Rock are ready when you need them."

I push her face away, laughing. "Those are the same person, genius."

For a few seconds, I do actually consider telling her about Everland.

Everywhere I look, there are reminders of it: the Sailor Moon badge on Aimee McDougall's school bag; "Heroes" playing on the radio in the canteen; Rongrong Li's royal-blue duffle coat, the exact same shade as Nico's nails . . . It's been hard keeping it to myself all day, and even harder focusing on our mostly one-sided conversations when all I want to do is think about next Thursday.

I could at least tell her about Nico. Megan's a huge gossip, but she knows how to keep a secret when she needs to—she's the only person I've told that I'm gay. Besides, it'd prove that there's more to my life than drumming and my cat. Megan's always texting or dating or breaking up with some guy. She asks me if I like anybody all the time, but I've never had much of an answer to give. The only person I've ever even kissed was her, and that was just an experiment when we were thirteen. (Not a successful one—my lip got caught on her braces, and apparently I tasted like chicken Kiev.)

As I open my mouth, Megan's phone interrupts. She pauses the show and flips to her messages. Her eyes go wide. "Oh my God, listen to what Adam just sent me."

She starts reading out some long, rambling message from her latest crush. By the time the bell rings, I know the guy's mum's name (Linda), his star sign (Taurus), and how many times he's been to Lanzarote (twice). The urge to talk to her about Nico has long fizzled out. Besides, if I tell her about him, I'll end up telling her about Everland. And if I tell her about Everland, she'll invite herself along next week—if only to make sure that I haven't gone nuts and started hallucinating secret villages hidden behind Calton Hill.

I don't want that. I love Megan. She's loud and funny and always knows just what to say. Most of the time, that's a good thing—means it's easier for me to slip into the background. But sometimes it's suffocating. Whenever she's around, I become the one-line bit part to her leading role. I can deal with that at school or at parties, but not around Nico. Not in Everland.

But by the time school ends, last night is already slipping

away from me—the way dreams fade as you go about your day. I can remember Nico's smile as the fireworks exploded above us, the people I met, the conversations I had, but the places and the atmosphere have started to dim. Doubts are starting to creep in. That door. The rivers. The trees . . . Everything.

I need evidence.

I've run out of data on my phone, so I have to wait until Jake goes out to his friend Amir's house before I can get on the PC and start my search. I type *everland calton hill*, but all that come up are TripAdvisor reviews and something about a theme park in South Korea. *Everland edinburgh* isn't any better, or *everland national monument*. Nothing.

A shiver runs over me. It's a bit creepy, all this. The monument was all sparkly colors and golden unicorns; not exactly subtle. There must be some mention of it online: a tourist asking about it on a forum, or even one of the old guests boasting about it on Reddit. I trawl through pages and pages of search results, but there's nothing. It's like I dreamed the whole thing.

If I can't find Everland, maybe I can at least find Nico. I remember Kasia mentioning his surname during one of the scoldings she gave him last night: Clark Calderón. After about twenty goes at spelling it, I eventually find him: a Twitter feed that hasn't been updated for three years, and an Instagram account. There are only a handful of photos on it, but Zahra and Kasia are in one of them, all dressed up in strange costumes, the outline of the monument's pillars behind them. They're real, and so is Everland.

Maybe I should have told Megan about it, I think as I wipe the search history from the PC. Maybe sharing it with someone from my normal life would make it feel less dreamlike.

But I already have to share my room with Jake, and the drums with every wannabe Dave Grohl in school. I can keep this one thing for myself.

SEVEN

MAM'S NOT SUPPOSED TO BE WORKING THE FOLLOWING THURSDAY.
Luckily, one of her colleagues comes down with food poisoning
after eating an out-of-date prawn cocktail, and Mam has to go in
to cover for her. I sneak out at quarter to eleven, silently thinking my stars for dodgy shellfish and Margaret's weak stomach.
I can feel Jake's eyes on me as I tie up my shoes, but he doesn't
ask where I'm going. I add *whatever boring essay's keeping him
distracted* to my list of things to be grateful for and slip through
the door into the fresh night air.

Although it's cold out again, Leanne and Michelle are sitting on the swings, their faces ghostly blue in the light of their
phones. A familiar sense of dread settles over me. I pull my hood
over my head and pick up the pace, but Michelle jumps off the
swing and runs toward me.

"Where you going, Fairy?" She plants herself on the path between me and the gate, her arms folded across her baby pink jumper. "Lost Tinker Bell again?"

"Piss off, Michelle." I try to move past her, but she steps to the left to block me. I switch to the right and find Leanne in my way.

"Must be past your bedtime," she coos. "Does your mum know you're out this late?"

She reaches over to ruffle my hair, but I slap her hand away. I barely touch her, but the girls fake a gasp. Like *I'm* the one who's crossed the line here.

"You gonnae hit me, Brody?" Leanne says, grinning. "Go on, then. Try and hit me."

I'm not, and she knows it. I've never hit anybody, unless all the scuffles Jake and I had when we were younger count. Sometimes, though, I feel like that's Leanne's aim. Because she knows she's a crappy person, that the stuff she's said and done to me is messed up—but if I hit her, it would erase all of that. It'd put me in the wrong, make me the bad guy. And it would. No matter how much of a nightmare she's been over the years, there'd be no excuse for hitting her.

So I won't. Instead, I sidestep to the right, trying to dodge past her. Leanne's too quick and blocks me again; Michelle grabs my bag and pulls me back, laughing and asking what's the rush. The number 22 bus is turning onto our street. I wriggle my arms away from the straps, ready to sacrifice my school bag and my costume—an Anubis mask that Keira had for her fourth grade

Ancient Egyptians project, jazzed up with black felt tip and gold nail polish—if I have to. The bus slows down, pulling up to the pavement. Shit. *Shit.*

"Oi!"

Nine floors up, Jake's head appears at our bedroom window.

"Piss off, Leanne," he says, sounding more bored than angry. "Let him go."

Leanne and Michelle aren't scared of Jake, but they do respect him. Somehow, despite going to a posh school and wearing a uniform that makes him look like an Enid Blyton character, he still gets some kudos around here. I don't understand it.

Leanne steps back, laughing lightly, and Michelle lets go of my bag. I run through the gate and toward the bus stop, arriving just as it starts signaling to pull away. Leanne's voice calls after me.

"Always need somebody to come to your rescue, don't you, Fairy?"

Her mouth keeps moving, but the bus doors slide shut behind me and block out her words. I flop into the first seat available, my heart pounding. I should be grateful that Jake helped me escape, but I'm more pissed off that he was spying on me from our bedroom window. Clearly, he's not as distracted as I thought.

Nico and the others are already waiting for me at the monument when I get to Calton Hill. Tonight, his face is painted like a cat's, only in different shades of pink, orange, and yellow, and he's wearing this amazing headpiece of huge neon-colored feathers. When I take out the Anubis mask, he holds his hand up for a high five.

"That's awesome!" He lifts it up, turning it to see it better in the dim light. "You could give me a run for my money, Brody, honestly. This is so good."

"Hardly." My eyes run over his dark eyelashes, the curve of his lips, the freckles faded beneath streaks of orange face paint. I'm trying not to smile too much, but I can't help it. "I like your feather . . . thingy."

"It's supposed to be a mane. I was going for a neon lion look—Aslan at a rave."

We have to wait a minute for the door to appear. Even after seeing it last week, it still makes my head spin: the way the colors slowly seep out of the dark sky between the pillars, how the hazy blur of gold and green thickens and solidifies as it turns into the door. I can see every knot and bump of the wood, every thin line etched around the unicorn's horn. I reach out and touch the stained-glass windows; they're hard and cold and wet. This is real.

"Do you no' end up with random people wandering in here, when they see the door?" I ask as Zahra turns the unicorn's horn.

"Sometimes," says Kasia—this week, wearing a dinosaur onesie. "Remember that German tour group who wandered in after us last year? They left when we told them it was a private function, but they seemed a bit bewildered."

"But how come more people havnae found it?" The door opens, and I follow Zahra inside. "It's pretty noticeable."

"You can only see it from a few meters away," Zahra says. She's dressed as No-Face from *Spirited Away*, one of Megan's favorite films. "People do see it, but they tend to assume it's just an art thing—some sort of projection."

Nico follows me through the gap. "If they're curious enough to come back, or imaginative enough to think it's something more than meets the eye, that usually means they're the right type of person to be here."

The door closes behind us, and a pinkish light floods the sky; the sun is setting behind the mountains, turning the clouds a blazing orange. We must take a different route down the hill, because tonight we arrive at a different square. This one is bigger than the last, with a large, round fountain, pale cobblestones, and old stone buildings with brown shutters over the windows. A few people are clustered around small patio tables, reading or watching the sky. Dani sits alone at a small table in the corner, scribbling in a notebook. The air is balmy, almost warm. I've never been abroad, but I imagine this is what Italy or Greece feels like.

Nico claps his hand onto my shoulder. "I need to talk to Dani for a bit. You'll be all right to explore on your own, won't you? I'll catch up with you later."

"Oh, right." It's a bit of a kick in the teeth after waiting a whole week to see him, but I nod. "Aye, I'll be fine. Where'll I find you?"

He grins. "Don't worry—you just will."

I watch him jog across the square toward Dani, whose face lights up as he sees Nico coming. Nico kisses him on the cheek, then flops into the seat opposite. His hands move in the air as he chats in rapid Spanish, probably filling Dani in on the week since they last saw each other. Dani leans forward and brushes something from Nico's face; Nico catches his hand, linking their fingers together.

There's another stab of disappointment in my chest, but I push it back. Nico and I are friends. Not "just" friends— friends. That might not be exactly what I was hoping for, but it's not any lesser, either.

Last week, when I was with him, we kept winding up in crowds: parties, concerts, that busy market. Tonight, everything feels calmer. I head out of the square, down a wide alleyway lined with orange trees on either side, and end up walking along one of the rivers. The tiny blue fish swim just beneath the surface, moving like cobalt lightning bolts under the water. I pass people dipping their feet, swimming, rowing small boats downstream. Most of them smile and wave as I walk by. An old lady offers me a mint, and a young guy on a raft starts talking to me in a language I don't recognize. We can't understand each other, but it doesn't seem to matter. Somehow, we end up laughing anyway.

It feels like having the whole world to myself. And the farther I walk, the more at home I feel.

After a while—I have no idea how long—a voice rises out of the silence. It's the same one I heard singing Bowie last week, this time doing an amazing rendition of "Sweet Dreams (Are Made of This)." I follow the sound and eventually find a crowd of people watching a band on a small wooden stage. The singer, a tall black woman wearing a red dress and long gold earrings, leans into the mic with her eyes closed, the words pouring from her mouth. A fat white guy in a Pink Floyd T-shirt strums the bass, and a petite Asian girl is on guitar. Bare light bulbs hang from the top of the stage, casting them all in a yellowish glow. And behind them, empty and glistening, is a drum kit.

It's a vintage Gretsch set from the 1970s—a thousand times better than the piece of crap we have at school. My hands start to twitch. Before I can even think about it, I'm edging my way through the crowd. I climb the wooden steps to the stage just as the song finishes. The musicians look around—my cheeks start to burn.

"Uh, hi. I'm Brody. Do you . . ." The words get knotted in my throat, but I force them out. "Are you needing a drummer at all?"

Three faces light up at once. The singer claps her hands together.

"This is perfect! Our drummer stopped coming a little while ago." Her speaking voice is lighter than her singing one, with a South African accent. "I'm Esther. This is Arnau and Sandhya."

"Go on—take a seat," Sandhya says, nodding to the kit. "We're playing one of Esther's own songs next, so just pick up the beat when you can."

"Um, okay, cool. Cheers."

I can feel people in the crowd watching me. I can hear whispers. I pull the Anubis mask over my face and quickly sit down, but the nerves vanish as soon as I pick up the sticks. Whether here or in the outside world, I always feel at home behind a drum kit.

I started playing when I was seven, the day Jake tripped on a step and split his chin open, and my parents left me with a neighbor while they rushed him to hospital. Heather was a blue-haired stoner with mermaid tattoos and no idea what to do with a wee kid, so she plonked me down behind the snare and went to find me a snack. I started to play. My feet couldn't reach the pedals, and I'm pretty sure I held the sticks the wrong way, but I just went for it.

Most kids would love bashing up a drum kit for a few hours. But for me, it was something more than that. The drums were so *loud*. Everyone was always telling me I was too shy, too quiet; asking why didn't I say hello, why didn't I run and make friends with the other kids . . . This—*this* was control. It was power. It was a voice.

When Heather came back, holding a can of tinned peaches and two Kit Kats, she stared at me like I'd morphed into Meg White herself. She asked me if I'd played before, and when I told her no, she shook her head for about two minutes straight. I thought she was mad at me until she came around to my side of the kit, adjusted the seat for me, and starting explaining how to hold the sticks properly and what the different parts were called.

After that, she let me come around to play a few times a week; when she wasn't too high to function, she'd even give me lessons. Sometimes, we'd lie on her carpet and listen to vinyls on her record player. She taught me about Sheila E. and Keith Moon, Questlove and Janet Weiss. Being seven, I didn't exactly have the best taste in music, but she never took the piss. She'd let me play along to anything I wanted. We had to leave that flat when I was eleven, and my lessons with Heather with it. The music room at school is the only place I get to practice now, so I take every chance I can get.

But it's got nothing on this one. This kit reminds me of Heather's, and how I felt playing it: like everything in the world could be divided into bars and beats; like fitting in was as easy as finding a rhythm. We play the strangest mix of music: everything from disco and reggaeton to jazz and Bollywood songs. I don't know ninety percent of it, but I improvise, and somehow it seems to sound all right. Better than all right, even. I could do this the whole night. I could do it forever.

When I look up a few songs later—or maybe more than a few (I lose track somewhere between Johnny Cash and a Malian song)—Nico is in the crowd, his lion's mane swaying as he dances. When Esther calls for a break, he climbs onto the stage to give me a high five.

"That was amazing!" he shouts. "You're so good! You're like—um—who's a famous drummer? Ringo Starr! You're like a young Ringo Starr."

"More of a Sheila E. fan, but cheers." I push my mask up and smile at him. "I'd be better if I had my own kit to practice on."

"You have this one now." Esther grins at me from across the stage. "You play really well. Come back soon, won't you? It's much better with a beat."

Nico hops down from the stage, and I follow him through the crowd. I'm sure we walk back the way I came, but when I turn around to take one last look at the stage, it's already out of sight. Instead of the meadow I came through, we're now in a long, barren landscape filled with enormous metal animal sculptures. The change of scenery is so disorientating, it makes me dizzy, but I follow Nico past huge steel elephants and rusty bronze giraffes, half listening to him talk about a tarot reading he got at one of the markets as we walk.

All the questions I pushed out of my mind last week are resurfacing. There are things that I can't ignore anymore: the fact that the scenery seems to shift every time we go from one place to the next, and the whole time situation, and—

"Nico." I stop, breathless, and stare around me. "What *is* this place?"

He turns around, following my gaze around the makeshift metal zoo. The animals' trunks and horns gleam in the dim light; above us, the sky is still the same shade of sherbet, even after all the hours we've been in here. Nico sits on a copper lion's paw and kicks his boots out in front of him.

"So. The first night I came here, I'd had this massive fight with my stepmum: something about getting nail polish on the settee, I think. I can't remember." He pulls his legs toward him and loops his arms around his knees. "My dad kicked me out of the house. We argue all the time, but that's the only time he's ever told me to leave. I didn't have anywhere else to go, so I went wandering, and somehow I ended up on Calton Hill. Right in front of the door."

His eyes shine. "That night was amazing. I don't know if I can call it a "night," really—it felt like forever. Like I'd been there for days. I stayed because I wanted to, not to teach my parents a lesson . . . though I did think they'd be relieved to see me when I turned up after being missing for a few days. But when I got back, it was only quarter to twelve. I'd only been gone around forty minutes."

I blink at him. "Like last week. I got back just before midnight."

He nods. "It's always like that. We timed it once. Technically, we're only in here for a minute—that's how long the door stays open. Sometimes it feels like hours, sometimes like days, but barely any time has passed on the outside at all."

"What—like some . . . knockoff Narnia?"

"Kind of, yeah." He laughs and points to his lion's mane headdress. "See, I've already got the outfit and everything."

I shake my head. I'm still waiting for him to admit he's pulling my leg, even though I know that can't be the case anymore. Instead, he slides his hand into the pocket of his jeans, takes out a plastic lighter, and flicks it on so the flame jumps up.

"I don't actually know what this place is," he says. "Nobody does—or at least no one that I've asked. All I know is that time works differently in here. You don't need to eat or drink, though you can if you want to. You don't need to sleep. I've heard people say you can't even die. Nothing can hurt you at all."

He puts his hand over the flame, letting it lick at his skin. After ten or fifteen seconds, he holds his palm up to show me. There's not even a smudge of ash there. He hands me the lighter to try myself. I do the same, biting my bottom lip as I wait for the pain. It doesn't come. I keep the lighter pressed against my hand for thirty seconds, then a minute, then two. The fire doesn't burn. Other than a faint tickling sensation, I can't feel much at all.

"Don't ask me how it's possible," Nico says, "but I think . . . I think we're not in the real world anymore."

I sink down onto the lion's paw beside him. My head is spinning. It was confusing enough when I couldn't work out how normal logic applied to this place. Now that I know it doesn't, it's mind-boggling . . . and a wee bit scary. There's part of me that wants to turn around and run back home. Back to my life of drumming and documentaries and things I understand; back to a world that was linear and logical.

But then Nico leans toward me, a faint smile on his lips, and the feeling fades.

"That first night, when I got home," he says, "nothing had changed. My dad was still pissed off; my stepmum was still scrubbing at the sofa like a lunatic. But I'd calmed down enough to apologize, even if I didn't really think I needed to. This place gives me time to work out my anger or my energy. That's really all I know about it—it gives you what you need."

And for some reason, that's when it clicks. There's this world, and there's that one; there are the rules out there, and there are the rules in here. Damned if I know how it's possible, but it is. I'm here. This is my normal now.

And even if it makes my brain hurt to think about it, it's the best kind of normal my life has ever been.

EIGHT

I LIKE SATURDAY MORNINGS. THEY'RE THE ONLY TIME I HAVE THE living room to myself. Keira goes to a musical theater group on the weekend, Jake usually spends Friday nights at his friend Amir's, and Mam and Dad always have a lie-in if she's not working. That week, I decide to start making another mask: Animal from the Muppets. Seems fitting if I'm going to be Everland's resident drummer.

I look up a YouTube tutorial, where an enthusiastic American lady tells me to start by making a papier-mâché head. We don't have any balloons, so I make two half-circles using Pyrex bowls from the kitchen. I find an old Comic Relief red nose I can glue on, cut a Ping-Pong ball in two for eyes, then rip the leg of an ancient soft toy badger for the character's bushy unibrow. It's pretty satisfying, making something like this. Something out of nothing.

At around ten, my parents' bedroom door opens, and Dad emerges. He blinks at the scraps of fabric scattered across the living-room carpet and at Tink wrestling with the amputated badger on the sofa.

"What you making, Brodes?"

"Uh, just a mask. Megan's having a party," I say quickly. "It's Muppets-themed." Megan actually does love the Muppets, for some reason.

Dad picks up the half-made Animal head. "You used to love dressing up," he says. "Remember the Tinker Bell wings you had when you were wee?"

"No," I say. But they come back to me as soon as Dad mentions them: dainty wings made from pale green mesh fabric, with bright pink lines curving out from the center. They came with a matching wand shaped like a star. It fills me with embarrassment, remembering my five-year-old self bouncing around our old flat dressed up like that, but the shame fades a wee bit when I think about Nico. He was probably the same. He still is, kind of.

"Aye, you do," Dad says, chuckling. "You didnae take them off for weeks! Wore them to McDonald's once an' all."

"Dad, shut *up*."

"There's no need to be embarrassed! I loved seeing you charging about with your wings on. You didnae give a damn what anybody else thought. Best way to be, Brody."

Then this sad look falls over his face, the way it always does when he talks about the past. Back when his life was more than four rooms and a TV screen.

My dad has agoraphobia. It showed up six years ago, but in a way it's been around much longer than that—since he quit the army, back when I was three. I don't know anything about what he did there because he never talks about it. There are a few photos lying around—one formal portrait and a couple of snaps from Iraq and Afghanistan—but it's like looking at another person. The young guy in the helmet and camouflage doesn't fit with the man who makes our tea and can quote Werner Herzog films by heart.

Between those two versions of him, there was another one. When we were wee, he was just like any other dad. After he left the forces, he got a job as a painter and decorator. He would take us for pizza or to the beach, sometimes to Hibs football matches or the swimming pool; he'd go out to the pub with his friends or for meals with Mam. He was loud, funny, sometimes grumpy. Fearless.

One night when I was ten, he was walking home from the pub and saw three men beating the crap out of some kid round the back of Tesco. If there's one thing Dad can't stand, it's an unfair fight; he even gets agitated watching animals gang up on weaker creatures in nature documentaries. He held the men off long enough for the younger guy to get away, but once he did, they turned on Dad instead. That's even weirder to think about than Army Dad: faceless people kicking his head, stamping on his chest . . . as if he weren't a person at all.

He was in a coma for two days. Broken ribs, bleeding on the brain. I remember low voices and serious people in white coats, machines beeping, and a too-smiley nurse rushing us out of the ward, asking us if we'd like a hot chocolate. I remember Mam's face being all tight, yellowish, until my gran walked in, and Mam finally broke down, tears and sobs bursting out of her in a way I'd never seen before.

But then I remember her rushing into our bedroom to tell us that Dad had woken up. I remember the car ride to the hospital in our pajamas, and that giddy mix of relief and joy and nerves when we arrived to find him sitting up, bruised and bandaged but smiling. It was in the papers and all: "Brave Father Makes 'Miracle' Recovery after Intervening in Leith Attack."

I thought that was it. I thought Dad was better, that everything was back to normal. But when he walked through the front doors of the hospital the following week, before we'd even reached the car, he had a panic attack.

Doesn't sound like much when you say it like that. It doesn't sound the way I remember it: Dad gasping for breath, eyes wide and face pale, clammy hands tugging at his collar as if his clothes were suffocating him. It doesn't sound like the horror in his face, or the fear that seeped out of him and snatched my own breath away. It doesn't sound like Keira crying, or Jake asking over and over what was wrong.

The attacks kept coming, worse each time. One day, I walked out of our old flat to go to school and found him in his van, clutching the steering wheel and hyperventilating. Another time, he crumbled outside the newsagent when he was taking me and Keira to the park. I remember people walking their dogs or going to buy milk on one side of the street, Dad slumped by the trash cans on the other. Just a normal Sunday, but to him the world was ending.

He started making excuses to avoid going out. He quit his job, or maybe lost it—I was never totally sure. Soon, he stopped leaving the flat altogether. Apart from a few hospital appointments, he hasn't gone out for years now. The broken bones healed, and the bruises faded, but Dad never really recovered from that attack outside Tesco. It triggered something in him. Some fear that he'd buried long ago.

When I was younger, I used to be so angry at him. I was mad that we had to move flats when we couldn't afford the rent, away from my friends and my drumming lessons with Heather. I was mad every time that I asked him to come outside Mackay House with me, knowing Leanne and Michelle wouldn't pick on me with my dad there, and he made up some excuse to stay indoors. I was mad the time I worked up the nerve to play the drums in the school talent show, and he wasn't there to see it. Mam took a video on her phone to show him, but it wasn't the same.

But now I know all that anger was pointless. He has an illness, a disability. It's not a choice. Now, what makes me mad are the people who think he's faking—the people who can't hear *disability* without *benefits* and *benefits* without *fraud*. Especially if it's a disability you can't see, like Dad's. And while it's a bit annoying never being able to watch what I want on TV, I get why he's so obsessed with documentaries: It's his way of seeing the world.

The look only lasts for a few seconds, then he blinks and it's gone. He spins around to the bedroom. "We must still have some photos of that—do we, Sal? Of him in his wings?"

Mam doesn't reply. I lean past Dad to look at her. She's sitting on their bed, one hand on her forehead, reading a letter.

"What's wrong, Mam?" I ask.

"What? Oh, nothing." She slips the piece of paper into a brown envelope and smiles at me. "The photos? They're in one of the albums somewhere, I think. That'll be one to embarrass him with when he starts bringing girlfriends home."

I bite back a smile at that. "All right, Mam—whatever."

They're trying to wind me up, but they don't mean it in a bad way. I don't remember my parents ever having a go at me for liking Tinker Bell or *Hannah Montana* or my cousin Leonie's Bratz dolls. It was Jake who had the issue with it; Jake who was always telling me I needed to play with "boys' toys." In one way or another, Jake has always managed to make me feel crap about myself.

Mam takes the Animal mask from me, turns it around to look at it, then plonks it on my head. "This is so good, Brodes! I think we've got some pipe cleaners you can use for his hair; Keira used to like playing with those. I'll go have a look."

"What's Megan going as?" Dad asks as I pull the mask off.

It takes me a moment to realize he's asking about the party I made up and not Everland. "Um . . . Gonzo."

Dad bursts out laughing. "Brilliant. I'd have gone for the Swedish Chef myself. Or one of the grumpy old guys."

I grin at him. "You wouldnae even have to dress up."

"I'm forty-six, you cheeky bugger!"

He picks up one of Jake's textbooks and pretends to bop me on the head, laughing. Mam comes out of Keira's room carrying a handful of orange, pink, and yellow pipe cleaners.

"Here you go. You could cut some holes in the mask and poke them through, bit like whiskers."

"You need a chain, too! Remember he has a chain round his neck?" Dad says. "Ask Ahmed downstairs—he'll have one for his bike."

It sounds pathetic, but I'm kind of enjoying this. I can't even remember the last time Dad talked to me about something other than his documentaries, or Mam asked me a question that wasn't about school or homework. They probably tried, to be fair, but there's always some distraction—some drama of Keira's, or Jake announcing he's won a bloody Nobel Prize or whatever. It's nice having their attention for once.

But of course it doesn't last.

The front door opens, and Jake walks in. He never usually comes back from Amir's until the afternoon, but today it looks like he's sprinted up the stairs. He holds his phone out in front of him, a huge grin spilling over his bright red face.

"I got an interview," he says, panting. "For Cambridge. History and Politics."

The textbook slides out of Dad's hand. Mam just about hurdles over the sofa to grab the phone from him; her hands shake as she reads the email, her lips mouthing the words. She can't have got to the end before she throws her arms around Jake's neck.

"Oh, Jake, you genius! I'm so proud of you!"

"I haven't got in yet," he says, as she smacks a kiss on his cheek. "And even if I do, I'll need a scholarship to actually go. But it's something."

And you know what? I am actually proud of him. I've never met anybody who works as hard as my brother. If he's not up till the wee hours working on essays or exam revision or the school newspaper, he's at debate club, Model UN, volunteering for his Duke of Edinburgh Award . . . anything that'll get him closer to where he needs to be. He's earned this. He really has.

But everything is always, *always* about him. It would've been nice to have my parents' attention for another ten minutes. Even for another two.

Still, as Dad goes to hug him, mumbling something in a choked-up voice, I give him a thumbs-up from the door.

"Nice one, man. You deserve it."

He smiles. I haven't seen a proper smile from him in forever. "Thanks, Brodes."

After she's read the email another hundred times, Mam gets out her phone and starts calling my grandparents and aunties to tell them the news. Dad decides we need a toast and goes off to see if there's anything in the fridge. Jake sits back down at the computer, casting a glance at the Animal head in my hand.

"What are you making?"

I look down at the mask. Its gap-toothed grin beams up at

me. The halved Ping-Pong balls are squint, the plastic nose is falling off, and the mouth is lopsided. I feel my face go red. My brother is on his way to Cambridge, and what have I achieved? A stupid Muppet mask that'll probably fall apart halfway up Leith Walk. And to think, just a few minutes ago, I felt almost proud of this piece of crap.

"Nothing. It's rubbish."

"No, it's—" Jake starts to say, but Dad comes out of the kitchen holding a tray with half a packet of Pink Panther biscuits and some fizzy drink from last Christmas, cutting him off with a cheer.

I scoop up the leftover bits of fabric and the pipe cleaners and dump them with the mask on my bed. He didn't mean to. He really didn't mean to. But my brother has managed to make me feel crap about this, too.

NINE

IN A WAY, JAKE'S INTERVIEW DOES ME A FAVOR. MAM AND DAD ARE too focused on him to realize that I'm spaced out all week, and he's been so busy preparing that he'll probably be too distracted to notice me slipping out to Everland again.

When quarter to eleven comes around on Thursday, I shoulder my backpack, the Animal mask safe inside. But as I kneel down to put on my trainers, Jake's voice makes me jump.

"So who's the girl?" he asks. "Or is it a boy?"

My head snaps up to look at him. My brother's looking at me with this wry grin, like he's caught me doing something I shouldn't.

"What are you on about?"

"Come on, Brody. This is the third time you've snuck out like this. I know you're not going out for some *fresh air*." He spins around in his chair to face me. "Why so late, though? And why always on a Thursday?"

My hearts starts thumping. Jake never asks me anything about my life, just like I never ask him anything about his. For a second, I want to slap the smirk off his lips. He's laughing at me. He's ruining everything. Like he always laughs at me. Like he always ruins everything.

"There's no boy. I'm not—I dunno what you're talking about." I try to tie my shoes, but my hands are shaking. "Just piss off, okay?"

Anger flashes across Jake's face.

"For God's sake, Brody, I'm only asking," he snaps, his voice rising. "I just don't get why you're going out at quarter to eleven every Thursday. Obviously, I'm not, like—I mean, it's fine if you're gay, I'm just—"

"I'm not—"

I can't get the word out. I don't mind being gay. I wouldn't change it. I even kind of like it—or at least, I think I will once I get to the having-a-boyfriend-and-sex part. But actually saying it, having other people know it . . . that's different. That scares me, and it can't be dissolved with an offhand *It's fine*. This is typical of Jake: taking something that I've thought about and worried about since I was eight years old and making it out to be a piece of cake. Like when I used to get stuck on my Maths or Spanish homework, and he'd swan over and explain it in this irritating children's TV presenter voice, going on about how "obvious" it was.

"Just leave me alone," I tell him, as I snatch my jacket from the hook on the wall. Dad grunts and shuffles on the sofa, so I lower my voice. "It's none of your business. I'm just—"

Mam's bedroom door opens.

"What's going on?" She rubs her eyes and looks at Jake, but he's gone back to his essay as if nothing's happened. She sees the jacket in my hand. "What are you doing, Brody?"

"Nothing." I gently let my backpack drop to the floor. She'll know something's up if I take it with me. "I'm just going out for a walk."

She squints at the computer screen. "It's ten to eleven!"

My stomach lurches; if I don't leave now, I'm going to miss the bus. "I'll only be a few minutes," I say. "I just need some air, Mam."

I'm out before she can answer, shrugging my jacket on as I race down the stairs. As I reach the eighth floor, I hear our door open above me. Mam's voice bounces down the stairwell, shouting at me to come back. I can hear Dad sleepily asking what's going on behind her, and Mrs. McAskill shuffling around in her flat. I'm never going to hear the end of this when I get back, but right now that doesn't matter. I just need to get—

The number 22 bus.

Which is early. And outside our block. And pulling away from the pavement.

"Shit!"

I sprint through the gates and chase it down the street, but the roads are quiet, and it quickly slips out of my reach. I run back to the bus stop and frantically check the timetable: there's a 16 coming, but it's delayed by eight minutes—it won't get me to the top of Leith Street until around half eleven. I'm too late.

Swear words burst out of me like hornets from a nest. I kick the bus shelter wall, startling a drunk guy stumbling home from the pub who tells me to "calm doon, laddy." Part of me wants to head up to town anyway, just to piss my parents off, but Nico'll be gone by the time I get there. I've missed my chance.

I storm up to Tesco and back—killing time to fake this "walk" that I went on about needing—then reluctantly trudge back up to our flat.

Mam is sitting on the arm of the sofa talking to Jake while Dad looks on. They all glance up when I come in. Jake swivels back to the screen, like he hasn't just been grassing me up.

"What the hell was all that about?" Mam's voice is mostly steady, but she's furious. I can tell from her folded arms, the thin line of her lips.

"Nothing," I say. "I told you, I just needed some air."

I head toward my room, but she holds out an arm to stop me. "No, you don't. Sit."

"Mam, I'm tired—"

Dad stands up. He spends so much time sitting down to watch TV that sometimes I forget how big he is: almost six foot, with bulky arms and a bit of a belly. "Sit down, Brody."

I grit my teeth and roll my eyes but slump onto the sofa.

Mam moves to the coffee table, where she can look me in the eyes. "What's going on?"

"*Nothing.* I told you—I was just going out for a bit of fresh air. I've been cooped up in my room all night; I needed to stretch my legs."

Jake's shoulders twitch. I wait for him to tell her about my longer disappearances over the past few weeks, but he keeps his mouth shut and carries on typing.

Dad shakes his head. "At this time of night? I wasnae born yesterday, boyo."

Mam's eyes narrow. Keira's got Dad's eyes, a watery blue; mine and Jake's are the same deep brown as our mother's. Maybe I should feel guilty about lying to her, but I don't. Not even the tiniest bit. Everland is too important for that.

"I swear to God, Brody, if you're using drugs—"

"Drugs? What are you on about? Of course I'm no' on drugs."

So that's why I'm getting the whole Spanish Inquisition. Nothing scares my mam more than drugs. Her sister, Carol, died of an overdose when she was eighteen, and her brother's been in and out of prison for the past twenty years for dealing. She's terrified we'll end up the same. It not like it's hard to get ahold of them around here. I've never been that interested, though. I did have a draw of a joint once, at one of Megan's brother Harry's parties, but it just made my eyes prickle, and my head feel like somebody was squeezing it like a lemon. That's about as *Trainspotting* as my life has gotten so far.

Then it comes to me. My excuse. It's embarrassing as hell, but it'll shut them up. It might even convince Jake.

"It's, like, the only time Leanne and Michelle aren't around," I say, pushing out the words before I can change my mind. "That's why I've been waiting until this late to go out."

There's a long silence.

My cheeks are burning. Even if it's not true . . . it's sort of true. I do try to avoid going out when Leanne and Michelle are in the courtyard. I rush home from school so I don't bump into them. I was once an hour late to go to Megan's because they were sitting on the swings having a smoke and I couldn't face walking past them. Sometimes the thought of having to deal with their bullshit . . . it's too much. Easier to just stay inside.

My parents look at each other.

"Brody . . ." Dad sighs. "You cannae let those lassies get to you, son."

Mam pats my knee. "I'll talk to Kath and Paul."

Kath and Paul are Michelle's parents. They're actually really nice—I don't know what went so wrong with their offspring—but grassing up their daughter definitely wouldn't help. I open my mouth to protest, but Jake gets in there first.

"That's literally the worst thing you could do, Mam." He clicks and drags to highlight something on the screen. "I've told him before—he just needs to ignore them."

"Right, thanks," I snap. "Like I havnae tried that."

Mam gives me a stern look, then reaches out to touch my cheek. "Either way, you can't be walking about by yourself in the dark. It's not safe. Mind that lad who got stabbed back in July?"

That was some gang thing, not a random attack, and it

happened at three in the afternoon. I nod anyway. "Yes, Mam, I'll do my best not to get murdered. Can I go to bed now?"

Dad pats my shoulder. "Aye, go on."

I start to stand up, but Mam puts her hands on either side of my face and kisses the top of my head. "Just tell us next time you want to go off wandering, okay? If it's this late, Jake or I can go with you."

The idea's laughable—as if Jake would take ten minutes out of his schedule to do anything for me, and hanging out with my mam would do nothing to get Leanne and Michelle off my back—but it's easier to agree. "Yeah, fine. Night."

The conversation worked as a stopper, but when I flop onto my bed and take my phone out to text Nico, the realization that I've missed my trip to Everland finally hits me. Another week to wait until I get to play those drums. An entire week before I can hang out with Zahra and Miyumi and the others. Seven days of school and home and boredom before I can finally get back there, that place that makes me feel like me.

And one whole week until I see Nico again.

TEN

NICO DOESN'T REPLY TO MY TEXT UNTIL FOURTH PERIOD THE NEXT
day. And when he does, he doesn't comment on my long, ranty
explanation about why I missed the bus and how it was all Jake's
fault. All he asks is what school I go to.

I'm in English, half listening to Mrs. Davies talk about rhe-
torical devices, but I text Nico the name of our school under
the table. I can feel Ryan Martin shifting in the seat beside me,
trying to sneak a look at the screen. After a few seconds, a second
message pops up.

Good. In that case, I'm outside ☺

I look out of the window. At the end of the courtyard, a tall
figure in a denim jacket is standing by the school gates. Almost
without thinking, my hand flies into the air. Mrs. Davies breaks
off and looks at me, blinking. I never put my hand up in class.

"Yes, Brody?"

"Can I go to the toilet, miss?"

The hint of hope in her voice vanishes. "Go on, then."

I force myself not to hurry—that'd be asking for Leanne to shout something about me having the runs—take the stairs down to the Tech department and slip through the exit beside the gym. I loop around the back of the school rather than cutting across the courtyard, where I'm more likely to be spotted, and jog down the street toward the front gates. Nico turns around, his face breaking into a grin.

"Thank God I got the right place," he says. "I'd have looked like a total weirdo hanging outside the wrong school all afternoon. Then again, I probably look like a total weirdo hanging outside the right school, too."

"What are you doing here?"

I almost can't believe it's him. He looks younger in his school clothes: black trousers, a school jumper, a denim jacket with a couple of buttons pinned to the collar, and a dark blue tartan scarf. His eyes are free of makeup, but his nails are painted pale orange, probably left over from his latest costume.

"You sounded upset about not making it last night. Thought I'd come and check on you." He glances toward the dull gray school building. "You fancy an afternoon off?"

My face hurts, and I don't know why. I put my hands to my cheeks and realize that it's from smiling. "Aye, all right, then."

Thoughts of English and food and the drumming that I'd planned to do at lunchtime float away like leaves on the breeze.

It's a surprisingly nice day for the middle of October, so we follow the Water of Leith, the river that runs up to town. I want to ask what I missed at Everland, but Nico starts telling me about the club he went to on Wednesday instead. As he talks, I send Megan a message asking her to pick up my bag from Mrs. Davies's classroom and to tell her I've gone home sick. She replies after about half a second.

Okay . . . on the condition you tell me who that guy is.

Another split second later, a line of emojis pops up: curious face, winky face, heart eyes, eggplant, screaming face, blushing face, detective. She's not even in my English class! I swear she's working for MI6 or something, the amount she knows. I shove the phone back into my pocket without replying. I'll make up some story to tell her later.

We walk for ages, through Stockbridge and the Dean Village and toward the modern-art gallery. Nico tells me about a documentary that he watched called *Kiki* (I make a mental note to mention it to Dad) and the girl in his art course who threw her sculpture out the window in a fit of frustration this morning. He asks how Tink is getting on, what I was doing at school before he whisked me away, but he doesn't mention Everland. By the time we eventually stop for a break and for Nico to have a smoke, talking about it almost feels like something taboo.

"Sorry to be such a wannabe artist cliché," he says, dumping his bag on a bench, "but I'm going to do some drawing. And so are you."

He sits down, opens the bag, and pulls out two sketchbooks.

In front of us, a bronze-colored statue of a man stands ankle-deep in the water, and a row of large redbrick houses lines the banks of the river to the right. Nico pushes one of the sketchbooks into my hands, then starts rummaging around for pencils, his cigarette balanced between his lips.

"Uh, okay," I say, sitting down on the bench next to him. "I cannae draw for shit, mind."

"Who cares? You're creative." He flicks through the sketchbook—past illustrations of an ashtray, a cuckoo clock, Dani, Zahra, a caravan—until he arrives at a blank page. "I've seen those masks you made; they're awesome."

He starts making sweeping lines across the page, the pencil moving fast and free. The scene quickly starts to take form: the grassy banks, the houses, the tall trees sloping toward the water.

Rather than drawing the whole scene, I decide to focus on the statue. There are a few of them like this at different points along the river, each looking in a different direction. They used to really creep me out when I was younger, but now I quite like them. There's something calming about their quiet, blank expressions.

"So," I say as I draw the rough outline of the man, "what did I miss last night?"

It's a relief to finally bring it up: There's part of me that, when I'm out in the real world, still doesn't totally believe that Everland is real. Nico glances across the water, then adds a window to one of the houses with a few strokes of his pencil.

"Not much. The band was wondering if you were coming back, and Zahra and everyone. Miyumi kept asking about you, too. Think she's got the hots for you, Brody."

He grins at me. I swallow and draw the outline of the statue's facial features.

"She's cute. No' really my type, though."

"Oh yeah? Who is your type?"

My cheeks instantly go Sahara-level hot. I look down at my page, trying to hide the blush that always turns my spots from pink to red. I mumble something about not being sure and ask the first question that comes into my head. "So, eh, how long have you and Dani been together?"

"Uh, I don't know if we are, really. It's complicated." He outlines the statue in quick, free strokes. "We're together when we're in Everland, and in there it's perfect—it's the rest of the time that's the problem. We used to speak online sometimes, but he doesn't have internet at home, so that made it difficult. Even when we did, it just didn't feel the same. It's like talking to somebody you met in a dream, you know? It doesn't feel real." He shrugs slightly.

"Then there's the issue that neither of us can tell our friends or families about each other. His parents are cool with him being bi, but the sort-of-boyfriend-in-an-alternate-reality part is harder to explain."

I smile sympathetically. Put like that, it does sound pretty nuts.

"Do your parents mind?"

"That I'm gay? My mum's fine with it. My dad doesn't care,

either." He takes a pink pen from the packet and pulls the cap off with his teeth. "It's everything else about me that disappoints him."

There's an edge to his voice that I haven't heard before. He draws a cluster of tiny stars just above the statue, his hand tight around the pen. Then he looks at me and smiles, and the brief flare of anger is gone. Still, it bothers me. I can't imagine how anybody could be disappointed by Nico.

"We've talked about trying to meet somewhere in the real world. Dani and me. He doesn't have the money to come here, but I could probably go to Argentina." Nico pauses, his hand hovering over his drawing. "It makes me nervous, though. What if he hates me or something?"

Even if it's hard to hear about it, I'm glad he's telling me all this. It shows that he trusts me. "Why would he hate you? Dani's crazy about you. It's obvious."

"Is it? Maybe." He sits up straight, like he's shrugging off the low mood and smiles. "I mean, I *am* pretty fabulous. Even in another dimension."

Sitting by the water with him that afternoon feels almost like being back in Everland. Everything else in my life floats out of my head, and the time flies by. He tells me more of his stories from his past trips there: the tiny island that he and Zahra came across one night, which they've never been able to find again, and what they think might be the remains of a pyramid. After half an hour, his drawing looks amazing: a detailed, super-realistic grayscale sketch of the river and houses, dotted with starbursts and shimmers of bright colors. Like a layer of magic superimposed over the real world.

And mine . . . looks more or less like a human being, I suppose.

"That's good!" He bumps his shoulder into mine. "'Ah canny draw,' my ass."

I roll my eyes at his terrible attempt at my accent. "Last time I came here, somebody had put a bikini on him," I say, nodding toward the statue. "He looks a bit chilly without it."

"I was gonna say, he must be freezing his balls off," Nico says (though as far as I can see, the sculptor didn't bother to add those). "Maybe we should help the poor guy out."

He unties his boots, rolls up his jeans, and strides into the river. The minute his foot lands, he explodes into swear words and jumps about six inches into the air, soaking himself up to the knees.

After a moment, I pull my own shoes and socks off, hitch up my school trousers, and follow him in. The water is bloody Baltic—I haven't been this cold since the time Dad took me and Jake camping in November, and we got caught in an early snowstorm. Still, I clench my teeth and wade toward the dead-eyed statue. Nico pulls his tartan scarf off and wraps it around its waist.

"There. Protect his modesty," he says, tying a knot in the material. He cocks his head to one side. "He's a modern man; I think he'll be all right with wearing a skirt."

"A skirt? Come on, it's obviously a kilt." I click my tongue at him, faking outrage. "God, no respect for the culture."

Nico laughs. For a moment, I forget about the ice-cold water threatening to gnaw my toes off. It feels good to make somebody laugh like that . . . the kind of laugh that transforms his whole face, crinkling at his eyes, making his freckles dance.

I already knew how much I liked Nico. But it's only now that I've realized something else: When I'm with him, I like myself more, too.

We manage another minute or so in the water before I actually start to worry I might not make it out of there with all my toes intact. By the time we've waded out of the river and our feet have dried, we're both shivering and starving. Nico tucks the sketchbooks back into his bag, and we carry on along the water until we find a cafe. I don't have any money on me, just my lunch card, but Nico insists on buying me a sandwich, a chocolate crispy cake, and a Coke.

"You can get me next time," he says, shoving the food and the can into my hands.

Normally, it bugs me when people do that—it just makes me stress that they'll ask me to pay them back later, and I won't be able to. It's always a bit irritating seeing people toss about money like it's nothing, too—it'd probably take my mam a couple of hours to earn the amount Nico's spent on all this, and he clearly hasn't given it a second thought. But right now, I'm too happy that he said there'll be a next time to let it bother me.

It's starting to get dark when we leave, and my teeth are beginning to chatter again. We're over an hour away from Mackay House, but Nico walks me all the way home, telling me about some Korean TV show Zahra got him into and the costume he's making for Everland next Thursday.

Arriving back in Leith, my stomach tightens with nerves, the way it always does when I'm just a few minutes away from another interaction with Leanne and Michelle.

"Are those girls still bothering you?" Nico asks as we pass the play park around the corner. "The ones who kidnapped your cat."

The question takes me aback; it's like he's read my mind. I give a knee-jerk response. "No. Well, yeah. Sometimes."

"Idiots. Let me guess: Everyone tells you to 'just ignore them.'"

"Aye. Kind of hard when they do stuff like that, though." I force a laugh, but Nico doesn't join in. "That's no' even the worst thing they've done. My dad's got agoraphobia—he cannae really go outside—and this one time, they told everybody that he's faking it for benefits. Another time, they said he was under house arrest for drunk driving."

I've never told anyone that before. It would have upset Dad, obviously, and Mam would have stormed down to 3C to have a go at Leanne herself. Nico's looking at me with a funny expression. It's not pity, exactly—I can't stand people feeling sorry for me. More like he understands.

"*Qué cabronas,*" he mutters, which I'm guessing is the Spanish way of calling them total bitches. "People like that are just pathetic."

"That day in the car park," I say, slowing down before we reach the pedestrian crossing, "you said it happened to you, too."

Behind the railings, a tired young mum is pushing a toddler on the swings. The kid gurgles happily, his chunky legs kicking in the air. Nico gives a small smile.

"Yeah. Not surprising, really, given what an obnoxious little kid I was. I was always putting on one-man musicals or giving impromptu dance performances . . . basically showing off to anyone who came within a hundred-meter radius. I went to this tiny alternative school in Madrid, and it was all right there; I had lots of friends, and people seemed to get me. But then my dad met Jenny and decided to move back to Scotland. The first few years were a nightmare. Everything I was, everything I liked and was good at, was used against me. My accent, too. I couldn't go five minutes without somebody making fun of the way I walked or talked or what I was wearing."

He turns his head suddenly, as though trying to shake the memories out. It's like he's describing *me*. Not the show-off side—I was really shy as a wee kid, and I doubt I'll ever be described as talkative, even if I live to be a hundred—but the rest of it. That feeling that no matter what I do or don't do, people are going to ridicule it. That it's easier just to bury parts of myself than let them see the sun and risk getting burned.

"The worst thing is how it lingers on you, don't you think?" Nico says. "Those kids went home and put the TV on and forgot about it in five minutes, but I worried about it all the time. It wouldn't have been so bad if I'd been living with my mum. She was a weirdo, too—she'd have known how to take my mind off it. My dad just kept telling me to stick up for myself."

"So what changed?" I ask.

"I found Everland. I found my people." He smiles and gives my shoulder a little push. "And now you have, too."

Hearing that, the nerves float away. We cross the road toward Mackay House and pause by the corner. Nico stops far enough away that no one'll be able to see us if they look out from the flats.

"Thanks for today," I tell him. "Really. It was fun."

"A pleasure, Mr. Fair." He doffs an imaginary cap. "Will we see you next week?"

"Definitely." I don't care if my parents try to stop me again. I'll rip up my bedsheets to make a rope and climb out the window if I have to, all nine stories down.

"Good. See you—Oh, wait . . . your drawing!" He starts to tear the page out of the sketchbook, then pauses. He pulls his own drawing from the book, tearing a bit off the top-left corner, and hands it to me. There are wee details I hadn't seen before: a Coke can floating at the edge of the water; a plastic bag caught in the branch of a tree; *Kevin is a prick* spray-painted on the edge of the bridge . . . I don't know if they were actually there, and I didn't notice, or if Nico added them in later somehow. They sink into the grayscale, all but invisible beneath his strokes and swirls of brightly colored ink.

"Let's swap," he says. "I like yours a lot better, anyway."

I watch him walk away before I head back toward Mackay House. The courtyard is empty, but right now I wouldn't care even if Michelle and Leanne were lying in wait—they could bombard me with jokes and jibes, and it would all slide off me. It doesn't matter what they think. I've found my people.

I've found Nico.

ELEVEN

"THE TIME HAS COME FOR YOU TO LIP-SYNCH . . . FOR YOUR LIFE."

It's half past eight on Thursday, and Megan and I are sitting on her bed with a Hawaiian pizza between us and an old season of *RuPaul's Drag Race* playing on her laptop. School's closed for the October holidays, so I told my parents I'd be staying over here tonight—partly because I've hardly left the flat all week, and partly because it'll be much easier for me to get to Everland this way. Mam normally gets funny about me staying at a girl's house (cue awkward pauses, Jake smirking into his spaghetti, etc.), but right now she's still too busy obsessing over his whole Cambridge thing to care. I even found her gushing to the mail carrier about it yesterday.

"Come on, Monét!"

Megan thumps the duvet in excitement. We've already

watched this season twice; we both know who'll be asked to sashay away at the end of the song, but Megan likes to relive each episode as if it were the first time. She stretches her leg out and nudges my foot with hers.

"So where are you going with Nico tonight?"

On the screen, Monét X Change fakes out a death drop. The judges are in hysterics. "That really is a class move," I say.

Megan pokes me in the rib. "Stop changing the subject."

I can't stop the smile tugging at my lips, but I don't answer. She sighs and flops onto her back, kicking her feet against the drawings of Alaska and Chi Chi DeVayne on her wall.

"I don't get why he can't just come here. That way I could meet him!"

I take a hasty bite of pizza. By the time I got home from my day out with Nico on Friday, I had twelve messages and three voice mails from Megan, all demanding to know who the guy was and where we had been and what we'd done. I told her that he's my friend, that it definitely wasn't a date, but she refuses to believe me.

"Your dad might wonder why some random guy's turning up at his house at eleven o'clock," I say, though her dad's not actually home yet. He started his own online advertising business a couple of years ago, and he's always traveling or at meetings. Megan's mum still lives in Manchester, so she and Harry have the house to themselves most days. They order so much takeout they know most of the Deliveroo couriers by name.

"Fair point," she says, picking a piece of pineapple off the bottom of the box. "Well, you need to tell me everything when you come back."

"Aye, I will."

"No, I don't mean the usual Brody-style four-word summary. I mean *everything*. I want details, descriptions. Adjectives, Brody—adjectives! I'm not letting you sleep until I get at least ten full sentences."

I grin. "I'll give you five."

"Seven. Final offer."

The episode ends in the usual flurry of wigs and sequins. Megan clicks onto the next one, then slides the pizza box toward me. "Finish that before I do, will you?"

There are three slices left. There were eight to begin with, and I think I had five of them. "Have you actually eaten anything, Meg?"

"I had two slices! I'm still full after lunch, anyway. Harry ordered burritos."

"All right, then. If you're sure." I pick up another slice and take a bite.

Megan watches me for a moment, then turns back to the laptop. "When are you gonna let me put you in drag? You'd look *so* good. I've thought of a name for you and everything: Rhythmisia. Get it? Cos you're a drummer."

I almost gag on the pizza. "Sounds like a skin disease."

"It's perfect! *Please?* Just a bit of eyeliner."

She's asked me this, like, a thousand times. I always say no. For the first couple of seasons, just watching *Drag Race* felt like a weirdly guilty pleasure—I could always picture Jake sneering at the screen, and at me for enjoying it. It's not like I'd ever want to be a full-on drag queen myself (drumming is the only type of performing I'm up for: People can only half see you behind the kit, and there are no talking or dancing or sewing challenges required), but I am a bit fascinated by it. It's like a window to another world—one where you can put on makeup and high heels and still be a guy. No dickheads like Leanne and Michelle to make you feel like crap. No older brothers telling you to *man up*, whatever that means.

My eyes glide toward the piles of makeup on Megan's dresser. Maybe I should give it a go. Nico wears nail polish, and eyeliner sometimes. It's not like anybody at Everland would take the piss. And it'd be a way to cover up my crappy skin.

I take a deep breath. "Go on, then. Not the full shebang, though."

Megan's face lights up.

"Seriously? Now?" She bounces off the bed and scoops up an armful of products from her dresser. "Yas! Come through, Rhythmisia!"

"Keep talking like that and I'll definitely change my mind," I say, but she just laughs and dumps the bottles, tubes, and palettes onto the duvet. My stomach squirms with nerves, a dash of regret—and beneath it all, a tiny, guilty bit of excitement.

Two episodes later, I leave Megan's house feeling like there are neon arrows hovering over my head. My makeover turned into something of a battlefield. Megan would have gone full-blown

Trixie Mattel on me if I'd let her: a kilo of foundation, more blusher than the downstairs floor of Boots . . . I had to actually wrestle some glittery lipstick out of her hand before she attacked me with it. In the end, we settled on eyeliner, mascara, green nail polish, and a layer of foundation to cover up my spots.

The whole time, I sighed and rolled my eyes and acted like I was doing Megan a huge favor, but when I turned around to look in the mirror, my jaw dropped. I didn't look that different—my skin was clearer, and my eyes looked bigger—and yet it was like looking at an entirely different person. Like with this face on, I could be whoever I wanted to be. Somebody confident. Somebody who could stand up for himself.

Even so, I walk up Leith Walk with my hood up and my chin tucked into my collar. Nobody looks at me, luckily—or if they do, they don't say anything. I pick up the pace as I reach Waterloo Place, the nerves dissolving into the excitement of getting to Everland again. The lights of the National Monument haven't come on yet, but everyone's already waiting by the steps. Nico starts walking toward me, then stops in his tracks.

"Oh my God, Brody. Your face."

I put my hands to my cheeks, stopping just a millimeter from my skin in case I smudge anything. "Does it look stupid? My friend made me do it."

"Are you joking? You look *amazing*!" He pulls his phone from the back pocket of his jeans. "We need to take a selfie immediately. This has to be documented."

He spins around so we're facing the monument, slides his arm around my neck, and pulls me toward him. My whole body goes hot. Just before he taps the screen, the gaps between the stone pillars fill with color. Blue and green light falls onto my face, orange and yellow onto Nico's.

"Perfect." He shows me the photo—I have to admit, Megan really did do a good job—and slides the phone back into his pocket. "God, I can't believe how much it suits you."

"Nico! Come on!"

Zahra, dressed as a green-haired anime character, beckons us toward the monument. Nico grabs my hand and pulls me along the grass and up the steps, sliding between the doors just as they close with that familiar sucking sound. He and Zahra keep going on about how good the makeup looks, and even Kasia nods. The neon arrows are still hovering, but I don't feel so self-conscious behind the door. Not with my friends around.

The band is waiting for me when I get to the bottom of the hill, this time on an old vaudeville stage with thick velvet curtains. Esther is doing some vocal exercises, and the others are tuning up their instruments. I don't want to leave Nico so soon, but somehow I find myself climbing onto the stage anyway. Sandhya's face lights up when she sees me.

"Woah! Nice makeup." She gives me a high five. "It's good to see you again, Brody. I wasn't sure you would come back."

"Really?" I sit down behind the drums. A shiver of excitement runs over me when I pick up the sticks. "How come?"

She turns one of her tuning pegs and shrugs. "It seems to

scare some people off, this place. It's too much to take in. We're gonna start with 'Let's Twist Again'—you know that one?"

I don't, but I pick up the rhythm soon enough. The playlist is just as eclectic this week: Nina Simone, the Black Eyed Peas, songs in Zulu and Xhosa. After a while, I lose track of time and how many songs we've played. I just keep drumming, tune after tune, until I'm nothing but hands and feet and the beat juddering in my bones.

Nico, Zahra, and Kasia have all long disappeared to their different spots, but when I look up during Fleetwood Mac's "Go Your Own Way," I see Dani in the audience. He waits until the end of the song, then weaves through the crowd and leans on the stage, doing a tiny double take at my makeup.

"I'm going up to the hills!" he shouts to me over the hubbub. "Do you want to come? Nico and Miyumi and Zahra are already up there."

Sandhya's gone to join her friends, and Arnau's taking a break, so I wave goodbye and jump down from the stage. As my feet hit the ground, I'm suddenly very aware of the fact I have makeup all over my face. Dani grins at me.

"*Re guapo*," he says approvingly. "I like it."

We take a right out of the square, and suddenly the stage is far behind us and we're climbing the hillside on the east of the valley. It's the first time I've hung out with Dani on my own, but it's not awkward. I get what Nico sees him in. He has this chill vibe that can't help but make you relax; he smiles a lot and laughs in all the right places. He tells me about a Russian couple he got talking to down by the river and the bracelet he bought from an Armenian woman at the market, then breaks off as we turn past some pine trees.

"Look, another door!"

Higher on the hill, a red door has appeared on a rocky crag facing the sea. Dani runs toward it—he's surprisingly fast—and touches the knocker. It's gold and shaped like an eagle's head with a hoop in its beak.

"I have never seen this one before!" he shouts. As I catch up, he reaches out to touch the bird's head. "From Mexico, maybe? Or the United States."

"What are you talking about?"

He looks at me, his thick eyebrows raised. "All the doors go to different places. You didn't know?"

As soon as he says it, I feel stupid for not having worked that out. There are thousands of people in Everland, far more than could come from Edinburgh. People here don't usually talk much about their lives outside, so I guess I just thought . . . I dunno, that they lived here, or that they were part of the scenery.

Dani spins around, then points to a stretch of forest at the foot of the hill.

"You see that blue one, between those trees? It opens in the basement of a music school in Tokyo. Miyumi comes here before her violin class every Friday morning." He spins around, scanning the skyline, then finds a white door in a meadow of purple flowers. "That one is mine. It goes to my village in the south of Argentina."

As I look around, I notice more of them: a yellow one lodged between two tents; an orange one in the middle of a market; a deep red one squashed between the walls of some ruins in the distance. It sounds impossible. It *is* impossible. But after everything I've seen in here, it's not quite so hard to believe anymore. A doorway to Japan. Sure, why not?

"Have you gone through any of them?" I ask.

Dani tugs on the hoop, but it doesn't budge. "Nico tried, but you can only leave by the one you came in. But it would be cool, no? To be able to go to New Zealand or Mongolia or Kenya any time you want?"

There's something wistful in his voice. I get the feeling that, like me, he hasn't seen much of the planet beyond his village. It makes knowing there are other worlds behind those doors even more frustrating.

"When did you find this place?" I ask him as we carry on up the hill.

"Three years ago," Dani says. "It was the day I decided to kill myself."

The shock must show on my face, because he gives a small, sad smile.

"I don't know why I decided to do it that day. I woke up and knew it was time. It had been with me for so many years, and I felt like I couldn't do it anymore. I went for a long walk by the river near my house. I had walked there a million times before, but now there was this white door, standing there in the middle of nothing. I opened it and . . . suddenly I was in here."

"And that's when you met Nico?"

He shakes his head. "He arrived a few months after that. The first person I met in here was a Canadian girl, Olivia. We started to talk, about everything. I told her all about the bad thoughts, the sadness. It was the first time I had talked to someone about my feelings. I thought, *Well, obviously I'm dreaming; it doesn't matter what she thinks*. Plus, my English wasn't so good back then. Speaking about it in a foreign language made it feel . . . less personal, maybe. When I returned home, I changed my mind—I wanted to go back the next Thursday, learn more. So I did, every week. And little by little, life became a bit better."

I don't know what to say. "Are you all right now, then?" I ask quietly.

"Yes and no. It's difficult. I still have the bad days, the bad thoughts. I'm not . . ." He searches for the word. "*Cured*. But I can see a future now. I want to go to university and become a doctor. I want to travel, if I can. I want to live."

I look at Dani and notice his easy, open smile and his shiny brown eyes. Just a few minutes ago, I was thinking how calm he seemed, how settled. Sometimes you just have no idea what's going on in someone else's world.

By now, we've climbed so high that we can reach up to touch the clouds as they float by. We find Nico, Miyumi, and Zahra sitting in the branches of a huge gnarled oak tree, swinging their legs beneath them. Nico waves and jumps down to meet us, knocking Miyumi's violin case out of the tree. Dani leaps forward and catches it before it hits the ground.

"Sorry!" Nico yelps, as Dani passes the case to a ghost-faced Miyumi. "Wait . . . Can things actually get smashed in here? If we can't get hurt, our stuff shouldn't be able to, either, right?"

"Uh, let's maybe not test that out with a million-pound violin," Zahra says drily.

My eyes widen. "A *million* pounds?"

Miyumi wraps her arms around the case. Her cheeks are pink. "Maybe. I only know the price in yen."

"It's a Stradivarius," Dani says. "It costs an eye from the face."

Nico laughs. "I think you mean an arm and a leg." He shuffles over on the branch to make room for him, then turns to me. "Miyumi's famous in Japan. She was a child prodigy . . . You were so," he says as she starts to protest. "I've seen the videos. You're something else."

"You should come play with the band." I climb onto the tree's roots, and Zahra offers me a hand to pull me up. "Esther would love that."

Miyumi shakes her head. "Thank you, but . . . every day I play very long hours. It's a lot of work: waking up at five in the morning, rehearsals, school, more practice. Everland gives me a rest."

"Fair enough," I say. "Well, you know where we are if you change your mind."

I'm starting to see that all of us get something a bit different from this place. A break for Miyumi; time to read or study or whatever it is that she does over in the library for Kasia; a space to work through his feelings for Dani, one he probably couldn't get in the real world. I'm still not sure about Zahra yet, or even Nico.

For me, it's two things. One is the drums and the band. And the other is just this. Just sitting here, with people who listen to me, who make me feel wanted, who won't care if I turn up with a faceful of makeup on. Together, looking down at a world that's all for us.

WINTER

TWELVE

THE MORE I SNEAK OUT TO EVERLAND, THE EASIER IT GETS. I GO out the next week without my parents noticing, and Mam is on night shift again the following Thursday. Jake sees me leave both times, but he's stopped asking where I'm going. It doesn't feel like I'm breaking the rules anymore; now, going to Everland *is* the rule.

I'm still never sure how much time I'm spending in there, but it feels like each visit is a wee bit longer than the last. Most of that time is spent exploring and hanging out with Nico, Zahra, and the others, but I've been with the band a lot, too. I can feel my drumming improving with each set. It's a weird thing, being able to get better at something without spending any time on it in the outside world: Dani massively improved his English in here, and Kasia's apparently worked through the equivalent of a first-year university course in Physics.

"I practiced guitar in here for four years before I showed anyone back home," Sandhya tells me one night. "This guy at a party saw me looking at his and offered to teach me how to play a few chords . . . *very* patronizing. I let him, pretending I'd never picked one up before, then casually played the most complicated solo I could manage. His face! It was so funny."

We're getting ready for our set, this time on an old-fashioned bandstand by a quiet lake. Unusually for Everland, the sky above us is bright blue and cloudless. It feels like a warm May day, rather than late November.

"You've been coming here awhile, then?" I ask Sandhya. Even though I've been playing with them for around a month now, I still don't know that much about the band members. Music always takes over.

She counts back on her fingers. "Five and a half years now. There was a break in the middle. The first door I found was in south Kolkata. I used it for about a year, but then it vanished. I was locked out for eight months, until I came across another one near my friend's home in Kumortuli, in the north."

"Seriously?" I've never heard of anything like that before. Makes me wonder if there are any other doors around Edinburgh. There could be—this place is so big, you could go forever without bumping into anyone from home.

"What about you?" I turn around to Esther, who's doing her

vocal exercises on the other side of the stage. "When did you start coming here?"

"I found the door when I was . . . twenty-one, I think," she says. "I don't know how many years ago that was. I've lost track of time. I stopped going back quite early on. It's all been a blur since then."

She opens her mouth and sings a few more notes. I stare at her for a moment as the words sink in. "You mean . . . you stopped going home? Why?"

An uncertain frown appears between her eyebrows. "I wasn't happy there," she says slowly. "That much I do remember. I'm better here."

There's a strange look on her face, like she's struggling to remember something. Nico told me that people can't die in Everland, but I'd never really thought about how that works before. What if Esther stayed in here another few decades then decided to go back—would she still look twenty-one? Or would her body fast-forward a decade until she caught up with all the people she'd left behind?

The thought sends a shudder running through me. I put it out of my mind, pick up my sticks, and get ready to play.

After Dad had to stop working, it took me a while to realize that my parents didn't have much money anymore. It's hardly like they were rolling in cash to begin with, but suddenly they had one slim salary and even slimmer benefits to cover three kids and the rent. Looking back on it now, I know they must have stressed about it. It must have kept them up at night.

But Mam never let us see that. When they couldn't afford to go up to the Highlands like we usually did in the summer holidays, it was an excuse for our grandparents to come to Edinburgh instead. When they had to sell the car, it was a way for us to walk more, do more exercise. By far the worst thing for me was having to move to a cheaper flat, away from Heather and her drum kit. But Mam even managed to pitch that as something positive: It'd be closer to my new school; there was a park around the corner, etc. As if a rusty swing set could make up for everything we were leaving behind.

The look on her face when I get up on Sunday reminds me of that. Like she's about to serve us a microwave meal and say it has a Michelin star.

"Morning, love," she says, in a too-bright voice. "We all need to have a wee chat. Get yourself some breakfast and come sit down."

I know it's serious because she forces Jake off the computer and goes to wake Keira up, too. I give Dad a questioning look, but he just sinks down on the cushions and keeps flicking through the TV channels.

Nerves start to wriggle around my stomach as I make my toast. Maybe Mam's found out about Everland. No, that's not possible—but maybe she's found out about Nico. She wouldn't call some awkward family meeting for that, though, would she? Christ, I hope not.

When I go back to the living room, the three of them are sitting at the table: Mam looking nervous; Keira and Jake tired and confused. She glances over at Dad and calls his name, but he flicks onto an antiques show and turns up the volume. After a moment, Mam clears her throat.

"You know I haven't been getting as many shifts at work as I used to on this zero-hour contract," she says. "And your dad . . . We found out a couple of weeks ago that your dad's been sanctioned."

Jake looks down at the table, muttering something under his breath. Keira asks out loud exactly what I'm thinking. "What's that mean?"

"It means his disability benefits are going to be stopped." Mam's voice is steely. "Basically it means they think he's fit for work and that he needs to get a job."

"What? But . . ." Keira looks over her shoulder. Dad is still staring at the TV, acting as if we're not there. Keira leans forward on her elbows and lowers her voice. "He's not, though."

Mam strokes her hair. "I know, pet. Don't worry—we're going to try and sort it out. I'll see if I can pick up some other work, too . . . Kath downstairs said she should be able to get me a few cleaning shifts. It just means we're going to have to cut back on some things for a while."

Things are starting to slot into place. The letters. The hushed conversations. The fact there's been less food in the fridge lately. Looking at my mam, I see the bags under her eyes and feel a stab of guilt. She looks exhausted. I probably would have noticed sooner if I hadn't been so caught up in Everland.

Jake raps his fingers on the table.

"Mam, you *have to* let me get a job." The way he stresses the words, I get the feeling this isn't the first time they've talked about this. "It's ridiculous. I could help out. I could—"

"No! I'm not having you mess up your exams. Not after you've worked so hard. You're so close, Jake."

"This is more important. You know it is."

Keira nods. "We have to eat, Mam."

"Don't be so dramatic," she says, scoffing.

She looks over to Dad for backup, but he's too busy watching an umbrella stand shaped like a greyhound being put up for auction.

"We'll be fine. I don't want you getting distracted, Jake. Especially not with your interview coming up. That's final," Mam says as he opens his mouth to protest.

My gran told us once that Mam had planned on going to university. She'd got a place and everything. She was going to study geography in Aberdeen. Her parents didn't have much money, but back then there were more grants available, and the cost of living wasn't as high as it is now. But a couple of months before she was supposed to leave, her sister's overdose happened. And then, while the rest of the family was at the funeral, her brother, Andrew, broke into their house and stole my mam's bike, the family TV, and all of my gran's jewelry. That was the start of a career in crime that led to a few long stints in prison. Really, they lost two kids at once.

My mam couldn't leave her parents with all that going on. Or maybe she could have, but she didn't want to. She turned down her university place, got a job in a care home in their village, and either got used to working or forgot about studying or something in between. By the time she met my dad eight years later, both of them drunk and dressed up at a wedding in Inverness, her family's wounds had started to heal. She moved down here to be with him, got a new job, had the three of us. She's never mentioned the other life that was almost hers; I had no idea she was even interested in geography until my gran brought it up.

Maybe that's why she's so focused on Jake getting where he wants to be: because she couldn't.

"I can get a job," I say. I'll be sixteen in a few weeks, old enough to work in a supermarket or a cafe or something. "I'll start applying after my birthday."

Mam swallows. She's working out how to tell me yes, without making it sound like my future doesn't matter as much as my brother's. I realize with surprise that I'm not mad about that. I want to help. And besides, I'm used to it by now.

"Well . . . if you want to, Brody." She lets out a long breath. "Just the weekends, though. And only a few hours, okay? You've got exams, too, mind."

"Aye, I know."

Jake throws his hands up. "You're seriously telling me it's all right for *him* to get a job and not me? He needs the study time more than I do!"

"Oh, cheers," I mutter.

"It's true, though, Brody," Keira says. "Your spelling's even worse than mine."

I glower at her. "A few hours is no' gonnae make any difference," I tell Mam. "I'll try the supermarkets. They're always looking for folk."

She looks relieved. Relieved, and also sad. "Thank you, darling." She puts her hands on my ears and kisses the top of my head, holding her face against my hair for a long moment. When she stands back up, her eyes are shiny. "That'll be a big help. Won't it, Rob?"

Over on the TV, the umbrella stand has sold for a hundred and twenty quid. Its owners are disappointed. Mam shouts Dad's name again. After a pause, he glances over his shoulder.

"Uh, aye. Good lad, Brody."

He spins around and flicks onto the next channel. Out of nowhere, this blast of anger hits me, the kind I haven't felt since we had to move when I was eleven. It's so bad that I have to get up and go into the kitchen, just to get away from him. Mam's trying to talk to us about something, and all he can do is sit there and watch *Antiques Roadshow*. Pathetic.

Mam hisses something at him while I'm filling the kettle. There's a long sigh, then Dad calls out again: "Thanks, son. Really."

I don't want a thank-you. And I don't expect him to stroll out of the flat and get a job in five minutes, either. I know this is a real problem; I know there's no magical fix. I just want him to try. Not to settle for this half-life filled with hours and hours of other people's adventures. Just to try.

THIRTEEN

MY BIRTHDAY TURNS OUT A LOT BETTER THAN I EXPECTED. MAM
buys a chocolate cake from Asda, and she and Dad get me a
book about the world's best drummers as a present. Jake gives
me a Joy Division T-shirt, which is actually pretty cool, and
Keira buys me a huge multipack of lollies, only two of which
she eats herself. (It's an improvement on last year's present: a
Broadway Hits CD from the pound shop that's lived in her bedroom ever since.)

My best gift comes from Megan, who makes me an amazing pop-up card: It's got drawings of all our favorite *Drag Race*
queens all over the front, and when I open it, a cardboard RuPaul
springs up and confetti falls out. The janitor is in a crappy Monday mood and forces us to pick every last bit up off the corridor
floor, making us both late for English, but it's worth it. All in all,

it's a good day. Not exactly the kind of radge sixteenth birthday party you see in American films. Just nice.

By the time I get to Calton Hill three days later, I've forgotten all about it. But as soon as I reach the monument, Nico and the others burst into a rendition of "Happy Birthday." Zahra is holding an enormous cake with burning blue candles on the top, and Kasia looks surprisingly enthusiastic as she waves sparklers around.

"There he is!" Nico pulls me into a hug and kisses my cheek. "Happy birthday, mister."

I can't believe he remembered—I only mentioned it in passing. "You didnae have to do all this," I stammer.

"Of course we did. This is your Everland birthday! You get two now, like the queen." Nico ruffles my hair. "Come on—everyone'll be waiting."

Beyond the door, the moon is so low and full that it casts pale gray shadows over the grass. When we cross the bridge, we find ourselves in a sort of clearing, lit by old-fashioned lanterns hanging from the branches of trees. Esther and the band are there, and Miyumi and Dani and a few of their friends. They start singing "Happy Birthday" again, this time in a mix of languages and keys. It's mortifying—I have to shove on the dragon mask I made over the weekend to hide my scarlet cheeks—but pretty nice, too.

Zahra holds the cake up toward me. "Make a wish!"

I lean in to blow out the candles, but I don't wish for anything. Right now, I can't think of anything else I could want.

Nobody's got a knife, so we have to dig into the cake with our hands. Someone appears with tea and lemonade, and Dani finds an assortment of jam jars from a nearby cottage for us to use as cups. Nico moans that we don't have any champagne, but nobody knows where to find some. Being in Everland is a bit like being tipsy, anyway—drinking on top of that might not be the best idea.

Once we've finished, I play a set with the band. Esther tells me to choose the first song, so I pick "Born to Hand Jive" from *Grease*. Keira's theater group is doing it next term—she's been playing the soundtrack nonstop to get ready for auditions, and it's got a great drum part. The others stick around to watch us play, and afterward, we end up wandering to the market, talking to the vendors and sampling tiny sugared biscuits and sweet honey cakes.

As far as birthdays go, it's pretty perfect.

Still, a tiny part of me wishes I had Nico to myself. Just for a wee while.

As soon as I think that, everyone suddenly disperses: Dani decides to find some of his friends, Kasia heads to the library, Zahra and Miyumi to the gardens. Nico and I end up walking through a stretch of wild woodland, scrambling over thick briar and tangles of strange orange and purple plants. It takes us a while: Nico's dressed as a phoenix, a red-and-gold headpiece and trailing veil of flame-colored feathers, and his costume keeps getting snagged on the branches.

"Thanks so much for tonight," I tell him again. "The cake and everything . . . You really didnae have to."

"We wanted to, Brody." He lifts up his trail of feathers and clambers over the knotted roots of an oak tree. "How was your actual birthday, anyway?"

"Uh, it was all right." I hold back a low-hanging branch to help him past. "My parents are a bit tight for money right now, so, like, nothing major. It was fine, though."

I don't know why I told him that. It's not like I wasn't happy with what they got me. My birthdays are always quiet—I don't like the fuss—and other than a drum kit and a phone that doesn't look like an antique, there's not much I'd really want anyway. I just wanted to talk to him about it, I guess.

He looks at me for a long moment, his eyebrows raised. I can tell that Nico's family doesn't have these issues. It's in the way he dresses, the type of phone he has, the way he spends money. Things he's never even thought about.

"Well, I'm glad it was okay," he says hesitantly. He looks like he's searching for something else to say, to move us away from the money topic. He taps the dragon mask, now balanced on the top of my head. "You know, you should think about going to art school. Seriously. Try for costume design; I bet you'd get in."

"Hardly. I just copied it off the internet; it took me about twelve goes to get it right. Besides, I cannae sew."

He fakes a gasp. "Brody, you can't go on *Drag Race* if you don't know how to sew."

"I've got no intention of going on *Drag Race*, dummy. Or to art school."

"I mean it, though. You could do it, if you wanted to. Or music school! Become a drummer."

"Maybe." I have thought about going to college, but I'm not sure I'm cut out for more education: I like *playing* the drums, not writing essays about them. Besides, I can't imagine my parents would be over the moon at the idea—not exactly the best job prospects. Dreams are for people like Jake and Nico. I need something more realistic.

"Well, think about it." He turns around and grabs my arm. "Oh my God—look!"

Bobbing on the river at the end of the forest, its mast peeking out above the tops of the trees, is a ship. Nico breaks into a run, dodging through the remaining trees. I jog after him, then stop in my tracks when the boat comes into view.

I once went on a school trip to the *QE2*, that massive boat the Royal Family used to take on their holidays. It was all right, but this . . . *this* is a proper *Peter Pan* situation. A real, actual pirate ship. There's a wooden steering wheel on the upper deck, lines of sturdy canons on either side, complicated ropes and sails hanging from each of the three masts—even a Jolly Roger and a plank for wayward sailors to walk. It's obviously seen some drama, too: There are two huge holes near the stern, as if cannonballs have ripped right through it, and there's a dark stain on one of the sails that looks like it could be old, dried blood.

"This is unbelievable!" Nico scrambles up the ladder, landing on the deck with a bump. "Do you think it's legit?"

I clamber up after him, almost falling into another hole where a cannonball seems to have bitten into the deck. It definitely looks like the real deal. All that's missing are Captain Hook, Smee, and a ticking crocodile.

Nico begins scaling the central mast toward the crow's nest. My heart in my mouth—I'm not good with heights—I follow him up the ladder and onto the narrow platform. He leans against the wooden barrier and lets out a low whistle.

"Man, I wish my phone worked in here so I could take a photo of all this. Can you imagine the likes on Instagram?"

I grip the mast, trying to ignore the wobbling feeling in my legs, and focus on the view. It is beautiful. From up here, you can see the length of the river winding through the valley; a silvery mist hanging over the forest; the full moon tucked into a nook between the mountains.

"How long do you think it goes on for?" I ask.

"Dunno. Maybe Everland is like space. Just stretching on and on and on forever."

I feel dizzy with the scope of it all, or maybe just with the fact we're thirty-odd feet above the deck. I wonder how the ship got in here—there's no way you could squeeze something this big through one of the doors. Maybe there really are pirates some-where in here, just like in Neverland. Anything seems possible on this side of the green door.

"We should fix this thing up." Nico stretches the Jolly Roger out; the fabric has frayed so badly, it's eaten into part of the skull. "We could sail it out—find out what's at the other end of the ocean. Maybe there's a whole other world out there."

I lean against the mast. "It's so far, though. What if the door closed before we go back? Or what if we got lost?"

"We'd just stay in here, then, wouldn't we?" A gust of wind whips around us, making the tattered flag ripple. "We could be pirates!"

"No school," I say. "No having to worry about jobs or money."

"We'd never grow up," Nico says. "We'd never die."

The tiniest hint of an idea sparks: I *could* stay in here. I could stay in here like Esther did. I wouldn't need to worry about what I'm going to do with my life—*this* would be my life.

But then the tug begins, that feeling that tells me it's time to head back, and the idea is snuffed out. Nico lets out a long breath. It's time to go. He feels it, too.

"Maybe one day," he says with a smile. "Come on. Time to get back to reality."

FOURTEEN

DECEMBER'S USUALLY MY FAVORITE MONTH. NOT BECAUSE OF Christmas itself. I just like the way the city looks: all frosty nights and shimmering lights. I like all the cheesy music and the look of that German-style market up in town, even if it is too busy and way too overpriced to actually buy anything. I like the idea of the year coming to an end, too. Always the chance that the next one will be better.

Can't imagine that'll be the case this year. Right now, everything is a bit crap. I apply for a bunch of part-time jobs—a few more supermarkets, some cafes and restaurants, and this amazing record shop called Rusty Records (on the off chance they can afford more than one employee)—but nobody gets back to me. Jake spends the run-up to his Cambridge interview stressing about his presentation, then comes back stressing that he messed it up. Mam's tired and snappy, and Dad's pretend-to-be-oblivious-to-everything-that's-going-on act is starting to get really old. Even Tink's grumpier than usual, and Megan's not herself, either. She's weirdly quiet, and there are bags under her eyes that not even multiple layers of her beloved Touche Éclat can cover up.

"Are you all right, Meg?"

We're sitting at our usual table in the canteen, surrounded by chattering sophomore girls. Apparently Rhona Lewis loudly broke up with Toby Harris in the middle of Biology this morning. Megan loves gossip, but she doesn't even seem to be listening.

"I'm fine." She pushes her barely touched portion of lasagna away. "Do you want the rest of this? I can't eat it."

"You've hardly eaten anything, though."

She shrugs.

"Go on, then," I say. "If you're sure."

I slide it onto my plate beside my tuna-mayo baguette. I'm starving: Keira finished the last of the bread this morning, there was nothing else for breakfast, and after our talk I didn't want to ask Mam for money to get something on my way to school. "Is your dad away again?" I ask.

Megan leans back, twirling a lock of hair around her finger. "Yeah. Moscow this time."

Sometimes, when I've had to wait what feels like five hours for Keira to get out of the bathroom or for Jake to get off the computer, I get jealous of Megan having her house to herself so much. But it seems a bit lonely, too, especially as Harry's out a lot. I can't imagine eating all those meals alone. Having nobody to say good night to.

"Can I come over tonight, then?" I realize, with a pinch of guilt, that it's been a few weeks since we hung out at her house. In fact, not since the night she did my makeup.

Megan's eyes brighten. "Yeah, definitely. There are, like, six new shows you need to catch up on." She leans toward me, her voice picking up into its normal tone. "You still haven't told me when I'm gonna meet Nico, by the way."

"Soon," I say. "Probably."

"When's soon? This week? This month? You've been seeing him for ages now!" She leans closer, her long hair almost sliding into the lasagna. "Have you slept with him yet?"

The sophomore girls are still at the other end of the table. I take a sideways glance at them, but they're lost in their conversation and don't look up.

"I told you, it's not gonnae happen," I say. Quietly. Begrudgingly. Because it's not like I haven't thought about that. Honestly, I think about it every few minutes. That's maybe a bit wrong. He's my mate, and he has a sort-of boyfriend—I probably shouldn't be picturing him naked quite so much. I can't help it, though.

"Why not? You waiting till you're married or something?"

I scowl at her. "Gonnae keep your voice down?"

Nobody's listening, but my pulse starts thumping in my throat all the same. Coming out isn't always a trauma at my

127

school, but it can be. Nobody batted an eyelid when Piotr Lisowski did it, but Thomas McInally got beaten up after somebody found out he had a boyfriend in East Kilbride. People hardly even mention that Louisa Walsh in junior year is gay, but when she started going out with Millie Yung, everyone said Millie was faking being bi for attention. (People still say that, and they've been together *two years*.) It depends on who you are. How much people like you. If that's not very much, it's just another weapon in their arsenal.

I know I wouldn't get a good reaction. Leanne and Michelle have taken the piss out of me for the stupidest stuff: getting 2/20 in English, getting 18/20 in English, laughing too loud, talking too quietly, wearing the same T-shirt to PE three weeks in a row. They might have guessed that I'm gay—judging by some of the jokes they've made, they definitely suspect it—but my actual coming out would be like an early Christmas present for them. It'd be like being transported into that crappy educational video about homophobia from the 1990s they showed us in Social Ed: broken noses and spray-painted lockers, hallways full of people pointing and laughing in slow motion. Only worse, because now we have the internet, too.

"Okay, okay—sorry." Megan rolls her eyes, like I'm overreacting.

I feel a stab of irritation. She just doesn't get it. Megan's pretty and popular and confident; she gets cute boys, good grades, and invitations to all the best parties. She doesn't know what it's like to feel like you don't fit in.

That's one of the things I like most about hanging out at Everland: My friends there do. I stab my fork into the soggy lasagna, sinking back into silence. Everland is only a couple of days away, but at times like this, the distance is almost unbearable.

"What do you think—hummingbirds or toucans?"

It's Thursday, and I'm at one of the Everland markets with Zahra, searching for presents. Her family is Muslim and doesn't really celebrate Christmas, but she's looking for some little gifts to take to her cousins down in England. Nico was supposed to come with us, too, but when we got through the green door, he said he had to talk to Dani about something. I felt this weird tension between them: Dani was all fidgety and nervous when he met us at the bridge, and Nico's smile didn't quite reach his eyes.

"Brody?" Zahra holds up two pairs of earrings and shoggles them in front of my face. "Help, I can't decide."

"Toucans," I say. "Got more personality."

"You're right. Two toucans, please."

She rifles in the pocket of her Russian ice-skating jacket (tonight, she's cosplaying Victor Nikiforov from *Yuri on Ice*) for some coins to give to the seller. This market isn't like the ones I've been to with Nico. It's large but calm, full of artisans quietly working on crafts behind stalls packed high with all sorts of trinkets: Russian matryoshkas and Japanese beckoning cats; snow globes and teapots; necklaces and bracelets made from blue and green sea glass, all strung like algae over pieces of driftwood. I'm guessing some people come here for more time to work on their craft, but others seem to have set up shop years ago. One guy has a newspaper called *O Globo* tossed to the side of his bench, as if set aside to read later. It looks brand-new, but the date on the front page says 1986.

Zahra rushes toward a stall selling bright embroidered blankets and cushions. The table is covered with piles of tiny hand-woven people not much bigger than my thumbnail. She picks one up, lifting it higher to see it better in the light cast by the lantern hanging from the roof of the hut.

"Worry dolls! You know these? You put them under your pillow to take your troubles away. From Guatemala, I think. Maybe I'll get some for my cousin Salima. She's doing a PhD; she's constantly stressed."

"My brother could do with some of those, too." I clear my throat, trying to think of a way to frame my question without sounding totally nosy. "Eh, speaking of trouble . . . what's up with Nico and Dani?"

Zahra glances at me while she counts out her coins.

"No idea. Relationships are always complicated in here. Especially with people from different places—makes it harder to bridge the gap between Everland and the outside world, you know?"

"Right." I remember what Nico told me that day we went sketching. "Well, I hope they sort it out."

Zahra gives me a knowing smile. "Do you?"

"Aye, course I do." My cheeks start burning. "Why?"

"Come on, Brody. You're not the most subtle," she says, grinning. "I mean, I get it. Nico's very charming."

Something in her voice tells me she's not finished. "But?"

"But . . ." She smiles at the seller sitting behind the stall and pockets the worry dolls. "He's complicated."

"How d'you mean?"

Zahra presses her lips together. "I mean, he has his issues. I'm pretty sure everybody in here does. Just don't put him on too much of a pedestal, you know?"

I want to ask what she means, but Zahra quickly moves on to a stall trading telescopes and binoculars and other types of optical instruments. She pays a few pounds for a tiny golden kaleidoscope, then trades some pens for three clay egg cups. Payment is a bit of a free-for-all here. Some people have set out tins or jars full of coins—maybe collecting for when they go back to the real world, though there's so many different currencies mixed together, I don't know how useful that'd be. Others are trading for different items, or even giving things away for free.

While Zahra's looking at colorful glass bottles filled with tiny village scenes, the stall owner, a gray-haired man with pocked skin and a couple of teeth missing, holds one out to me. I shake my head.

"Sorry, I've no' got anything on me."

The man smiles. "I have a lifetime's worth of work here," he says, in an Eastern European accent. "I will never sell them all. Please, take one."

He pushes it into my hand: a long, thin bottle with a miniscule model village inside. Tiny people walk down a tiny street of thatched cottages; a miniature streetlamp glows at one end, casting a yellowish glow on the snowy ground. It's amazingly detailed—a little world trapped inside the glass. I thank the man, wishing I had something to give him in exchange. There's nothing in my pockets except my phone and Jake's bus pass.

By the time we've looped around the whole market, I've picked up enough freebies to cover all my Christmas shopping: a bright pink purse decorated with tiny mirrors for Keira; a sculpture of a typewriter made from yellowing book pages for Jake; and for Mam, a little pocket watch encased in a bronze locket decorated with a sparrow on one side. I'm tempted to keep the village in a bottle for myself, but I'll give it to Dad. Seems like the sort of thing he'd like.

I don't know how long we shop for, but eventually the market slides behind us, and we arrive in a wide field where yellow-tipped grass reaches past our knees. There are mountains to the north and east, a waterfall in the distance. Silence all around. It's funny how Everland changes depending on who I'm with. When I'm with Nico, we always end up in crowds, at parties or celebrations or festivals. With Zahra, there's always so much space. When I mention this, she smiles.

"That's what I love about this place. The freedom."

Farther ahead, two deer are lazing under a cherry tree. Zahra pauses for a moment, watching them.

"I haven't told you about my mum, have I?"

I shake my head. "No?"

Zahra takes a deep breath: The air tonight is crisp and smells of pine and woodsmoke. "She has MS—multiple sclerosis. My dad works abroad, and now that my sisters have moved out, I'm sometimes the only one around to look after her. I get a lot of help from our neighbors and our community, but still. It's a lot of pressure."

"Wow. I bet," I mumble. I've had to look after dad a couple of times, when he's had panic attacks and that. But that's not the same as being an actual caretaker.

Zahra runs her fingers across the top of the long grass. "I found this place after one of Mum's bad episodes. She'd fallen in the kitchen and hit her head, and I had to call an ambulance. My dad was in Texas for work, so it was the first time I'd had to do that by myself, and it was . . . pretty overwhelming. She was okay, but they kept her in overnight just in case, so one of my aunties came to get me and took me back to her house for the evening. I couldn't sleep, so I went for a walk and somehow ended up on Calton Hill. I noticed Nico and Kasia by the monument, saw the door appear, then followed them in. I've been here every week since. I felt bad about it at first, but it's not like I'm doing anything wrong. Our flat is only a four-minute walk away, so I'm never gone long."

"I had no idea," I say quietly. "I'm sorry, Zahr."

She smiles. "Thanks. I'm okay—this place gives me the space I need. I think I might have gone a bit off the rails without it."

We walk in silence for a while, watching the deer graze.

I didn't know about any of this, just like I didn't know about Dani's story. It makes me even more grateful for Everland: that so many people can find what they need here.

Some time later, we arrive back where we originally set off from—a wide square dotted here and there with palm trees, and a red door with a silver moon tucked between rustic white buildings. Miyumi is sitting cross-legged under one of the trees reading a book, and Esther and the band are setting up to play on the other side of the square. Just seeing it makes my chest swell with contentment. I don't care about Kasia's theory that you're supposed to find this place yourself. This is where I belong.

I turn to Zahra, about to ask her to keep hold of my gifts while I play. Then I hesitate.

"I cannae actually give my family any of this," I say. "It all looks too expensive. They'll wonder where I got the money to pay for it."

It's only once I've said it out loud that I realize it's true. Mam already thinks I'm some sort of junkie—don't want her to add theft to my supposed life of crime. To my surprise, a lump rises in my throat. I would have liked to give her and Dad something nice for Christmas. Especially with all the crap they're going through at the moment.

"You could say you made them," Zahra suggests. "I've seen your masks. They're well good."

"Bit of a jump from that to this," I say, holding up the bottle.

"Well, hang on to them anyway. Maybe you can give them as

134

gifts another time." She holds out her arms, and I gently place the presents in her hands. "Things won't always be like this, Brody."

I nod, but it's not until I'm halfway across the square that I realize I don't know what she means: life, or Everland, or both.

FIFTEEN

WHEN I GET HOME FROM SCHOOL THE FOLLOWING THURSDAY, OUR living room is being torn apart by Hurricane Keira. I've seen my sister pull some Category Five tantrums before, but this is a whole new level: Her face is streaked with black mascara tears, and her screams are so hysterical, I can't make out a word of what she's saying. This is way past the point where either Mam or Dad usually loses their rag and starts yelling back at her, but tonight both of their faces are stony. Dad's eyes are firmly on the TV, and Mam keeps shaking her head and saying she's sorry.

". . . no choice," I hear her say, when Keira eventually pauses to take a breath. "I wouldn't do it unless—"

Mam takes a step forward, her arms outstretched in the offer of a hug, but Keira bats her hands away. Her blue eyes are icy with anger. Even Jake has stopped typing to watch. He usually treats Keira like an annoying puppy, but right now he looks almost sorry for her.

"I hate you," Keira says, her voice bubbling up. "I *hate* you."

She storms off to her room, slamming the door so hard the walls shake. Mrs. McAskill instantly starts banging on the ceiling; Jake stamps his foot on the carpet in reply. Mam sinks onto the sofa, her head in her hands. After a moment, Dad reaches over and squeezes her knee.

"She'll come around, Sal. Give it two weeks—she'll have found some new hobby and forgotten all about it."

"No, she won't. She loves those classes."

She rubs her eyes and pinches the bridge of her nose, clearly trying to fight back one of her headaches. I look at her, and it's one of those weird moments when you realize that you've seen someone every day for months but haven't really seen them at all. She looks different. Older. There are flyaway gray hairs framing her face that weren't there before, and the lines around her mouth have deepened. When she looks up and sees me standing by the door, her face freezes.

"Brody—when did you get home?"

"Uh, just now. What's going on?"

She takes a long breath, steeling herself for something. Dad folds his arms, his attention fixed on the TV again. I look at Jake, but he's already gone back to his essay. Mam nods toward the table.

"Sit down, love."

I sink into the nearest seat, letting my school bag drop to the carpet. This is starting to feel . . . oddly familiar. Mam takes the seat beside mine and leans forward, her elbows on the table, a worried expression on her face. She's always been good at hiding how she feels about stuff. Like when Dad was in hospital. Like the past few years, with his agoraphobia getting worse and worse. Maybe it's because we're older now that she feels she can finally be honest about what's going on. Or maybe it's because things are getting too bad for her to hide anymore.

The thought scares me a bit.

"Mind I told you that we'd need to cut back a bit, until we get this issue with Dad's benefits sorted out?" she says. "Well, we can't really afford Keira's musical theater classes right now."

"Oh. Right."

That explains the dramatics. Keira lives for that class. She's good at it, too. We went to see their production of *Annie* last term. Keira played Duffy, one of the orphans, and she was brilliant—totally over-the-top but really funny. She redid the whole thing as a one-woman show in the living room for Dad afterward. She knew every single line—her Miss Hannigan was better than the film version, if you ask me.

"It's just so expensive, and we've got other things to worry about." Mam's gaze drops to the table. She scratches at a bit of dried ketchup on the wood. "I know it's hard, but we all need to make some sacrifices."

"Just give her some time." As usual, my sister is acting like a total diva, and a bit of a brat, but she's a good kid deep down. Her temper never lasts long. "She'll be fine."

Mam keeps scratching at the ketchup. There's a long pause.

I swear Jake's typing gets faster and louder, like he's trying to fill the silence. Eventually, Mam sighs and looks up at me.

"Brody . . . I think we need to find a new home for Tink, love."

For a second, I don't get what she means. Like a moron, I actually think she means we're all going to have to move flats again. When I realize what she's actually saying, my jaw drops.

"What? Mam, no! Why?"

She wrings her hangs together. "We're not even supposed to have pets in this flat, Brodes. We should really have given him away before we moved in here, but you were so attached to him, and you were only eleven . . . I couldn't bring myself to do it."

"So, what? That makes it okay that you're doing it now? I've had him long enough, is that it?"

Dad turns the volume on the TV up. Jake's shoulders twitch, but he doesn't look away from his essay. Mam shakes her head.

"I'm sorry, Brody. I really am. We'll keep him until the new year, but after that, he'll have to go."

"But I told you I'll get a job. I've applied for tons of stuff," I say. It's true—I haven't had a single reply yet, but I'll keep trying. "I can pay for his food with the money from that."

"Food's not really the issue. Tink's getting old. What if he needs an operation or medicine, something like that? Besides, we can't risk being made to leave this flat for a pet."

We've had a handful of inspections since we moved in here. Each time, we left Tink with Keira's friend Amanda upstairs, hoovered up the cat hairs, and hid his bowl and litter tray under the sink. The guy from the letting agency barely stayed five minutes, let alone long enough to go hunting for evidence of animal contraband. I remind Mam of all this, but she just keeps shaking her head.

"Brody, this is serious. I've asked and asked, but I'm just not getting the hours at work that I need. I've had to go to the food bank twice. The only reason we had anything to eat last night is because Mrs. Adebayo upstairs brought us some of her curry."

Her voice wobbles, and something inside me with it. I knew things were bad, but not that bad.

"What the hell are we going to do if the landlord chucks us out for breaking his rules?" Mam asks. "We've got no chance of finding anything cheaper around here, and it'd be years before we could get a council house. I'm sorry, but Tink is a luxury that we just can't afford right now."

"A *luxury*?" I can't even look at her. There's too much whirling around my head. I stand up and snatch my bag off the floor. "This is bloody ridiculous."

Finally, Dad decides to chime in. "Don't talk to your mother like that. She's doing her best."

That's all he says. He shuffles on the sofa and goes back to his TV show, like all this has nothing to do with him. And for a second, I hate him for it. I know that's unfair. I know it's a disease, that he's sick, that he can't help it, but lately it feels like he's not even trying to get better. That he'd rather sink into his documentaries—get swept up in true-crime stories or deep-sea explorations—than take any interest in what's going on around him.

"Fine," I say. "Give him away. Do what you like."

Following Keira's lead, I go to my room and slam the door like I haven't since I was about eight. Tink is stretched out on the square of sun pouring in from the window, his ginger fur fiery in the afternoon light. I flop down on the carpet beside him. Anger is throbbing at my throat, my chest, my wrists. This is the worst thing they could have taken away from me.

Well, no—Everland is. But Tink is a close second.

"This is bullshit," I tell him. "Fucking bullshit."

I stroke his back, but he's not in the mood. He gives an angry yelp and makes for the door, scratching at the wood until I open it and let him into the living room. That's not unusual; he's always in a bad mood. But today, it actually hurts.

It's not even four o'clock yet, but I'm too pissed off to stay in. I get changed and head out before supper, ignoring Mam when she asks me where I'm going. I wander through the streets for a while, kicking at stones and litter on the pavement. Mam's words echo in my head, with all the arguments I could have made to keep Tink coming to me too late. After a while, I text Nico and ask if he's about. He calls me back. Nico's the only person I know under forty who prefers to call rather than text.

"Brody! I was just thinking about you."

Hearing his voice makes mine choke up. I don't know why. It's just nice to listen to him talk, even if I can't get any words out in response. Nico says my name a few times, but I can't answer.

"Where are you?" he asks. "Come to mine. I'll text you the address."

* * *

It takes me half an hour to walk up to New Town. Nico answers the door wearing Adidas trousers and a paint-stained white T-shirt. Before he says anything, he gives me a hug. I let my hands linger around him just a beat too long, my face pressed against his shoulder, his hand rubbing my back.

"This is a surprise, Brody," he says gently. "What's wrong?"

"I'm fine. It's just . . ."

My voice fades out again. I don't know what's wrong with me. Nico's face falls, but he doesn't ask any more questions. He moves aside to let me in.

"Come up. My dad and Jenny are still at work; they won't be back for ages."

I shuffle in and kick my shoes off. Their flat is like something off *Grand Designs*: shiny wooden floorboards, high ceilings with those carved wooden edges, a skylight. Nico grabs two Diet Cokes from the kitchen—the fridge alone is about the size of Keira's bedroom—then leads me upstairs. There are two paintings on the walls—a still life and a seascape of the Firth of Forth—but no family photos.

"Sorry about my room. I'm finishing up a piece for my portfolio." Nico nudges a door at the end of the corridor open with his foot. "So it's a bit of a mess."

It's not what I'd expected. I'd pictured Nico's bedroom to have cobalt-blue walls, clothes and costumes scattered all across the floor, an entire wall covered in sketches and pages cut from fashion magazines. It's nothing like that. There are pencils, paints, and sketchbooks on the desk, but the only drawings and photos are contained within a white-framed pinboard. His wings are propped up by the wardrobe, and there's some pale gold material spread across the bed, but not the piles of costumes I'd expected. The walls are cream, the blinds beige, the duvet and carpet different shades of gray. It doesn't feel like Nico at all.

"I know what you're thinking." He pushes the fabric aside and flops onto the bed, sending roses falling to the carpet. "It looks like a three-star hotel. All that's missing is a mini kettle and two packs of shortbread on my desk."

"At least it's big." It's *massive*—almost twice the size of the room I share with Jake. You could practically fit our whole flat in here. The garden outside is double the size of the courtyard by Mackay House, too. "And . . . eh . . . the view's no' bad."

Nico gives a short laugh. "I hate this room. I painted it purple when I was fifteen, but I went to visit my mum for a few weeks in the summer, and when I came back, Jenny had done it up like this. *More mature*, she said. *More appropriate*. I thought about changing it back, but she'd just do it all over again." He stretches his arms out over his head. "I can't wait to go to art school. My room's gonna look like Matisse and Miró had a paint fight in it."

I sit down on the bed beside him. "Where are you applying again?"

"A few different places: London, Paris, Barcelona, Berlin. London's my first choice."

It stings that he's not even considering the art schools here in Edinburgh, but I nod and listen to him ramble about the different courses. His voice changes when he's talking about it. It's not like the way Jake talks about Cambridge, when his pitch gets higher, and his words get faster. Nico sounds way more relaxed, as if he knows it's a home he hasn't found yet. It makes me feel a bit uneasy. It must show on my face, because he smiles and taps the back of his hand against my knee.

"I'll still come to Everland, Brodes," he says. "There must be doors in all those cities. I'll find one, and we'll be able to hang out every Thursday, just like we do now."

He sits up and pulls the gold material toward him. It's a sort of cloak, with long sleeves and a hood embroidered with delicate floral patterns. "Hey, do you mind giving me a hand with this? I've got about a hundred roses still to attach, and the deadline's next week."

Turns out, he's not exaggerating. He goes to his desk and comes back with a whole box full of roses, all made from gold satin. I can't sew to save myself, but he's marked little dots around the hem of the cloak where they need to be attached, so it's not too difficult. It's pretty relaxing, actually. Nico puts some music on, and we sit in a comfortable silence for a little while, stitching and watching his creation take shape.

"Are you gonna wear this to Everland tonight?" I ask.

"Nah, have to take photos of it for my portfolio first." He ties a knot in his thread and looks up. "I need to go to Kasia's and help her finish her costume before we head up there. Do you want to come with me? She lives off Leith Walk—you know, the flat where we first met."

My heart gives a pang thinking about that day. Tink hiding underneath the wheels of the car; the way he sat in the crook of Nico's arms as he carried him across the courtyard.

"Do you think she'd mind?" I ask. "She's no' gonnae chuck me out like she tries to push me out of Everland every week, is she?"

Nico laughs.

"Oh, come on. Kasia likes you fine. She's just obsessed with these rules that she's invented." He grins and flicks a rose at me. "It'll be fun. I'll get us a pizza or something. That way you won't have to suffer through the hell that is dinner with my dad and Jenny."

"They cannae be *that* bad."

Nico gestures around him. "Brody, look at this room. You think anyone with even a modicum of personality would choose this?"

"All right, then," I laugh. "I'll come to Kasia's."

"Cool." He smiles and takes another rose from the box. He turns it in his fingers for a moment, then glances up at me. "So . . . Do you want to talk about what's up?"

I swallow.

"It's nothing. Just, uh . . . My mam's giving the cat away."

I try to make the story sound funny, like I'm not that bothered. I make a joke out of the way I reacted. Nico laughs in the right places, but his eyes are all soft and sad. He actually looks slightly heartbroken.

"God, Brody," he says, once I'm finished. "That really sucks."

"Aye, it does." My throat's gone all tight again. There's pressure building behind my eyes. As I reach for another rose, Nico touches the tips of his fingers to mine.

"I'd take him here if I could, but Jenny'd actually murder me. She'd probably murder Tink, too—I wouldn't put it past her, to be honest."

"Thanks. I know." I bite my lip. "It's no' just that . . . I dunno."

He waits, quietly stitching as I work out my words. I'm not good at this. Not good at saying how I feel, or even really thinking about it properly. I stare at the wings by the wardrobe, letting the different shades of blue grow hazy in my eyes.

"I'm just a bit sick of everything," I say finally. "I'm sick of feeling second best to my brother, and people walking all over me, and nobody ever listening. I'm sick of those girls at school taking the piss, and I'm sick of feeling shit about myself because I *let* them take the piss. I'm sick of being treated like a kid—I know my mam wouldnae say we have to get rid of the cat if she didn't have to, and I know it's no' their fault they've got no money. But it's the fact they just made that decision for me without even asking me what I thought. Everything in my life feels like it's out of my hands. I've got no say over anything, no control over anything. School's a mess; I doubt I'll pass any of my exams; I don't know what I'm gonnae do afterward. Seeing you at Everland is the only thing that keeps me going, but there's a whole week between each visit, and it's getting harder and harder to get through it."

By my standards, that's like a dramatic monologue. When I

look over, Nico has sat up and is staring at me. My cheeks start to burn.

"Sorry." I pick up the needle again and begin to attach another rose. "That was stupid."

"No, it wasn't," Nico says quietly. "I get it, Brody. Seriously. All of us in Everland have felt like that at some point. I feel like that all the time."

I find that hard to imagine. Nico's so himself, so comfortable in his own skin. Then again, he's obviously not comfortable in this room, in this house. That can't be easy, either.

He shuffles across the bed to sit beside me and pulls me into another hug, his skinny arms holding me close. Despite all the anger and frustration of this afternoon, my stomach fills with butterflies.

"That feeling you were talking about . . . it's why you found Everland. Even if it was via me. It's why you belong there." He leans back to look at me, smiling, and the tightness in my chest starts to unravel. "The rest of the world doesn't matter. You've got us now. We're a family. No matter what happens next year, I promise that won't change."

SIXTEEN

THAT NIGHT AT EVERLAND FEELS LONGER THAN USUAL: LONG ENOUGH for me to angry-drum my way through five or six sets with Esther and the band; long enough for me and Nico to go exploring until we find an old water park and a street full of china shops. By the time I finally feel the tug to go home, Zahra and Kasia are already long gone. Even Miyumi, who always stays behind after the rest of us, is getting ready to head back.

But at the end of it all, nothing has changed. It's still Thursday. It's not even midnight.

Everybody's awake when I get home. That's no surprise where Dad and Jake are concerned, but Mam's usually in her bed long before now if she's not on night shift. She's sitting at the table going through some papers, but she puts her pen down when she sees me come in.

"There you are."

I'm expecting an instant bollocking and a hundred questions about where I've been all evening, but instead she sounds relieved.

"Put the TV off, Rob, will you?" she says.

A long, slow shot of some tropical rainforest pans across the screen. Dad reaches for the remote, but I tell him not to bother.

"There's no point talking about it." I hang my jacket up and kick off my shoes. "You've obviously made your minds up."

Mam stands up, fiddling with the rings on her left hand. "Listen, love, Jake's had an—"

A small starburst of anger flares up inside me. I don't *care* what Jake thinks. Haven't heard about many "sacrifices" on his part. Still, I force myself to keep my voice steady. My night in Everland may not have changed anything, but it gave me some time to calm down. None of this is my mam's fault. I'm not going to pretend I'm okay with it, but I don't need to make it worse for her.

"Mam, I'm tired," I say. "I'm off to bed."

Instead of going to my room, I go to Keira's. She doesn't answer when I knock, but the light is still on, so I step inside. She's tucked up in bed, her purple duvet pulled over her head. Now her rage has finally died down, she's crying into her pillow.

The throb of pain in my chest takes me by surprise. My sister is loud and obnoxious and bossy and thoughtless, and she loves attention, but she's not one for crocodile tears. If she's still crying, it means she's really upset.

"Hey." I sit on the edge of her bed, gazing at the photos of her friends on her pinboard, the posters of musicals and pop groups on the back of her door. Her room is so small, I can stretch my legs out and touch the wall. "Well, this is shit, isn't it?"

The duvet shuffles. Suddenly, Keira sits up and flings her arms around my neck. I can't even remember the last time we hugged, but I wrap my arms around her and pull her close. She's tiny enough that my elbows almost meet around her waist.

"Here." I reach for Barry, the soft toy bunny she's had since she was two, and nuzzle his face against her cheek. "Tell Barry about it. Barry's a good listener."

"Piss off, Brody," she says, laughing, but she takes the bunny and hugs him against her chest. Under the makeup and the jewelry and the high heels she borrows from her friends, I sometimes forget how young Keira actually is. I think she does, too.

She sits back against the wall, pulling her knees toward her chest. Her eyes are blurry black with mascara. She wipes them on the sleeve of her pajama top.

"This is so unfair. I know they don't have a lot of money, but I love performing. They think it's just some stupid hobby, but I'm *good* at it."

"I know. You're really good." I squeeze her toes, tucked up in striped pink-and-green socks. "I get it, Kei. Honestly."

And I do. Our parents see my drumming the same way— something fun, but far from a priority. Jake's hobbies are a priority because they'll help him get into Cambridge. They'll help him "realize his potential." If I'd had private drumming lessons or my own kit, maybe I could have made something out of it, too. I know my parents can't afford any of that, so I can't be angry with them about it. But it still sucks.

"It'll probably just be for a wee while, till Mam gets more hours at work," I tell Keira. "I bet you'll be able to go back after the summer."

She pulls a face. "But we're doing *Grease* next term. I wanted to be Frenchy."

"There'll be other shows."

"Yeah, but no' this one."

I hold back a sigh. Keira might get to carry on with her classes eventually, but I won't get my cat back. I'm the only one giving something up for good. Me, and Tink himself.

Still, for all she annoys me, Keira and I are in the same boat. Deep down, she probably knows she's got hardly any chance of making it to Broadway or the West End, just like I had to admit a few years ago that there was no chance I'd ever become a professional drummer. We can't all be exceptional, and our family already has one genius. Jake wants to go into politics. In twenty years, he'll probably be living down in London, or in some fancy mansion here in Edinburgh. Keira and I will still be living in places like this, working jobs that barely pay enough to live on, scraping by like our parents always have. Given the way things are going in the world, we might even be worse off.

I lean back, staring up at the magazine posters stuck on Keira's wall. "Anyway, this doesnae have to stop you. Could you no' start a musical theater group at school or something?"

She raises her eyebrows at me. "What—like *Glee*?"

We both grin. Our school isn't exactly a jazz-hands-and-show-tunes sort of place. If anyone tried bursting into song in the canteen, they'd probably get a kick in the baws.

"No—like a school show or something," I say. "You should talk to Miss Patel about it. She loves all that stuff."

Keira sniffs. She wipes Barry over her tearstained face, leaving a black smudge on his nose. "Maybe. Would you join it?"

"Aye, sure. Here, we can do my audition now."

I start singing "Defying Gravity" from *Wicked* (another one of the soundtracks she plays on repeat; I'm pretty sure half of Mackay House knows the words by now), exaggerating just how crap my singing voice is—though, to be honest, I don't have to exaggerate that much. Keira suffers through two lines before covering my mouth with one hand, Barry's ears with the other.

"Never mind, never mind! You can play the drums if you like, though." She rests her chin on her knees. "Sorry about Tink. It's gonnae be weird without him around."

My throat gets tight. I'd been so angry with Mam for saying she was going to get rid of him, I hadn't really stopped to think about what it'll be like when she does. Tink's been in our family for eleven years. I can't remember a time when he wasn't there to slink around my legs, or sit on my lap as I do my homework, or wake me up by rubbing his head against my jaw and meowing for food.

Keira holds her toy bunny out to me. "Do you want tae take Barry tonight, Brodes? It helps."

If Jake had asked me that, I'd tell him to piss off and stop patronizing me. But as it's Keira, and I know she's not taking the mick, I just smile and gently toss it back at her.

"Think I'm a bit old for Barry, Kei. Thanks, though." I ruffle her hair. It was already mussed up, but she scowls and smooths it down. "Get some sleep."

I go to brush my teeth, ignoring Dad's "good night" as I come out of the bathroom, then head to my room. Jake is sitting on my bed, stroking Tink for the first time in about a decade. The lump in my throat swells. The thought of having to say goodbye to that stupid grumpy face, of having to drop him off in some animal shelter where nobody'll know that he likes having his whiskers stroked with a toothbrush or that his favorite food is cheese . . . it shouldn't bother me this much, but it does.

Jake stands up. His hands slide into the pockets of his school trousers.

"I talked to Amir," he says, rolling back on his feet. "They can take Tink after New Year's, if you're okay with that. His mum's been wanting to get a cat for ages, anyway, and they've got a huge garden. That way you can still visit him."

His voice is all slow and steady, like he's been rehearsing what to say. That just pisses me off even more. I can picture him and Mam scheming behind my back, discussing how to manage my reaction as if I'm some temperamental toddler.

"Fine," I say. "They can have him. But I'm hardly gonnae get the bus up to Morningside to go visit a cat."

"You could come with me. I'm there all the time."

"Aye, like that won't be weird." I sit down and scoop Tink up. He wriggles in my arms a bit, but he doesn't jump away. "Besides, wouldnae want to embarrass you in front of your friend."

"What are you talking about? You wouldn't embarrass me," Jake says, but I know it's not true. He's never brought any friends home, and he gets all stiff and awkward when we go to his school for his plays or concerts or awards ceremonies. "For God's sake, Brody, will you just . . . I'm just trying to . . ."

He breaks off, mumbling something under his breath, then throws up his hands and goes back to the computer. He doesn't get it. He never has. His life is on one track, and mine and Keira's are on another. As the years have gone by, they've overlapped less and less.

Soon, they're barely going to touch at all.

SEVENTEEN

AROUND CHRISTMAS, REAL LIFE GETS IN THE WAY OF OUR TRIPS TO Everland: Nico's going to his mum's in Spain for the holidays, Zahra to visit her cousins in Birmingham and London, and Miyumi to perform in Saint Petersburg, so they won't make it there for a couple of weeks. We decide to throw a winter party on the last Thursday before they leave—or rather, Nico decides, Zahra and I agree, and Kasia reluctantly promises to make an appearance.

When we walk through the door that Thursday, it's like falling forward six months: The sky is bright blue, and the air is so warm that I have to peel off the arctic fox mask I made over the weekend. But as soon as we cross the bridge, this time into a wide square with a decorative fountain of carved stone fish, it starts to snow.

It's never snowed in Everland before, or at least not when I've visited. The flakes are bigger than I've ever seen—perfect white circles the size of bottle caps, spinning in quick spirals toward the ground. Nico takes a step forward, beneath one of the streetlamps, and holds his palms up. He's dressed up as one of the three wise men, though to me he's more like a young Dumbledore: a long, wine-red cloak embroidered with stars, moons, and suns, and a bushy brown beard, which he has to keep pulling down to talk. It looks like a movie scene: Harry Potter meets Narnia meets *Miracle on 34th Street*.

"Snow," he says, beaming. "This is actual snow!"

It's only been a few seconds, but already a thick, white blanket is covering the square. I haven't seen anything like this since one Christmas at my grandparents' when I was wee. And in the city, any snow we get mostly just turns to grayish slush pretty fast.

None of us are really dressed for winter weather; Dani's even come from South American summer in shorts and a T-shirt. But somehow, the snow here doesn't bite into your skin and leave you shivering like it does in the outside world. It just feels sort of tingly, a bit like pins and needles. When Miyumi appears around the corner, her face lights up.

"*Yuki!*" She squeals with joy. "Snowball fight!"

She drops her violin case—Dani and Zahra let out synchronized gasps, but the snowdrift is already thick enough to cushion it—and scoops up a handful of snow. Nico gets her with a blast to the shoulder first, but Kasia and I team up with Miyumi and pepper him with three-to-one snowballs.

"Brody!" he splutters. "You're supposed to be on my side!"

Nico leaps over the edge of the fountain and chases after me, tackling me into the two-foot-deep snowdrift. I wriggle onto my back, scrambling to make a snowball; Nico leans over me, picks up a handful, and smushes it into my face. I laugh, spitting out swear words and snowflakes, and get him back with a snowball to the right ear. He grabs my wrists and pins them over my head, grinning down at me, his breath a mix of mint and cigarettes. Something catches in my chest. Thick white flakes keep falling, gathering in his curls; dim golden light from the streetlamps slides over his face and casts shadows under his eyelashes. Around me, all the laughter and movement fades into nothing. I wish I had my camera. I wish I could freeze this moment—

Another snowball hits him in the jaw. Dani is watching us from behind the fountain, a wide grin on his face. I feel a stab of guilt, but he doesn't look mad. He just laughs as Nico scurries to his feet and chases after him, gathering snowballs as he goes.

By the time we're all snowballed out, a bonfire has appeared in a clearing just behind the square. We sit in the warmth eating Kasia's *kołaczki*, a type of cream-cheese dough filled with fruit, and the *pan dulce* that Dani brought with him. The coating of snow on the ground melts away, but the flakes keeps falling; they glow gold for a moment before they reach the flames and disappear.

I lie on my back listening to Miyumi and Zahra chatting about the shapes they can see in the fluffy clouds floating past, and to Nico and Kasia as they debate the benefits of Christmas in Spain versus Poland. But Dani is oddly quiet. When I look at him, he's lying back with his head in his hands and his eyes closed. I'd think he was asleep, but as far as I know, you can't sleep in Everland.

Suddenly, he sits up.

"So . . . I have two things to say."

Kasia and Miyumi turn to face him; Nico gets up, his eyes suddenly wide. After a moment, Dani's face cracks into a huge, bright grin.

"I applied for an athletics scholarship to university, and they gave it to me. I will move to Buenos Aires in March!"

Everyone bursts into cheers and clapping. Kasia hugs him, and Miyumi gives him a high five. Dani beams. He looks just like Jake did when he told us about his Cambridge interview: a mix of proud and bashful; excited that his life is starting to turn out the way he'd imagined.

As he starts giving us the details, Zahra claps her hands to her head. "Wait—is there a door from Buenos Aires? There must be, right? Have you asked anyone here?"

Dani's eyes flit to Nico. "Well, that was the second thing," he says gently. "I have decided . . . I will not come back here next week. Tonight will be my last night in Everland."

This time, his announcement is met with silence. Zahra's face falls; Miyumi lets out a faint "oh" of surprise. I look at Nico, but he's staring at the sleeves of his cloak, tracing one of the moons with his index finger.

"Never?" Kasia frowns. "Why not?"

Dani runs a hand through his hair. He looks north, to the mountains and the sea beyond them, and his eyes grow foggy. "I am so grateful to this place," he says quietly. "It saved my life, really. But it has *become* my life." He breaks off, looking to Nico again. "I need to concentrate on making a new one. A real one—in the world outside. It is my time to go."

There's another long silence. Sitting here, watching snow fall from a bright blue sky, it doesn't feel like this could be anything other than real. It's the world outside that seems strange and improbable now.

Nico claps his hands together. "We should have a toast." He pulls his beard down and raises an imaginary glass, a fixed smile on his face. "To Dani."

"To Dani," everyone echoes.

If I'd known this would happen a few months ago, I'd have thought I'd be happy about it: Dani not being here means I'll get more time with Nico, after all. But I like Dani. He's nice and smart and interesting, and obviously good for Nico. I don't want him to leave. Not for Nico, and not for the rest of us.

I shift over to sit beside him. "You're really not coming back?"

"It's the best thing for me, Brody. Every week, all I think about is here . . . about Nico. It's not healthy." He looks around, past the bonfire and toward the mountains in the distance. "It's my time to go. I feel it. This place is beautiful, but it's not real."

"Yes, it is," I blurt out. "If we're real, this place is, too. It has to be."

Dani opens his mouth, then gives me a sad smile. Almost

159

like he feels sorry for me. My cheeks flush. What's he got to be sorry about? We have Everland. That's everything. He squeezes my shoulder.

"Please, look after Nico," he says. "I worry about him. I'm going to miss him a lot."

"I will," I say, though to me it never seems like Nico needs looking after. "Promise."

That feeling begins: the feeling that tells me it'll soon be time to leave. Dani must feel it, too, because he gets up to start saying his goodbyes to Miyumi and the others. Kasia says something about having some books to give him and sprints off to the library. Nico doesn't move from the bonfire. He sits watching the flames, humming something into his fake beard.

"Are you okay?" I ask, sitting down beside him.

He nods. "He told me he was thinking of leaving a few weeks ago. Besides, I knew it was coming. He's been kind of distant lately. Hasn't been spending as long in here, either."

"I'm sorry," I mumble. "It sucks."

They could still meet in the outside world, but there are thousands of miles separating them. They'd never be able to see each other every week again, like they can in here.

Nico shrugs. "It's cool," he says, scratching at his beard. "I'm happy for him. Pretty jealous he's moving to Buenos Aires. Looks amazing there."

I nudge his arm. "Well, you'll be going to London. Or Paris or Barcelona or wherever. That's not so bad."

"Not if my dad has anything to do with it." He throws a

handful of grass into the bonfire. "He told me last week that he and Jenny won't support me if I decide to go to art school. They want me to do law or something. Can you imagine me studying law? I'd last five minutes."

"You could be a judge. At least you'd get to dress up," I say. "I can see you in a cloak and a white wig. You'd pull it off."

I'm just trying to make him laugh. He does, but it sounds a bit empty.

"You know, you're right—I totally would." He digs his hands into his pockets and shrugs. "It's okay. I'll talk to my mum about it when I go to Madrid on Saturday. She used to be an artist, too—she made pottery. She'll be on my side."

That tug toward the door gets stronger. Nico looks over at Dani just as Kasia comes back with an armful of medical books for his studies. Zahra is fighting back tears, and Miyumi looks miserable. Nico stands up, pulling his long sleeves over his hands.

"I guess this is it, then." Nico swallows. His eyes are misty. "I'll catch you outside, Brody, okay?"

Tonight, time in Everland feels like it's running away from us. I give Dani a hug, wish him luck, then the rest of us leave him and Nico to say their goodbyes. When Nico appears through the door, just a few seconds after us, his face is pale, and his eyes are red. I don't know how much longer he stayed behind with Dani. It could have been hours; maybe days, if they managed to fight back that tug drawing them home.

No matter how long they had, it clearly wasn't enough.

EIGHTEEN

MY PARENTS USED TO DRAG US OUT TO FAMILY PARTIES ON NEW Year's Eve, but since Dad's accident, they've celebrated with Pringles, wine, and *Hogmanay Live* on BBC2. This year's much the same, only Mam's downgraded to store-brand crisps and mimosas. Keira's upstairs at Amanda's, with a 12:15 p.m. curfew that she'll obviously stretch by about two hours, and Jake's gone to a party at Amir's. It's just me, my parents, and Tink curled up beside me on the sofa.

I'm sixteen, and this is how I'm spending Hogmanay.

Bit depressing.

It's like every other Hogmanay I've had for the past few years, really, but it never bothered me before. This year, though, I wish I had somewhere to go. None of my friends are doing anything. If Megan were here, we could probably have tagged along to some party with her brother, but they're both being forced to socialize with awkward uncles and second cousins at her mam's house in Manchester. So far, she's sent me four selfies, each one looking more despairing than the last.

But it's Everland that I'm missing the most. I've hardly even left the flat since Christmas; there's only one place I want to go, and I can't get there. If today were a Thursday, I could stretch the second between this year and the next into hours or days. I could be kissing Nico at midnight.

Well. Probably not. Okay, definitely not. Dani only just left, after all, and Nico's still in Spain. He hasn't called me since he left, and he's hardly texted. He's staying for his birthday and Three Kings Day, a big celebration there, so he won't be back until the seventh. The thought of another week without him is pretty unbearable, and the lack of communication just makes it harder.

By quarter past eleven, Dad's snoring, and Tink's skulked off to sleep at the foot of my bed. Mam zaps the TV in the middle of a folk tune from Phil and Aly and pushes herself to her feet. I turn to say good night, but then she picks up her coat from the back of the chair.

"Come on," she says, whispering so as not to wake Dad. "Let's go and see the fireworks."

I glance out the window. It's dry and clear, the sky an unusually deep black behind the top of the blocks opposite ours. I can't really be bothered moving, and going out with your mam on New Year's Eve somehow seems even worse than staying in with your mam on New Year's Eve, but she's got this tentative, hopeful look on her face that I can't say no to. Even if I haven't forgiven her yet.

Outside, music is thumping from a flat on the fifth floor, and the pub on the corner is so packed, people are spilling out the door. Three guys come staggering along the pavement, half singing and half slurring the Proclaimers' "I'm Gonna Be (500 Miles)." One points at us, trying to get us to join in, then swivels around and vomits on someone's front step.

"To be the man, who threw up a chip supper all over your door," Mam sings, laughing. She nudges me to join in with the next part, but I just give her a half smile. Her shoulders sag a little, but she puts her arm around me and gives me a squeeze.

"Nice to be just the two of us for a change. Been a while, hasn't it?" She sticks her hands into the pockets of her coat, her shoulders hunched up. "I know I've been a bit distracted lately, with work and your dad and all that. I'm sorry."

"It's fine," I say. "It's no' like I need looking after."

"I know. And I know you're still mad about Tink," she says. "I'm upset about it, too, love. I'm gonna miss the wee guy."

"Aye, I know." I kick at a piece of gravel on the pavement. "Doesnae mean I have to like it, though."

She sighs. "That's not what I'm saying, Brody."

We carry on up the road without speaking, past a lost-looking flock of girls shivering in tiny dresses and a couple having a screaming match outside a tattoo shop. The silence isn't awkward as such, but it doesn't feel totally normal, either.

I realize she's right. It *has* been ages since it was just me and her. When I was wee, we were always doing stuff together— baking or playing games or dressing up. During my *Peter Pan* obsession, she'd help me act out the whole story: me hogging the roles of Peter, Tinker Bell, the Darling kids, and all the Lost Boys; her playing Hook, Smee, and the crocodile. She'd laugh so much, it would make me feel like I was the funniest kid on earth. Her laugh is really infectious, too—this low, guttural chuckle that always makes you want to join in. I can't remember the last time I heard it properly.

Some of the anger thaws. None of this is her fault.

"Where you wanting to go, anyway?" I ask.

"Up to you," she says, her voice all bright and upbeat again. "North Bridge, maybe, if it's not too busy? Or we could try Calton Hill."

My stomach flips. It's a Tuesday, so there's no chance of getting through the monument, and obviously Nico and the others won't be around. Even so, it feels like a weird collision of worlds. Not just real life and . . . whatever Everland is. There are parts of me that exist in Everland that I can't show at home. I've gotten so good at hiding them, it doesn't even feel like I'm doing it.

"Calton Hill's fine," I mumble.

As we reach London Road, we get caught in a horde of drunk girls belting out a Taylor Swift song and find ourselves being swept up the path toward the hill. The monument has been closed off by a circle of tall metal fences, but there are color-changing lights turning the pillars green and pink and blue. It looks a wee bit like it does at 11:21 p.m. every Thursday, only without the stained-glass windows and the unicorn door. For a moment, I forget where I am—I really feel like I'm about to walk into Everland. It's the first time since our night in the snow that I've felt at home in the real world.

Then a tourist in a "See You Jimmy" hat bumps into me, and the feeling's gone. When I turn around, Mam is looking at me with a strange expression. There's no way she can have guessed what I was thinking about, but I still feel a jolt of panic.

"What?" Again, it comes out sharper than I meant.

"Nothing. I just . . . I never know what's going on with you. I wish you'd talk to me," she says. "I know it's hard to find the time, between Jake and Keira. But your dad and I are there, Brody, and we want you to—"

The countdown to midnight begins. I start shouting out the numbers, cutting her off. I don't want to talk to her about this. Not here. Not yet. I'd end up having to tell her some version of the truth, something about Nico. And even though I know she'd be okay about it, I'm not ready for that. The thought makes me feel itchy with nerves.

After a moment, she sighs and joins me in the countdown.

As the crowd shouts out, "One!" the sky explodes in blue and white fireworks. Mam pulls me toward her and kisses my cheek.

"Happy New Year, love," she says. "This one'll be better. I promise."

I'm not convinced—not when it's starting with giving Tink away. I nod and force a smile anyway. "Happy New Year, Mam."

Someone starts belting out "Auld Lang Syne." Mam joins in, crosses her arms, and grabs my hand. We end up in a misshapen circle with some Swedish tourists, three very drunk Geordies, and a Scottish couple with voices like foghorns. Nobody, including me, knows all the words, but they all give it laldy for a few verses anyway.

As the song ends, my phone buzzes. Nico's name appears. I quickly swipe to open the message.

Happy New Year, Brody ☺

I start to write back, but three dots come up on the screen. He's writing something. I wait for his reply, expecting some drunken rambling about the party he's at, or how he can't wait to get back to Edinburgh and to Everland.

Instead, he sends just one letter: *x*

Despite the cold, a warm feeling spreads through my body. It's stupid to read into it—he must be sending a bunch of messages out, and he was probably in a hurry—but the smile stretches across my face before I can stop it. Nico never puts kisses at the end of his messages. Not once in all the time I've known him.

It's not the kind I would have liked to get tonight, but for now, it'll do.

NINETEEN

WHEN KASIA TALKED ABOUT HER LIBRARY, I'D PICTURED IT TO BE like the one at school: shelves of old textbooks and dog-eared paperbacks, round tables in the center, and a handful of computers to serve a few hundred pupils on one side. But the building she takes me to on Thursday is a castle. Literally. It's like something straight out of *Dracula*: dark stone and gray slate perched on a huge crag of rock, with ivy-wrapped walls and pointy turrets piercing low-hanging clouds.

"Impressive, isn't it?" Kasia says. "It looks just like the castle in this book of Polish fairy tales I used to have. I almost thought I'd fallen into the story the first time I saw it."

We climb a long, narrow flight of steps carved into the rock face, toward an imposing set of wooden doors at the front of the building. I'm not totally sure what I'm doing here: I was about to go and find the band when Kasia asked me to come with her instead. Zahra and Nico still aren't back, and I haven't seen Miyumi around. We managed to keep the small talk going as we walked through the valley—Christmas, Hogmanay, the book on space she's reading—but it's starting to feel a bit awkward without the others to act as a buffer between the two of us.

"I've been meaning to bring you here for a while." Kasia turns around to look at me from the top step. We must be five hundred meters up, but neither of us is out of breath. "I found something I thought you might like."

She pushes open the huge wooden doors, and suddenly we're surrounded by books. Thousands, maybe millions, of books. The rooms are practically *made* from them: As well as shelf after shelf lining the vast hall in front of us, there are staircases built from encyclopedias, tables made from paperback novels, corridors between piles of catalogues and magazines. Even the floor is covered in newspapers, some of them dated from almost a century ago. Kasia leads me under an archway formed from *Beano* and *Dandy* comic book annuals and into a room so chock-full with books, you can't see the walls behind them.

"Quite a collection, right?" She smiles at me. Not the usual stiff half grin—an actual smile. "There are books from all over the world in here. Thousands of languages, every genre. It's probably the best library on the planet."

I stop by a huge pile of hardbacks. There are cookbooks, plays, picture books, anthologies of fairy tales . . . a proper mountain of them, at least ten feet tall. Some are so well-worn, the spines are falling off. I pick up the one closest to me—what looks like a Russian gardening manual—and flip through it.

"How many of these have you read?"

"Not enough. I could come here every Thursday till I'm ninety, and I still wouldn't have time to read them all." She picks up a hardback book with Arabic letters stencilled on the cover and runs her fingers down the spine. "Still, it's something. I'm doing an apprenticeship to become an electrician, and on the weekends I help my parents out in their shop. I hardly ever have time to read in the real world."

She leads me through another room and up the stairs, past wobbling stacks of medical journals and knee-high piles of Mills & Boon romance novels. Jake would love this place. He somehow manages to get through three or four books a week, most of them brick-sized tomes about politics or international relationships. My tastes are a bit more limited: Since *Peter Pan*, I've read a few books for school, a couple of sci-fi things my gran gave me for Christmas, and all the Harry Potter books five times each. Jake used to go on and on at me about branching out. That's probably what put me off.

After a few more turns through the maze, Kasia walks into what could be a bathroom, if it weren't filled with books: the tub and sink are overflowing with picture books, and there are stacks of newspapers piled up on the shelves. She fishes through the books in the bath and pulls out a blue hardback.

"Here it is," she says, handing it to me. "I thought you might like this."

I brush a layer of dust off the cover. There are vines of golden ivy around the edges, with fairies and swallows dotted between the leaves, and a delicate illustration of a boy, a crocodile, and two mermaids around the title. Written in the center, in bright gold lettering, are the words *Peter and Wendy, J. M. Barrie*.

I look up at Kasia. "How did you know?"

"Well, you have a cat named Tinker Bell. That was a clue." She smiles. "It's a first edition. Signed and everything. Makes me wonder if the author brought it here himself."

Wiping my hands on my jeans, I carefully turn to the opening page. *All children, except one, grow up* . . . Just reading that first line brings the story flooding back to me: the Lost Boys, the pirates, the ticking crocodile . . . Wendy sewing on Peter Pan's shadow, Tinker Bell sacrificing herself for Peter, then being brought back to life by kids who believed in fairies. For a few seconds, I'm five years old again, chasing after Tink and demanding Mam put the DVD on for the thousandth time.

"I used to love this," I tell Kasia. "I practically knew it by heart."

"You should keep it. Belated Christmas present." She sits on the edge of the bath, then reaches over to pick a large, tatty atlas from the shelf to her right. "There are millions of books in here. No one'll miss it."

"Are you serious?"

I don't know how much first editions go for, but it must be a fair bit. Probably more than what Mam makes in a month. I stammer out a thanks. Kasia nods, but her smile has disappeared.

She opens the atlas, absentmindedly thumbing the dog-eared corners. For a moment, I think she's forgotten I'm here, but then she begins to speak.

"Did Nico or Zahra ever tell you about Magda?"

I look up, surprised. "Is that your girlfriend?"

"Yeah. Well, my ex now." She turns the page, and her eyes haze over as she stares down at a map of the Middle East. "I found Everland two years ago. We were both going through a bit of a rough time. Magda has really bad anxiety, my dad kept pushing me to leave school and get a job, and my mum wasn't over the moon about me coming out as a lesbian. I don't know why or how I ended up on Calton Hill that night. It was like I was being pulled toward the door . . . like it was calling me.

"I brought Magda here the next week. For the first few months, everything was perfect. You know what this place does to you: It makes everything in your real life feel like it's behind glass, like it can't really touch you. We came every single Thursday, stayed as long as we could. But then it started to . . . leak into real life."

She turns the page of the atlas to a map of China. Her hands look older than her eighteen years: They're pale and bony, with bluish veins that poke out below her knuckles.

"How do you mean?" I ask.

"She couldn't concentrate on anything. She was spaced out all the time. You'd be talking to her, and she'd trail off in the middle of a sentence, just staring at nothing. Magda was never that academic, but after a while, she couldn't even focus enough to write more than a few words—I had to do all her homework for her. Her parents thought she was on drugs or something. They even took her to the doctor for tests, but obviously they didn't find anything. The only time she really seemed present was when we were on our way to Calton Hill, and she was only her normal self in Everland. I should have known she would decide to stay."

I lean back against the wall. "Stay in Everland?"

Kasia nods. "It happened four months after we started coming here. We were sitting up in the hills when the tug started, that feeling that it was time to go home . . . but when I went to leave, she didn't follow me. I fought with her, obviously—I even tried to physically drag her away, but I could feel the door starting to close. I had to leave or I'd get stuck myself. So I left her behind."

She falls quiet again. I can tell it's hard for her, saying all this. Reliving it.

"So . . ." I pause, working it out. "That means she was missing."

Kasia nods. "She was gone for a whole week. Her parents were freaking out. Especially after her weird behavior—they were scared she'd hurt herself or overdosed or something. I had to lie to them, to the police. Nobody believed that I didn't know where she was. Her mum kept phoning me, crying and begging me to tell her the truth. But if I had, they'd have thought I'd lost it. Or that I was trying to cover up something even worse.

"When I finally went back the next Thursday, I was ready.

Nico and I rounded up a couple of people from one of the squares and got them to help us carry Magda to the green door. It took four of us, and she kicked and screamed the whole way, but eventually we managed to push her through. It was like she was possessed—she almost shoved me down the steps of the monument trying to get back through the door. Even after it had disappeared, she kept pushing at the pillars, trying to find a way back in.

"She still had her phone on her, so I turned it on and rang my own number to make it look like she'd called me—I knew the police were going to ask how I'd found her. Then I called her parents. By the time they arrived on Calton Hill, Magda had stopped fighting, but she still wasn't right. She seemed terrified: She kept saying she didn't know where she was, that she wanted to go home. I remember her dad running toward us, shouting her name . . . Magda looked at him like he was a stranger. Totally blank."

My stomach lurches. "She didnae recognize him?"

"Or her mum. It was like she'd forgotten her real life altogether."

Kasia tilts her head to stare at the ceiling. Forcing her tears back. I don't know what to say. It makes me think of the first time Dad had a panic attack: all the confusion about what was happening, all the fear. I know how it feels to watch somebody come apart like that.

"God," I mumble. "That's terrible."

Kasia sniffs and looks back at me. "Yeah. It really was. Her parents had to take her to hospital. They wouldn't let me come, but they called me later demanding to know what she'd taken. Even when the tests showed up negative, they still blamed me. Eventually, they had her sent to a psychiatric hospital. Her parents haven't let me see her since. Her friends keep me up to date, and apparently she's doing better now. Most of her memories came back, but there are still blanks."

She falls quiet again, flipping through the atlas. The pages move down through Asia and into the South Pacific, but judging by the haze in Kasia's eyes, she doesn't see any of it.

"I think . . . I think it happened because I brought Magda here," she says quietly. "When I came to Everland, it was like I was being drawn here. Like it was calling to me. It was the same for Zahra and Nico, and everyone else I've asked about it. It wasn't like that for Magda."

A cold feeling comes over me. "So, what? You think Everland was punishing her or something? You think she didnae belong here?"

She pauses for a moment, thinking. "Not *punishing* her. I just think she couldn't handle it. Most people know when it's their time to stop coming here—like Dani did. If I hadn't forced her out, Magda would have stayed in here forever. Before you, and the other people Nico brought here, she was the only person I knew who hadn't found Everland on their own. There has to be a connection."

Blood starts to pound in my ears. Kasia's gaze remains impassive, knowing, and for a second, my sympathy for her is replaced with a blaze of rage. This is my place. I know it is. It gave me the band, didn't it? I feel more like myself in here than anywhere else. She can't tell me I don't fit.

"You just want rid of me," I snap. "You've been trying to shove me out since the first night I came here."

Kasia's eyebrows rise. "I'm telling you this because I *like* you, Brody. I don't want the same thing to happen to you."

My hands clench around the copy of *Peter and Wendy*. It feels like a bribe now—a souvenir from a too-short holiday. As if a book could be a fair trade for what this place has given me. I toss it toward the pile of books by the sink, but I miss, and it slips down to the floor, bending the pages in the middle. Kasia winces.

"You're wrong," I tell her. "I do belong here. Just as much as you."

I storm out of the bathroom. Kasia follows me down the corridor, calling my name. When I turn around, she's holding *Peter and Wendy* in her hands, straightening out the folded pages.

"Look, I'm not saying you have to leave. I just wanted you to know the risks." She holds out the book again. "It's up to you. Just promise me you'll tell somebody if you start to feel weird. If you start to feel like real life is . . . slipping away."

Her gray-blue eyes are wide and worried. She's doing what she thinks is best. The anger dims a little, but it doesn't completely disappear. I'm sick of people trying to make decisions for me.

"Fine. Whatever," I say. "That's no' gonnae happen, though."

Kasia presses her lips together. "I hope not."

Reluctantly, I take the book from her. I flip through the pages as I walk back through the valley toward the band, but after Kasia's story, the gift has lost some of its sheen. Reading about Neverland isn't enough anymore. Not now that I have the real thing.

TWENTY

WE HAVE TO BORROW A CAT CARRIER FROM THE FRASERS ON THE second floor to take Tink to Amir's after New Year's. Unsurprisingly, he hates it. Our flat isn't big, but it's much better than being shoved into what's basically a shoebox with holes and dragged across Edinburgh on a double-decker bus. He screeches the entire way up Leith Walk, only shutting up when I take a bag of cat biscuits out of my backpack and push some through the bars.

"Amir's mum's already bought a cat bed and one of those scratching poles," Jake says. "I think Tink'll like it there, you know."

As if Jake has any idea what Tink likes. Other than shoving him off the sofa or swearing when he gets under his feet, Jake hasn't paid him any attention for years. I don't answer, and eventually he shrugs and goes back to listening to his podcast.

We get off the bus in Morningside and walk up a long street of posh houses, most with a rotting Christmas tree dumped at the foot of the drive. Their gardens are massive: ponds and flower beds, trampolines and tree houses, all sprinkled with a faint coating of frost. I'm suddenly acutely aware of my ancient muddy trainers and my shabby jeans. Jake, on the other hand, strides along the street like it's his own. Not surprising, really, given how much time he spends at Amir's. Amir's family even took him skiing in Switzerland last year. *Switzerland.* I'd be lucky to get to the dry slopes at Hillend.

Amir's mum is waiting on the front steps when we arrive, rubbing her arms to stave off the cold. She's got neat black hair cut in a sharp bob, a heart-shaped face, and bright eyes that crinkle at the edges when she smiles.

"Hi, Mrs. Shah. Happy New Year," Jake says. His accent always changes when he's around his friends from school or their families. Like our gran when she answers the phone.

"Happy New Year, Jake. You must be Brody. Lovely to meet you," Mrs. Shah says to me, smiling. She leans toward the door of the cat carrier, her hands on her knees. "And *you* must be Tink! Let's get you out of that box, shall we?"

It's only when she puts her hand out to take him that I realize I'm really, *really* not ready for this. Still, I hand the carrier over. Mrs. Shah sets it down on the floor and opens the latch: Tink darts out, skeets out across the rug, then comes to a halt by the stairs, peering around at the shiny wooden floorboards and the mahogany chest of drawers covered with family photos from weddings and holidays.

"He might take a while to get used to you," I say. "Don't take it personally."

Mrs. Shah laughs and drops into a crouch, holding her hand out and making a high-pitched whistling noise. A tall kid with boy-band-neat hair and slightly protruding ears pads through from the kitchen eating a sandwich.

"Oh, hey. Hi, Brody." He holds up the sandwich in a semi-wave. "I'm Amir. I think we met at our awards ceremony freshman year, didn't we? Man, you two look even more alike now than you did then," he says, looking from Jake to me and back again.

"You think?" Jake smiles at him. "Don't see it, myself."

Amir asks if we want anything to eat, but I hardly hear him; I'm watching Tink explore his new home. Mrs. Shah has moved over to him and is stroking his back a little harder than he likes. I want to tell her to lay off a bit, and about the cheese and the toothbrush and all his other quirks, but my throat seems to have closed up. Tink slips out from under her hand and goes into the next room to check it out. Just a flash of ginger, and he's gone.

I swallow.

"Right. Well, thanks for taking him." I force a smile. "Uh . . . bye, then."

I don't know if that's directed at Tink or at Jake or at Amir and his mum.

Mrs. Shah stands up, brushing cat hairs off her sleeve. "You don't want to say goodbye?" she asks. "There's no rush! Stay and have some lunch."

I shake my head. "Nah, I'm all right. Thanks."

"Oh. Okay." She looks to Jake, a wee bit flustered, then back to me. "Well, you can come back to see him whenever you like."

Amir swallows another bite of his sandwich. "And Jake'll let you know how he's doing, too. We can email you some photos, if you like."

I force a smile. They're nice. Tink'll be happy here. He'll have more space, and there'll be no Leanne and Michelle around to kidnap him when they're bored. I should be relieved. It's ridiculous that I'm feeling like this, anyway—it's not like I'm giving a baby up for adoption. It just sucks. And no matter how much they offer, I know I'll never come back here. Who goes to a stranger's house to hang out with their former cat? Too weird.

After another thank-you and a goodbye, I hurry down the steps and along their driveway. Jake follows me out, closing the door behind him. He calls my name a few times before I turn around.

"Why are you running off?" he asks. "You should say goodbye to Tink properly."

"Why? It's not like he understands. He's just a cat."

But he's more than that, too. He's a link to my five-year-old self, that kid who loved *Peter Pan* and liked to dress up in fairy wings and named his kitten after Tinker Bell. He's a symbol of who I was before all those parts of me became tangled up with shame and embarrassment. Since Everland, I've felt like that knot inside me is slowly coming undone. But I still don't want to let him go.

Jake wouldn't get any of that. He'd probably tell me to man up, stop being such a drama queen, something like that. He looks at me for a moment, his lips pressed together, then shrugs.

"Okay. If that's what you want. I'm going to stay here awhile, work on some stuff for school."

"All right. See you."

I start to walk away, but he shouts after me again. When I turn around, his eyes are shiny.

"I did try to get Mam and Dad to change their minds, you know. They wouldn't have done this if things weren't really bad."

His voice cracks the tiniest bit. I can't tell if he's putting it on, and it doesn't matter: It sends another burst of anger surging through me.

"Why is it never you who has to give anything up? I don't see you volunteering to stop rugby or your violin lessons—"

"That's different," Jake says. "The school pays for all that; it's part of my scholarship."

"The school didnae pay for you to go to Cambridge for your interview, though, did they? How much did that cost, the trains and the hostel? Enough to pay another term of Keira's theater classes, I bet. Enough for a bit of cat food."

He gawps at me. I turn on my heel and walk away, fingernails cutting into my palms. After a moment, Jake's footsteps follow.

"What do you want me to do, Brody? You want me to turn down all the opportunities I've had because you and Keira don't get the same?" He grabs my arm and spins me round to face him. "I'm sorry you couldn't get a scholarship, okay? I'm sorry you weren't smart enough."

His face falls as soon as he says it. "I didn't mean that."

"Aye, you did." I shrug him off, slide my hands into my pockets. "And it's true. I wasn't. I'm not. But that doesnae—"

I stop. I don't know how to finish that. But that doesn't mean I *deserve* any less? But that doesn't mean I *am* any less? I think all of those things, but I walk back down the road and leave them unsaid. Because though I might know otherwise deep down, right now, it doesn't feel like they're true.

TWENTY-ONE

BY THE TIME THURSDAY COMES AROUND AGAIN, SCHOOL HAS started up. Our teachers won't stop going on about how our college prelim exams are just a few weeks away and how "vitally important" they are—as if the world is going to end if some of us don't scrape a pass in Maths—but I'm so desperate to get back to Everland, I can barely concentrate. Zahra and Kasia are waiting by the steps when I finally get back to Calton Hill, dressed up as Princess Mononoke and some weird ox creature, but there's no sign of Nico.

"He should be here by now," I say nervously. "He got home on Monday. He texted me a few times."

Kasia raises two fuzzy-felt eyebrows. "Well, he'd better hurry up if he wants to get in."

Just as the door appears between the pillars, we see a

thin figure running over the grass. Zahra yells at him to hurry. The three of us rush inside, holding the door back to let Nico in; I can feel it beginning to push back as he dives through the gap. It snaps with a bang, pushing me into Nico. He trips over my foot and spins away, his arms thrown out for balance.

"Sorry, sorry! I got a bit . . . sidetracked."

His voice is all blurry around the edges. He sways a little as he stumbles forward, and when he hugs me, he smells of something strong and sweet. Zahra watches him with an amused expression; Kasia looks thunderous. As the relief that he made it ebbs away, something else hits me.

"You're drunk!"

I don't mean to sound so scandalized. I'm just surprised. Not that he's drinking—he's just turned eighteen, after all—but that he's drinking before coming to Everland. He's never done that before.

"I went out for a drink. A few drinks." He puts his hands on his hips. His brown eyes are glazed. "What kind of welcome back is this? Didn't you guys miss me?"

"You know you're not supposed to come here drunk," Kasia says, scowling at him.

Nico pulls a face. "You and your rules, Kash." He spins around and takes off down the path. "You don't know anything."

"You also have school tomorrow," Zahra says, hurrying after him. "School? Education? Exams? You do remember what those are, right, Nico?"

"I'll skip it." Nico looks over his shoulder and shrugs. "It's just senior year."

Kasia's whole body tenses. I remember seeing her surrounded by all those books in the library, cramming in the education she wishes she could have in the outside world. I'm not surprised when, once we reach the end of the path, she storms off without saying anything. Nico mumbles something about her overreacting, and I have to bite my tongue to stop myself from snapping at him. Kasia and I might not see eye to eye on much, but I get where she's coming from here. It's "just senior year" to Nico because he has so much to fall back on: good grades, opportunities, parents who could pay for tutors if he needed them. Most people aren't that lucky.

"Let's find you some water," Zahra says wearily. "Maybe that'll help."

Turns out, Nico is even more talkative when he's wasted. He strides down the hill, blethering on about friends from back home in Madrid, from his art course, other things I can't keep up with. Zahra and I both watch him nervously. I've been drunk myself a couple of times, and I've been around other drunk people loads—family gatherings at my grandparents' are always a bit of a free-for-all like that. But it's different in here. Everland is already so unpredictable, and this gives it a strange new filter.

Crossing the bridge, we arrive at a small square with terracotta buildings, floral paving stones, and a bright yellow door standing upright near the center. Zahra pops into a cottage and comes back holding a mason jar full of water. Nico insists he's fine but reluctantly takes a few sips.

"You go do your thing," I tell her. She shouldn't have to take care of somebody in here, too. "I'll look after him."

"Are you sure?" The relief is clear on her face when I nod. "Thanks, Brody. Come and find me if you need me."

Everland feels chaotic tonight. Nico whisks us through bustling streets I've never seen before, into a sea of people milling around the metallic animal structures, into parties so loud the floor shakes and the sky vibrates with sound. It's only when I start actively wishing for things to calm down that the crowds slip away, and we end up wandering through a long purple meadow and into a woodland of thin birch trees. Tucked into a clearing among them is an old-fashioned funfair: a helter-skelter, a coconut shy, fun-house mirrors—even a giant carousel with sea monsters instead of the usual ponies.

"Oh my God! This reminds me of this place I went when I was little," Nico says. "I ate too much popcorn and *garrapiñadas* and threw up on the drive home."

He steps forward, and the funfair lights up. Golden bulbs flash around the helter-skelter; the carousel begins to turn, the monsters bobbing like boats on a choppy sea. It's a bit eerie without any music or kids running around stuffing their faces with cotton candy. Nico takes a run-up and grabs the pole protruding from a giant squid's back, swinging himself onto one of its tentacles. I walk past the mirrors. Different versions of myself stare back at me: some short and squat, some alien and elongated. Nico spins slowly past, gliding up and down with the movement of the monster.

"How was home?" I ask.

"It sucked," he says bluntly. "I told my mum about my dad and Jenny refusing to pay for art school. Turns out, she agrees with them. She thinks I should do something more useful, do my costumes on the side." He leans forward, resting his head against the carousel pole. "It's okay. I'll still go. I'll just have to get, like, three jobs to pay for it by myself. If I even get in."

He sounds pissed off. It's probably the first time Nico's ever had to think about money. I feel another quiver of irritation, but I push it down. I haven't seen him in weeks. I don't want to be mad at him.

I walk over to the coconut shy and pick up a beanbag. "You'll manage. People do it all the time."

"Yeah. You're right. I'm just being a *quejica*."

He mixes his languages more when he's drunk. It's cute. He slides down the squid's tentacle, still a little wobbly on his feet.

"Sorry, Brody. It's always a bit weird, going back there. My mum's husband is nice enough, and I love seeing the girls, but they have all these in-jokes, these little quirks and routines. Every family has a rhythm to it, you know? I can never seem to fall in time with them."

He grabs a beanbag and tosses it at the middle coconut, but his aim is just a little too low. I get what he means—my family marches to Jake's beat, even if no one else can keep up. But I've never thought about what it must have been like for him: being uprooted from his home, his country, sent across the sea to live with his dad and a woman he barely knew and still doesn't seem to like much.

"Sorry," I say gently. "That must be tough."

For a moment, Nico's face looks like it's about to crumple. But then he shakes his head and gives a bubbly laugh.

"I'm just being moany again. *Pobrecito de mí*, eh?"

He throws another beanbag, but this one is too high. He swears at it in Spanish, laughing, then hands me one to try. On my third go, I knock the middle coconut right off its stand. Nico throws his hands up and cheers. I grin. It almost feels like a date, something out of an American teen movie. For a second, I let myself pretend that it is. And that he's not drunk.

"First prize to the gentleman in the gray hoodie!" Nico waves one arm up and down, gesturing to an invisible row of prizes. "Giant teddy bear? Or how about a goldfish?"

I grin. I'm about to opt for the goldfish—a crappy replacement for Tink, but it'd do—but when I open my mouth, something else come out. Something I didn't even know I was going to ask.

"How are you feeling about Dani leaving?"

Nico blinks at me. He looks away, his eyes glistening like beetles in the moonlight.

"I miss him," he says. "I understand why he had to stop coming. I do. But it also feels like . . . I wasn't enough for him. Like I wasn't worth it."

"You know it wasnae like that."

Nico doesn't seem to hear. He wanders toward the mirrors, stepping back and forth to stretch and squash his reflection.

"I know it's not really about me. He was ready. They say there comes a point when you know it's time to move on from this place. For most people, anyway." He moves forward and his eyes swell in the mirror, deep and dark. "He sent me this really long email, talking about coming over here one day, when he has money . . . but I know it won't happen. He'll meet somebody else and forget all about me."

I tell him how ridiculous that is, but he shakes his head.

"No, seriously. Lots of people don't remember this place at all after they stop coming." He climbs back on the carousel, this time onto the head of a blue whale. "My friend Mark—the one from my art course that I brought here last year—he came here three times, but it seems like it's been completely wiped from his memory. I mentioned it to him once, and he looked at me like I'd said I'd teleported to Turkey for the weekend."

"Dani was coming here for years, though." I lean against the carousel, raising my voice as Nico spins away. "He'll no' forget about it that fast. And besides . . . he could still come back."

"Nah. He's gone, Brody. It's over."

There's nothing else I can say, so I don't try. Above us, the sky is changing color. I've never seen it do that in here before. The usual deep blue turns indigo, then violet, then dusky pink. And then, quite suddenly, a deep bloodred.

It's like a flash of rage on a passive man's face—just a split second, and then it's gone. Something about it snatches my breath away. Before I can point it out to Nico, it's already changed back to blue.

"What's wrong?" he asks. "You've gone all pale."

"It was . . . nothing. I'm fine."

He jumps down from the carousel, staggers a little, then throws an arm around my shoulders.

"You look like you're gonna throw up. I thought *I* was the drunk one."

The shakiness wears off, but it takes a while for the nervous feeling to fade. Nothing about tonight has been quite right. I feel like I've seen something I shouldn't have seen. A monster baring its teeth.

TWENTY-TWO

RUSTY RECORDS IS THE SORT OF PLACE THAT YOU WALK PAST AND wonder how the hell it manages to stay in business. It's a tiny shoebox of a music shop, packed full of vinyls and CDs—I even spotted a pile of dusty cassettes in one corner when I handed my pretty-much-empty CV in there before Christmas. I didn't think anything would ever come of it, but in the middle of January, some guy called Mark MacNeill phones and asks me to come in for an interview.

"Tomorrow morning," he says. "Around nine o'clock. Actually, make it ten; I've got a gig tonight."

I get to the shop five minutes early and have to wait another fifteen before Mark turns up. He's nothing like I imagined. I'd expected some aging rocker with a Ramones T-shirt and a hangover, but he's wearing a suit and carrying a large black briefcase. He looks me up and down as he unlocks the shop door.

"So you're over sixteen?"

I nod.

"Know much about music?"

"Um, yeah. More or less."

He pauses, his fingers gripping the door handle. "Name Pink Floyd's first album."

I know this. It's one of Arnau's favorites; we've played a bunch of songs from it at Everland. "*The Piper at the Gates of Dawn.*"

Mark grins and pushes the door open. That seems to be the extent of the interview.

He shows me how to work the till, which looks like it's almost as old as he is, then gives me a tour. There's not much to see: just a toilet, a very messy stockroom, and the shop floor itself. He claims that everything's sorted by category, but there seems to be a bit of genre-jumping going on; I see a Foo Fighters record poking out of the jazz section, and I'm pretty sure that Lady Gaga could never be considered punk.

Still, I love it in here. It feels like a film set. The back wall is covered with old gig posters—Led Zeppelin, the Cure, Shonen Knife—and stickers and gig stubs cover every available surface. There's a huge vintage record player in the corner, and a makeshift chandelier of cracked vinyls hanging from the ceiling. All the dust is going to have me sneezing nonstop . . . But getting paid to hang out in here? I can't really believe my luck.

As Mark's telling me about a shipment of new records that's due in the afternoon, the bell on the front door jingles, and a girl comes in wearing a green Rusty Records T-shirt. She's about my age, with light brown skin, glasses, and curly black hair, and she's using a wheelchair.

"This is my daughter Jett. Her sister used to help out in the shops, too, but she's abandoned us for Zara. Staff discount, apparently." Mark claps his hands together. "So, ready to start? It'll be minimum wage, nine or ten until five or six, Saturdays and Sundays, and you get half an hour for lunch."

The whole "induction" is over in about three minutes—and to think I wasted my precious computer time looking up job interview questions on the internet. Mark tells me to help myself to tea or coffee, shoulders the man bag, and hurries out, leaving me alone with Jett.

"I'll get you a T-shirt," she says, chewing on a piece of bubble gum. She disappears into the stockroom, coming out with a maroon version of her own shirt. "Sorry, they're about fifteen years old, and we've only got XXL left. I'll get my dad to order you another one."

She turns away to move a Blondie record back to the " '70s Pop" section. I quickly pull off my jumper and T-shirt and put the new one on instead. It almost reaches my knees, and I have to roll the sleeves up four times to get it past my elbows, but I quite like it.

"Um, I'm Brody, by the way," I tell her. "Is that your real name—Jett?"

She turns to look at me. Her bubble gum pops.

"Yup. With two *T*s. My parents have this weird thing with music surnames. My sisters are called Franklin and Lennox. They could have called us Joan, Aretha, and Annie, but they just *had* to be different."

Her tone is scathing, but I'd pick a rock-star surname over "Brody" any day. A dad who owns a music shop beats one who spends his whole life washing up and watching documentaries, too, though I feel bad as soon as I think that.

"I'll let you put the first disc of the day on," Jett says, pointing to the record player behind the counter. "No pressure or anything, but this is a test, and my entire and unchangeable opinion of you is riding on the results."

I laugh. Well, I try to. I flick through the records, trying to find something cool but not too try-hard, iconic but not too obvious—something that'll give the room a bit of energy without being aggressive. After a couple of minutes, I go for a Ben Folds Five album. Heather introduced me to them during our music lessons; I loved "Song for the Dumped" because of all the bad words.

Jett gives me a thumbs-up. "Good choice! I was only kidding about it being a test, but you would've passed." She grins, and I try not to show my relief. "Here, I'll show you how to put the record on. Not that I think you're incapable or anything—it's just a bit temperamental."

The aisles are a tight squeeze for her wheelchair, but she expertly maneuvers her way toward the record player. It takes her a couple of goes to get it working, but soon "Jackson Cannery" is playing through the speakers.

"So, um, what do you normally listen to?" I ask her.

"Lots of stuff. I like Dylan, the Doors, Nina Simone . . . I also like Beyoncé and Halsey and Harry Styles." She raises an eyebrow at me. "You're not some music snob like my dad, are you? He thinks nothing good was created after 1994."

"Uh, well, *I* was created way after 1994, so no. And I love Halsey. And Harry Styles. Well, I mostly like his face." I blink. There's no way I would have said something like that to a stranger a few months ago. "Sorry, that was a bit . . . gay of me."

God. I wouldn't have said that, either.

Jett just laughs. Her eyes are sparkling.

"Don't apologize. I'm pansexual, for the record, so gay away. Next question—do you play anything?"

"Drums. And a bit of guitar."

"You're a drummer! Nice. I'm a guitarist, mostly, but I play the piano and the violin, too."

We talk about music, TV shows, the festivals that she's planning to go to in the summer. She reminds me of Megan a little: She's open and talkative and asks lots of questions. When she mentions what school she goes to, my mouth falls open.

"My brother goes there," I say. "Jake Fair?"

It's her turn for her jaw to drop. "No way! He's in the year above me. God, it should have clicked you were his brother. You look so alike." I wait for her to ask why I don't go to their school, too, but instead she pulls a sad face. "Sucks about him and Amir, eh?"

I frown at her. "What do you mean?"

"Oh—nothing." She leans down to the nearest box and straightens the records inside. "I just heard they had a fight or something."

So that explains why Jake's been at home so much lately. I can't believe Jett knows him. I never, ever would have guessed that the owner of this shabby wee shop could or even would send his kids to a school like that. He must have another job, because there's no way this place is doing enough business to pay those fees.

Our first customer comes in at half ten. He's a regular, according to Jett, so she goes off to chat with him about the new Brian Eno album and the gigs he's going to at Celtic Connections. A few more customers come in after that: a Korean couple, a woman looking for a birthday present for her husband, and three almost-identical guys with long hair and Nirvana T-shirts.

Though nobody's asked me to, I start sorting through the boxes of records, sliding them into the right categories and arranging them in alphabetical order. In the first, I find RuPaul's *Supermodel of the World* on vinyl. I take a photo to send to Megan, telling her to come into the shop to visit me if she's around later. I haven't seen her much since she got back from Manchester: I've been busy with drumming, making masks, texting Nico.

When I start digging through the second box, I find an album by Manel, another of Arnau's favorite bands. That's when I realize something. I've hardly thought about Everland since I got here. I've thought about Nico a few times, but not about Everland.

That shouldn't feel weird, not when I've only been here a few hours. It does, though. It makes me feel sort of guilty, like I'm slipping away from the place. But that's daft. I'll be back there on Thursday, back where I belong. After working in here all weekend, I'll have loads more song suggestions for Esther and the band, too.

Everything until then is just a placeholder. Even this.

TWENTY-THREE

SOMETHING IS HAPPENING IN EVERLAND.

It clicks over the next month. Just little things at first, like the sky changing color again, or the stars disappearing as if they've been blotted out with dark ink. But soon it starts to feel like something bigger.

One night, I'm walking down the hill, and the river turns a deep burgundy, a shade of red wine, like blood—but when I move closer, it's back to the normal color of water. Another time, the white-spotted deer who graze around the hills charge across the valley in a thousand-strong stampede. It only lasts a few seconds, but it makes the whole ground shudder. And a week later, the usual balmy temperature shoots up so high, it feels like we've been transported into the height of a Mediterranean summer.

"This isn't normal," Kasia says. "The temperature has never changed so drastically. Not in all the time I've been coming here."

The five of us are lying out on a long stretch of sand near a bend in the river, parts of costumes scattered at the feet of the palm trees behind us. The sunless sky above is a perfect, cloudless blue; we keep having to dip our feet in the river to cool down.

"It could be like this all the time," Zahra points out. "We're only here on Thursday nights. Maybe it's Club Tropicana the rest of the week."

Kasia runs a hand over her forehead. "You know it's not just that. That thing with the deer . . . and the river . . . Something is happening in here. I'm telling you, it's not normal."

Nico rolls onto his side, scattering sand around him.

"Kash. For the thousandth time, there *is* no normal here. There are no rules." He lies back again, his arms stretched above his head. "You're gonna have to go back to dreich February Edinburgh in a bit. Just enjoy it while you can."

Kasia's not one for relaxing. She gets up and brushes the sand off her jeans. "I'm going to the library. Maybe somebody's got some information in there."

Zahra offers to go with her to help; Nico pulls a face at me and mumbles something about her being paranoid. Even if I don't want to, I agree with Kasia. It's as if tectonic plates are shifting below us, transforming the shape of Everland, altering how it works. It feels like something's about to change.

* * *

I wake up the next morning in a bad mood. That's been happening a lot after my nights in Everland, almost like it's leaving me with a hangover. Even so, the day gets off to an undeniably bad start. There's nothing but cornflakes for breakfast—I hate cornflakes; tastes like eating soggy leaves—and Jake has a go at me for nicking his socks. And since my prelims start today, things at school are even worse.

My first one is Spanish. The CD player won't start (big surprise, seeing as it's older than anybody in the class), so Mr. Velázquez has to run off to find a spare. He tells us to sit quietly and read over the questions until he comes back, which obviously nobody does: One-half of the class whips out their phones, while the other drifts across the room to talk to their friends.

Anton Akande, who sits beside me, pulls out his textbook to cram in some last-minute revision, so I do the same. *I should really practice this stuff with Nico*, I think, as I read over environmental vocabulary. All I've learned from him are swear words and *aguafiestas*, something he always calls Kasia when she's being a killjoy.

While I'm reading, the word *fairy* drifts out of the hubbub. Without meaning to, I look up. Leanne is watching me from two rows over, a wide smirk on her face.

"Heard your dad got his benefits cut, Fairy," she says, loud enough for the entire class to hear. "Is he gonnae have to *finally* get a job now?"

Thirty-odd faces turn to look at me. My body goes cold, but

an instant heat wave hits my cheeks. I sink down in my chair, my eyes fixed on the vocab list in my textbook.

"None of your goddamn business, Leanne."

Leanne laughs. She swings back on her chair, her trainers tucked around the legs of the table. "He cannae, though, can he? Cos he's mental. Hasn't left the flat in five years."

Beside her, Jamie Wight sniggers; Rongrong Li turns around and glowers at him. Anton mutters something about that word being offensive. I keep staring at the textbook, but the words on the page have become a blur. My pulse is racing. I open my mouth to tell Leanne to piss off again, but nothing comes out.

"Heard your mum got rid of your cat, too. Poor Tinker Bell!"

My cheeks flare even hotter. A few people laugh. Out of the corner of my eye, I see Leanne fake a pout.

"Aww, you gonnae cry, Peter Pan?"

Mr. Velázquez comes back into the room holding another CD player. Leanne twists around in her seat, the legs of her chair hitting the carpet tiles with a bump. Five seconds later, she's already blethering to Jamie about some boy she got off with over the weekend.

The listening test starts, but the blood is thumping in my ears so hard, I can hardly make out anything on solar panels or wind energy or whatever the hell the audio's about. Leanne's words keep looping around my mind. My own do, too. *None of your goddamn business, Leanne.*

That's all I said. I didn't even correct her. I didn't do anything.

By the time we get out for lunch, Megan's network of spies

have already informed her about what happened in Spanish class. I find her waiting for me outside the canteen, her arms crossed tight over her chest.

"I can't believe you never told me about your dad."

That's the first thing she says. Not, *God, Brody, that must be really worrying for your family.* Or even, *Leanne's such a bitch for telling everyone like that.* I grit my teeth to stop myself from snapping at her. This is typical Megan, making everything about herself.

"Aye, well. Didnae want to think about it."

I push past her and join the queue for lunch. Greasy shepherd's pie on the menu, watery custard for dessert. Today is not my damn day.

Megan grabs a tray and puts an apple on it. "How long has this been going on for?"

I keep my eyes on the food and don't answer. Megan lets out a long sigh.

"You never tell me anything anymore."

Maybe because this is how you react, I want to snap. Going on at me about how I didn't tell you, about how it makes *you* feel. One of the canteen ladies slides a portion of shepherd's pie onto my tray, her gaze lingering curiously on my stormy expression. I swallow and hand it back to her.

"No, thanks. I'm no' hungry."

I spend the whole lunch break angry-drumming in the music room, but even that can't get Leanne's—and now Megan's—words out of my head. They follow me around like a swarm of bees, buzzing and pricking at me all through my last two classes. By the time I get back to Mackay House, I'm hungry and tired and in an even crappier mood than I was this morning.

My parents are the only ones home. Mam's sitting at the computer, and Dad's doing the ironing and watching something about astronauts. He glances over as I come in.

"All right, Brodes." He slides the iron over one of Jake's school shirts, sending a cloud of steam into the air. "How'd the exam go?"

"Fine." I don't have the energy to tell them the truth. "It was just a prelim, anyhow."

I go to the kitchen to get a snack, but there's nothing except some tins and half a loaf of bread. I stick a slice in the toaster and make myself a cup of tea. There's no milk, either, so I put in extra sugar to make it taste half-decent. I slump down on the sofa, kicking my feet onto the coffee table. On the TV, a group of teenagers in blue overalls are exploring the inside of a spaceship.

"They're at a summer camp at NASA," Dad tells me. "Some of these kids might be the first people to live on Mars. Bloody mad, isn't it?"

I take a bite of my toast. "Mmm."

One of the American girls starts talking about how they're going to deal with the lack of water on the planet. Mam types slowly on the computer; upstairs, one of the neighbors is hoovering. Other than that, the room's weirdly quiet. Something's going on. I can sense my parents' gazes lingering on me, feel them silently communicating behind my back.

"So, Spanish went well, did it?" Mam asks in a too-bright voice. "Maths next, right? That'll be a tough one."

The screen cuts to footage of a woman floating around in space. Her long black hair stretches above her head, swaying like sea grass without the gravity.

I take another bite of toast. It's already cold.

"It'll be fine."

She gives an airy laugh. "Will it? Haven't seen you doing much revision, Brody."

They've planned this, her and Dad: They've discussed how to bring this up, the best way to raise it without me closing off. Like I'm some problem to be handled. The feeling in my chest—that tight, angry knot that's been there since this morning, steadily growing throughout the day—is ballooning.

"It'll be fine," I say again. "I told you, it's just prelims."

"We're no' trying to get on your back, Brody. Just wondering how you're getting on," Dad says. He picks up a jumper from the pile of clothes. "*You* might as well be living on Mars, the amount we've heard from you lately," he adds, in a jokey tone that's not really a joke.

And suddenly, the balloon pops.

I spin around to face Dad. "What's it like for you, watching stuff like this?" I say. "Do you no' find it weird, thinking about how huge the universe is, when yours is only a few rooms? That there are people out there planning on traveling to bloody Mars, when you cannae even walk down the street to buy a Mars bar?"

As soon as I say it, I wish I hadn't.

Mam splutters out my name, but Dad doesn't say anything. He just stares at me, his expression slowly morphing from shock to hurt. I've never spoken to him like that before. I know it's stupid, and mean as hell, and as pointless as telling someone with broken legs to just try walking. He's sick. It's not his fault.

Funny how I can know all that and still be mad at him.

The door crashes open. We all turn around, Dad brandishing the iron midair like he's ready to whack an intruder with it. Jake is standing in the doorway, his school tie loose, a baffled grin cracking over his face.

"I got in." His voice is shaking. "I got into Cambridge."

Just like that, the bad atmosphere evaporates. Dad leaps forward, almost burning Jake with the iron, and Mam trips over her handbag in her rush to go and give him a hug. My words are blown away in a flurry of cheering and congratulations; Dad starts asking a hundred questions, and Mam snatches up her phone to call everyone in a hundred-mile radius. Jake looks so happy he might burst. He even gives me a hug.

"Well done, man," I tell him, patting his back. "You deserve it."

He beams at me, his eyes bright. "Thanks, Brody."

I should be happy for my brother. I *am* happy for my brother. Relieved that he's taken the heat off me by distracting Mam and Dad from my outburst, too. But another part of me feels like this is just more of the same: like every time they really see me, something brighter and shinier catches their eye. I'm starting to feel like I could disappear, and they wouldn't even notice.

TWENTY-FOUR

MY DAD BELIEVES IN PREMONITIONS. NOT THAT HE'S HAD ANY himself—if he had, maybe he could have avoided what happened to him six years ago. He's been convinced they're real since he saw some documentary about people who refused to board the *Titanic* because they'd had a nightmare about it, or Twin Towers workers who followed some gut instinct and decided to stay home on 9/11. I always thought it was rubbish, the idea that your body or your dreams could somehow predict the future. But when I walk into Everland on the first Thursday in March, I definitely have a feeling.

Something bad is going to happen tonight.

On the surface, everything looks normal. It's felt that way for a while now. The temperature has dropped back down to its usual comfortable level, and it's been weeks since I've noticed anything weird going on up in the sky. After I play a set with the band, I find Nico and the others hanging out down at the river. Kasia's reading aloud the "best bits" from a book on medieval history, which only Miyumi is politely pretending to pay attention to, and Nico is sketching Zahra. It's just another night in Everland. Even so, I can't sit still. Everything feels wrong.

"What is up with you tonight?" Nico asks me, scratching behind his ear.

He's dressed as some sort of arty unicorn: this amazing cape cut out of material printed with a Renaissance painting, and a gold headpiece made from dozens of chocolate-coin foils. I don't have as much time to make new costumes anymore, now I'm working in Rusty Records on the weekends, so I'm wearing my jeans and an Adidas jumper that I nicked from Jake with my old Anubis mask.

"I dunno. I'm just feeling weird." My eyes skate over the sky. It's a purplish blue tonight, with strips of pale violet clouds just behind the mountains. "Like the atmosphere's different or something. Can you really no' tell?"

They look at each other, then shake their heads. Kasia's looking at me with this concerned expression that makes me grit my teeth. Probably thinking that this is a sign of something. That I'm going to refuse to leave Everland and have a breakdown like her ex did.

"It's probably nothing," I say quickly. "Forget I said anything."

Then, from somewhere in the distance, someone begins to scream.

Before I can think about it, I'm running.

Then we're all running, past the giant metal animals, through long stretches of meadows and into the gardens, the landscape shifting fast around us. We end up back in the square with the terra-cotta buildings and the floral paving stones, the same one we arrived in back in January the night Nico was drunk. But something's different. The door, the bright yellow door that stood between the buildings, has disappeared.

Standing in the space where it used to be is a man. I've never seen him before: He's tall and pale, wearing board shorts and a Nike T-shirt. He keeps pacing back and forth, babbling in a thick Australian accent about how *this can't be happening; this can't be possible.*

Zahra's hand clamps to her mouth; Miyumi whispers something in Japanese. I stare at the man for a few more seconds before it clicks.

That was his door. And now it's gone.

He's stuck here.

The man claws at his hair, frantically rambling to himself. Other people run around the square, checking in and around the buildings as if somebody could have hidden the door for a joke. "Try another one, Louis!" someone shouts. The man nods for a moment then takes off out of the square. With dozens of us following him, he moves through the market, through manicured gardens and into a meadow of flowers, where a white door is half-hidden in the long grass.

Just a few steps in front of me, Nico stops.

"That's Dani's door," he says. "*Was* Dani's door."

The Australian man, Louis, sprints up to it and pulls on the handle as hard as he can. The door slides open; a few people around us gasp. For a second, I think he's done it: He's opened a door to Argentina. Beside me, Nico tenses. He could run through there, I realize with a jolt. He could find Dani—

But the door only opens an inch before it slams shut again. Louis lets out a strangled cry. Two more people run up to help. With three pairs of hands on the knob, they yank the door open. The same thing happens: It only opens an inch before it's pulled shut.

Beside me, Kasia has gone pale. "It won't work. You can only leave where you came in. He won't be able to get out that way."

Overhead, the sky is changing again: Red clouds roll over the mountains, turning the sea the color of blood; in the distance, flashes of lightning whip toward the horizon. It starts to rain. I've never seen it rain in Everland before.

Louis staggers backward from the door, clutching his head in his hands. "What do I do? What do I do?"

A few people go to comfort him. Others hurry away, perhaps back to their own doors and their real lives, or maybe just to someplace they can pretend this isn't happening. Though we've only been in here a short while, or what feels like it, I already feel the tug pulling me back toward our own green door.

The others do, too. We all say goodbye to Miyumi and quickly head back up the hill. Everyone is quiet. I can't stop thinking about that guy, scouring the square for a route home that's not there anymore. He's probably got a family waiting for him back home . . . friends . . . a job. Will he just disappear from his real life, now he can't get back?

Beyond the pine trees, the green door is waiting for us as always. Zahra lets out a gasp of relief.

"This isn't supposed to happen." Kasia pushes the door open, her hands shaking. "It doesn't make sense."

"This must b-be a mistake," Zahra stammers. "It'll come back. It has to."

Nico follows them out into the cool, crisp evening. "It'll be back by this time next week. We'll feel stupid for panicking about it then. Bunch of drama queens."

He forces a laugh, but no one joins in.

I felt that change. I felt it coming. I sensed it with the changes in the sky and the running of the stags. And I don't think we've seen the end of it yet.

TWENTY-FIVE

IN THE GUIDANCE ROOM AT SCHOOL THE NEXT DAY, MRS. WÓJCIK slides five sheets of paper across her desk. Red circles and crosses are scattered over the pages. My prelim results, laid out like a bad poker hand.

"What happened here, Brody?" Mrs. Wójcik asks, pointing to the grades at the top of the papers. "Music is great—no surprises there! And English wasn't too bad . . . But what happened with Maths and History, eh? Or Spanish? You normally do quite well in Spanish."

"Dunno, miss."

I shuffle in my plastic chair and duck my head to hide a yawn. I hardly slept last night. I couldn't stop thinking about Louis, hammering on a door he couldn't get through. Trapped in Everland forever.

"It seems like you're struggling a bit taking five subjects."

Mrs. Wójcik leans back in her seat, smoothing her cream cardigan down over her stomach. "Any reason for that?"

There's no good excuse that I can give her. Obviously not that I've been too busy spending my Thursday nights in a secret world hidden behind Calton Hill to focus on school, and I don't want to tell her about what's going on at home.

"Nah, miss. Everything's fine."

She starts a postmortem of my prelims, dissecting the results, trying to establish the cause of failure. I stare at the postcards from Zante and Prague taped to her filing cabinet, my eyes hazing over. Soon my mind has wandered off again, thinking about what happened last night.

It's thrown up even more questions about Everland. About why that door disappeared, and whether it'll come back. I need to talk to Nico about it. My whole head's a tangle right now. He could help me sort through it.

"Brody?"

I look up. Mrs. Wójcik's looking at me like she's waiting for an answer, her overly plucked eyebrows so high, they almost meet her hairline. I didn't hear the question.

"Uh, sorry, miss?"

She makes a face—something between a smile and a grimace. "I said, how about dropping a couple of subjects? Concentrating on your best ones."

"I'll work harder before the actual exams." I squint at the papers, as if that could somehow transform the Fs and Es into Bs. "There's still time."

"Not that much time, though." She laces her fingers together and shifts in her chair. "How about we leave History and Maths for now—you can always take them next year if you want to—and focus on the other three. Sound good?"

I'm not dumb. I know what she's doing: They don't want me dragging down their exam results, so they're kicking me out of the classes that I'll fail. I probably wouldn't have passed Maths or History, true, but they're not even giving me a shot at it. Somehow that feels worse than failing them in the first place—the fact that I'm not worth the extra push, a bit of encouragement. The fact that their stats are more important than what I'm going to do with my life.

But I don't have the energy to fight it.

"Yeah, all right. Fine."

"Great." Mrs. Wójcik slides the papers back into a pile. For a second, she reminds me of the tarot reader in the market: gathering her cards, satisfied that she's dealt someone their fate. "Let's work on getting English and Spanish up to scratch, then. I know you can do well if you put your mind to it."

Megan's waiting for me outside in the corridor when I leave. Though I can't be arsed talking, I tell her what happened. She clicks her tongue, her arms crossed over her chest.

"That's well shan. It's like when Mr. Phillips picked me for that maths tournament in Perth, then Jamie Keir got *two points* more than me on an algebra test, and they decided he could go instead."

"That's no' the same thing at all." A surge of irritation flares

214

up inside me. "Christ, can you go five minutes without making something about yourself?"

There's a long, shocked pause. I push past Megan, heading toward the music room and the drums. After a moment, I hear her shoes clacking down the corridor after me.

"I'm just trying to help, Brody," she says, loud enough that a group of freshmen look up from their phones to stare. She grabs my sleeve and spins me around to face her. "What's the matter with you?"

"Nothing." I pull my arm out of her grasp. "Everything's great. Just leave me alone, will you?"

The words come out harsher than I mean for them to. Megan takes a step back. For a horrible second, I think she might cry.

"Sorry," I mutter. "I'm just tired."

"It's all right." She looks at her shoes and flattens the back of her hair with her hand. "Wanna go up the street for lunch? I was wanting to talk to you about some stuff."

"I've booked the drum kit." I don't have any money to go up the street, either, but I don't want to admit that here. "I need to practice. It's been ages."

I don't have time to listen to Megan's boy drama or whatever. It's not that I don't care; I just can't deal with it today. She looks hurt, which is enough to make me feel bad. It's enough to make me promise we'll hang out on Monday. But right now, it's not enough to make me go with her.

* * *

The yellow door doesn't come back. When we get to Everland the following week, another one has disappeared, this time leading to Bucharest. Two women are standing in a garden, where, according to a man in the hushed crowd of people around them, a bright blue door used to be. One is sobbing and shouting something in Romanian, totally inconsolable. The other seems oddly calm. A few people try to talk to them, but no one is rushing around trying to help this time. It's only been a week, but it seems already everyone's accepted that there's no alternate exit when a door disappears. It's gone for good.

Everyone except Nico.

"Maybe it'll pop up again," he says a bit feebly. "Maybe this is just a mistake."

Nobody replies. The calmer woman puts an arm around her friend and leads her away. I can hear her sobs long after they've left the garden. Kasia clicks her tongue and rolls up her sleeves.

"I'm going back to the library," she says. "There must be something in there that can explain all this. This place has existed for centuries—*somebody* must have left some notes."

The others get pulled off in different directions after that: Zahra says she's going to the river; Nico, to the largest and loudest party he can find, probably. I want to go with him, but somehow I end up going to find the band instead. Like everyone else around here, Esther and the others look a bit subdued as they tune up their instruments.

"You heard about the second door?" Esther asks as I climb

onto the stage. She nods toward Arnau. "This guy's thinking of not coming back next week."

Arnau grimaces as he loops the strap of his bass over his head. "It's dangerous," he says. "My mother, she will be very sad if I cannot go back."

"We don't even know what's happening yet, though," I tell him. "It could just be those two doors."

He shrugs. Behind him, Sandhya is biting her lip. I spin around to Esther.

"What about you? Are you gonnae leave?"

She shakes her head fast, making her long earrings jangle. "My home is here now. I barely even remember my life on the outside anymore. I remember songs and stories, books I read or films I saw when I was a little girl. But the people and the places are hazy. I hear their voices, sometimes, or I see faces I used to know . . . but when I try to latch on to them, they slip away. There'd be nothing for me to go back to now."

That night, I find myself getting pulled toward parts of Everland I've never seen before. I walk past a heart-shaped lake, through a never-ending meadow where wild horses roam through long grass, toward a cluster of run-down stone structures poking from the ground like rotten teeth. Music floats up from behind the walls—slow, sad strings. I move through a low archway and find myself in an ancient ruin of an amphitheater, a smaller version of Rome's Colosseum. Miyumi is standing in the center, playing her violin.

To say she's amazing would be an understatement. It's like the notes are moving through her: Her eyes close, her mouth twists, her body moves from side to side as if pulled by forces I can't see. When the music quickens, her fingers move so fast they're a blur of pale skin; when it slows, her chest swells with every vibration of the strings. It feels like all of Everland must be able to hear this. They *should* be able to hear this.

When the piece ends, I feel like I'm coming out of a trance. Miyumi stops, the hand holding her bow slowly falls to her side, and she opens her eyes. She doesn't look surprised to see me. I clap, but it doesn't feel enough, not when it's just me. She gives a small bow.

"Handel's Sarabande," she says breathlessly. "It is one of my favorites."

I walk down the steps to meet her. "I thought you didnae play in here."

She kneels by the stone seats, picks up the violin case from the ground and opens the clips. "Usually no. Things are different now."

"Well, I'm glad I heard it. That was unbelievable."

"Thank you." She smiles and nods her head. She nestles the violin in its case, her hand brushing the shiny wood for a moment, then slips the bow inside.

"I am very lucky," she says, standing up. "When I was young, all I wanted was to play music. I have performed in the Sydney Opera House and La Scala and the Bolshoi Theatre. As a musician, I have done all the things I wanted to."

I wait for the *but*. It doesn't come.

"I take it you're no' coming back next week, then?" I say.

She blinks at me, confused. I wonder if she's misunderstood— her English is great, but my accent's a bit thick for her sometimes—but then she shakes her head.

"Yes, I am. Of course."

We set off to find Nico and the others, and as we walk, I won- der about Miyumi and Esther, Sandhya and Arnau. About their lives on the outside, and what they have there that's too valuable to risk losing. Or what they don't have that'd make them decide to stay.

We end up back in the square where we arrived. Nico, Kasia, and Zahra are sitting on the edge of a fountain, staring at the space where the yellow door used to be. Around us, some people have already begun to say their goodbyes. Two men are standing by a pale orange door, holding hands and whispering; another couple are slow-dancing in silence under the starlight.

When she sees me coming, Kasia stands up and smooths her jeans down.

"We should go." She's looking at me like I'm a bomb that could go off at any moment. "Are you ready?"

I don't feel that pull drawing me back yet, but I nod and fol- low her up the hill, Nico and Zahra right behind us.

The walk back to the door is quiet tonight. Once outside, the four of us sit on the top step of the National Monument. It's raining, but none of us is in a hurry to get home.

"I don't think I can go back there again," Zahra says shakily.

"Not if the doors are really disappearing. It's too much of a risk. What if something happened to my mum and I couldn't get home? What if I got stuck in Everland forever? I can't do that to my family."

She looks like she's about to cry. Kasia slides an arm around her shoulder and squeezes. Nerves twist at my stomach. Zahra's right. It's a huge risk. Even coming here tonight was dangerous—what if our door had vanished behind us, and we'd all been stuck there forever?

But truth is, it hadn't occurred to me not to come. That's mostly because I thought the yellow door disappearing was a one-off. But even now that I know it wasn't . . . I can't imagine not coming back next Thursday. This place gives me the one moment in my week when I can breathe properly, when I can stop worrying about money and school and Leanne and Michelle and just *be*. It's the only place where I don't have to watch what I say or how I'm saying it.

It's the only place where I feel okay as I am.

And that feeling, it's a lot to give up. I almost feel like I'm addicted. The risk of getting trapped, being separated from my family forever, makes me feel queasy, but it's not enough to keep me away. I need Everland. I'll take the risk and keep going back as long as I possibly can.

Nico and I look at each other. He's pale and shaken and the quietest I've ever seen him, but he doesn't look scared.

I know he'll be back here next week, too.

SPRING

TWENTY-SIX

ZAHRA ISN'T WAITING FOR US WHEN I GET TO CALTON HILL THE following Thursday, but Kasia is. Even with the worries about what happened to her ex still gnawing at her, she keeps coming to Everland every week. I don't know if that's because she can't give it up, or because the doors disappearing is a riddle that she needs to solve. Nico and I barely see her; she spends her whole time cooped up in the library, emerging dazed and frustrated some time later. But after a few weeks incommunicado, one day she comes to join us in a garden behind the castle, carrying a large scroll of beige paper.

"I think I've worked it out."

Nico looks up. "The doors?"

We're sitting by the edge of a pond, watching strange white-and-blue birds glide across its surface. We said we'd go over

Spanish vocab for my exam next month, but Nico's in a weird mood, all quiet and distant. My head's not in it, either. It's hard to focus on what's going on in the outside world when I'm in here. When we came through earlier, some Peruvian guys that Nico knows told us two more doors have disappeared since our last visit—one leading to Shenyang, and the other to Uppsala. The week before, it was one to a village in Costa Rica. They all vanished just after their visitors went back through them, so fortunately nobody got stuck here this time. But they'll never be able to return to Everland unless they find another entrance.

I don't know which would be worse: being trapped here or never coming back.

Kasia drops to the grass and unfurls the paper, holding the corners down with books from her backpack. It's a map of Everland: the three rivers, the waterfall, the mountains in the distance . . . Nico's eyebrows rise.

"Did you draw this?"

"Nah, it was in the library. Took me forever to find it though. Look, it says it's from 1818." Kasia points to a scribbled date on the bottom left of the page. "But what I'm interested in are these."

Dotted around the page, drawn as small, sharp rectangles, are doors. There are dozens of them, each one with a number and a place name printed beside it. We kneel down to scan the page, looking for the green door we walk through every Thursday. Nico finds it before I do.

"Edinburgh," he says, pointing to a small mark up on the hill. He leans closer. "What's that say—1649?"

"I think that must be the year it first appeared." Kasia sits up on her knees and pushes her hair out of her face. "I've gone through them all. There are three hundred and eighty-one here. This one is the oldest."

She points to a mark near the right-hand side of the page: *Kingdom of Tlemcen, circa 1500.*

"This is the oldest door listed here, in what's now Algeria. I went to the place where it's marked on the map, but the door's not there anymore." She slides her finger across the page. "And this was the second oldest."

Kasia points them out one by one: dozens of doors, most leading to places I've never even heard of. Eventually, we come to the ones that have recently disappeared: Romania, 1609; China, 1610; Sweden, 1610. My stomach starts to sink. Nico sits back on his heels and rubs his palms into his eyes.

"So they're closing," he says dully. "The doors are disappearing."

We knew that, even if we didn't want to admit it. But for some reason, seeing it like this—on paper—makes it all the more real. It feels wrong to be applying logic to Everland like this. It feels wrong to apply time to it.

"I don't get it," Nico says. "Why is this happening? You think it's breaking down or something?"

Kasia shrugs. "Maybe. But for all we know, it happens all the time. This place is so vast . . . We only noticed the first door disappearing because we saw someone get trapped this side. Maybe this has been going on for ages."

I'm not so sure. Those weeks seeing the sky flashing, the stars blot out, the river turn red—that felt like something radical was changing in here. I don't think this is something that happens all the time.

"I made a list," Kasia says. "They seem to be vanishing in the order they appeared in. If I'm right, ours will go after this one," she adds, pointing to a door marked *Montreal, 1648*.

"But there's no way to know when," Nico says. "We don't know how often they're going. Or if there are others that aren't marked on here."

"Exactly. It could take months, even years, or ten could go all at once. Ours could disappear at any time." Kasia's face is tight. "I don't know what to do."

For a while, we just sit in silence. It feels like months have passed since Zahra left, but it's still weird without her. Our group feels incomplete. Out of the silence, the sound of Miyumi's violin drifts toward us from somewhere in the distance. For the past few weeks, she's done nothing but practice in here.

Nico pushes himself to his feet. "I'm going for a walk."

I stand up, too. "Want me to come with you?"

He doesn't reply, already walking away. Kasia shoots me a confused look, then nods at me to go after him.

I hurry across the moorland, following him to a strange, quiet stretch of houses I've never seen before. Nico takes a right into a long alleyway. It's eerily quiet and a million miles from the parties and festivals that he usually ends up in. I follow him through street after street, through shadows and puddles and occasional pools of light cast from the windows of houses. Inside, people are laughing, talking, playing card games. A few watch as we hurry past, but none of them invites us in.

What's going on here?

Behind the buildings, the pulse of Everland keeps beating: I can hear a song that I think might be Esther's, but it's too far away to tell. Something inside is urging me to get away from here and go and join them, but I ignore it and keep following Nico. Eventually, the streets widen, and we end up in what I can only describe as a wasteland. It's vast and empty, with only a few bare, withered trees breaking the panorama.

"What is this place?" I ask, though I don't think Nico knows, either.

He stares around, his face blank. He takes a few heavy steps, his boots kicking up clouds of dust, then stops.

"I got an email yesterday," he says. "I didn't get into art school."

"Which one?"

"Barcelona. Last week it was Berlin. I didn't even get interviews for London and Paris." He turns to look at me, and his face crumples. "I didn't get into *any* of them, Brody. Not a single one."

For a long moment, I just stare at him. I have no clue what to say. I never thought this would happen. His costumes are incredible. There is so much time and effort and love in every one of them. So much of him. How could they say no to that?

"My dad and Jenny are being so smug about it." He kicks at

a stone. "They're acting all sympathetic, but you can tell they're dying to scream, *I told you so.* My dad practically whipped out the champagne when I got my last rejection."

"You can try again next year . . ." I start to say, but Nico's already walking away. I run after him. "Hey, come on. It's no' like it's—"

"Stop trying to make me feel better, Brody," he snaps. "You can't make me feel better about this. This is all I wanted. This is all I *am.*"

He swallows, but he's not going to cry. All I see is anger. I get it. Dani left. His mum left. His dad doesn't want him, or at least that's what he thinks. Everland might be lost to us soon, and now this has been taken away from him, too. But he still has so much. He still has his talent, and his friends—and me. I start to tell him that, but Nico holds up a hand.

"I just want to be alone, Brody, okay? I'll talk to you later."

He walks off without saying goodbye. I watch him go until he disappears past the trees, into the haze of beige on the horizon, and out of sight completely.

TWENTY-SEVEN

A WEIRD RATTLING NOISE FROM THE LIVING ROOM WAKES ME UP ON Saturday. At first, I think our decade-old PC is breaking down again, but when I get up to investigate, I realize it's Jake. I've hardly seen him all week: Mam had to cancel our internet last Friday, so he's been spending more time at school, the library, or his friends' houses. It doesn't look like he's been to bed yet. He's sitting on the floor in his school uniform, breathing rough and fast, the way Dad does when he has an attack.

"I can't do this," he says in a voice all high-pitched and panicked. "I can't. I can't do it—I'm going to fail."

"What are you talking about?" I say. "Of course you're no' gonnae fail."

He tries to answer, but his breathing is coming too fast. I

run to the kitchen, pour a glass of water, run back, and push it into Jake's hand. It's been a while since I've seen Dad have one of these, so I'm a bit rusty on what to do, but it comes back to me. I get a flannel from the bathroom, soak it in cold water, and press it gently to his head.

"Just breathe," I tell him. "Count to ten."

I've never seen him like this before. And honestly, the first words that come to mind are *This is ridiculous*. He's not going to fail. *I'm* the one who actually has failed, so bad I'm not even allowed to sit the stupid exams. I shouldn't have to prop Jake up, tell him how smart and brilliant he is. He's got a room full of trophies and certificates to prove that.

But maybe it's like Dad's agoraphobia. Logically, he knows that the chances of anything bad happening are small, but he's still scared to step outside the flat. Just because Jake's success is obvious to everyone else, it doesn't mean he can see it.

So I don't tell him he's imagining things or that there's nothing to worry about. You wouldn't say that to someone with a broken arm or a bleeding leg—the feeling's just as real. Instead, I tell him to keep breathing, keep counting, until finally the heaving movements of his chest slow down. He wipes his face with the flannel and drinks the rest of his water.

"Thanks," he says, his voice shaking. "I just . . . I dunno— I'm just stressed."

"Seems like you're overdoing it a bit." There are books and notes spread across the floor, on the kitchen table, on the desk. I lean back on the arm of the sofa, putting some distance between us again. "Maybe you're just needing a break."

"I can't." He pushes himself to his feet and wipes his sweaty palms on his trousers. "I've still got to finish my Latin dissertation, and I haven't even *started* my English essay, and I've got volunteering for Duke of Ed this afternoon—"

I hold up my hands. "Jake! Christ, you can take ten minutes." I glance at the clock on the computer screen: ten to ten. I'm running late. "Look, I've got work just now. You can go with me to the shop, get some fresh air."

Though he looks horrified at the idea of leaving his revision, he nods and puts his jacket on while I quickly get ready. The lift's broken again, so we have to take the stairs down to the courtyard. There's a match on at Easter Road, and Great Junction Street is packed full of cars. Not exactly the zen atmosphere Jake needs, but at least I got him away from his books for a while.

"So . . ." I try to think of a subject that's not related to school and fail. To be fair, Jake doesn't give us much to work with. "What's your Latin dissertation about?"

"Uh, it's on the characterization of Nisus and Euryalus in Virgil's *Aeneid*."

He might as well have said that *in* Latin for all I understand. "Right. Sounds . . . fun."

"It's really not."

He forces a laugh. An awkward silence follows us to the end of the block.

"So, uh, how are you liking working in the shop?" he asks eventually.

"Aye, it's grand. It's pretty quiet, so we mostly just listen to records all day."

"Nice."

God. If there was such a thing as Advanced Higher Small Talk, my brother would get an F. It wasn't always like this. When we were younger, we used to talk all the time. We argued and fought and took the piss out of each other—he made me cry at least once a week—but at least we spoke. He was all right, sometimes.

I wonder what he'd make of Everland. I can't really imagine him there. Jake's so serious, so tied to the world and all its realities. So ambitious, too—he wants to be First Minister of Scotland, for crying out loud. I bet his brain just wouldn't let him believe what he was seeing. He'd find some rational explanation, the way I tried to the first day I was there.

By the time we arrive at the shop, he's calmed down a bit. He looks embarrassed now, and annoyed with himself. Dad gets like that, too, though there's no need for it. It's not like they can control it.

"Will you be all right getting back?"

"Aye, I'm fine. Thanks, though. I feel better now." He turns to go, then pauses. His eyes scan the door of Rusty Records.

"I know you probably think I'm not pulling my weight not getting a job," he says. "It's just until my exams are over. Obviously, I'll get one for the summer. You know what Mam's like, though . . . She'd kill me if I went behind her back."

"I hadnae really thought about it."

I really hadn't. If Jake spent all his time out with his friends or watching TV, I'd probably have moaned, but he's always studying. Too much, judging by today's episode. Asking him to add a job on top of that would push him over the edge.

"Stop worrying." I give him a push on the arm. "You're gonnae do fine. You always do."

It feels good to be in Rusty Records this morning. All I've thought about since Thursday is Nico and about everything that's going on in Everland. I like having something to keep me busy, even if it is just alphabetizing the boxes of dusty records Mark dumped on the counter earlier.

Around lunchtime, I'm sitting on the floor, sorting out a stack of seven-inch vinyls from the '90s, when I hear a voice above me.

"Excuse me. Have you got 'Sorry Seems to Be the Hardest Word'?"

I twist around. Nico is standing above me. He's wearing a faded gray jumper and jeans, his face is pale, and there are bags under his eyes.

"Eh, probably." I stand up, brushing the dust off my hands. "What are you sorry for?"

He shrugs and digs his hands into his pockets. "For being a dick. For being selfish. I shouldn't have just walked off like that."

I bite back a smile. "Bit of a clichéd choice, d'you no' think? I'd go for . . . 'I'm So Sorry' by Imagine Dragons."

"'El Perdón,'" Jett chimes in. "Nicky Jam and Enrique Igle-sias. It's a tune, man."

She's watching us from behind the counter, a wide grin on her face. There's nobody else in the shop—Gavin the Brian Eno fan came in at around ten, but otherwise it's been dead all morning.

"You can take your lunch early if you want, Brody," Jett tells me. "It's not like we're gonna be swamped this afternoon. Not in this weather."

It's a sunny day, which means everyone in Edinburgh has gone outside. Nico and I walk down to Leith Links and sit under some trees by the side of the path near a group of girls having a kickabout and an old man lying in the sun with his shirt off. I take a squashed ham sandwich out of my pocket; Nico extracts a pack of cigarettes from his. He takes a draw and collapses onto the grass, one hand over his eyes.

"You hungover?" I remember that look Dad used to get, from the days when he still went to the pub with his mates—like everything in the world was a little too sharp the next day. Nico looks just the same.

"A bit. Okay, a lot." He gives me a wry smile. "I threw up all over Jenny's geraniums. She's gonna kill me when she notices."

He flicks his lighter on and off. For once, there's no paint on his hands. Not even a line around the fingernails. "I really am sorry about Thursday, Brody. It was just a shock. Going to art school . . . It's all I've ever wanted to do with my life. It didn't really occur to me it might not happen. Pretty arrogant, I know."

"They're idiots," I say. "They must be. Your costumes are amazing."

"Clearly, they're not."

"It must be well competitive, then. They probably get thousands of applications." I shift toward him. "It doesnae mean yours are bad."

He doesn't reply. Obviously, there's no talking him out of this.

"Well, if it's any consolation, I failed half my prelims," I tell him. "I mean, I wasnae planning on going to uni, anyway. But now there's no way it's an option."

Nico looks at me. "You can still turn it around. You have time. Come on, pop quiz." He sits up, drumming his free hand on his knee. "Uh . . . when did the Byzantine Empire end?"

I laugh. "How the hell am I supposed to know? We're doing the Wars of Independence and Nazi Germany."

He doesn't know much about either of those, and he's worse at maths than I am. He makes me go over the dialogue for my Spanish speaking exam until it's almost perfect, though, and he's surprisingly well versed in *Othello* and *Hamlet*. But though we take our time, there's an undercurrent running through the conversation. Another, more important topic pushing at the surface.

"So"—Nico runs his fingers through the long grass—"I was thinking about what Kasia said. About how the doors are disappearing. About how ours is going to close soon."

"What about it?"

He flits his finger through the flame of his lighter, quickly, so it doesn't burn. "I think . . . I think I might stay. Like Esther and the others. I think I might stay in Everland."

Everything around me slows down.

"What are you on about?" I stammer. "What about your family?"

Nico scoffs. "They'll barely even notice. My mum's too busy with her new kids—she doesn't care. And I'll never be good enough for my dad."

His words are dripping with anger. You can almost see the stain it's left on him. To be honest, though, I find it hard to believe either of his parents could feel that about him. Even if sometimes I feel exactly the same way about mine.

"Look, I know things suck at the moment." I shift across the grass toward him and squeeze his shoulder. "But it'll pass, Nico. It's no' gonnae be like this forever."

"What if it is, though?" he says. "What if I never find anything like Everland again? What if this is it for me? Feeling out of place wherever I go."

If you'd told me, back in September, when Nico stormed out of that flat and ordered Leanne and Michelle to piss off . . . if you'd told me that he felt like this, too, I never would have believed you. Nico can walk down the street dressed as a fairy or a phoenix or in a coat of golden roses and not bat an eyelid. I thought sniggers and weird looks and insults slid right off him. I thought he was confidence personified. But maybe the costumes are a way of hiding something.

Suddenly, he lets out a laugh.

"God, I'm so pathetic. There are people in Everland escaping violence and abuse and persecution. Transphobia, racism, all sorts of discrimination. People who have been diagnosed with terminal diseases looking for more time." He looks down at his hands, picking at the skin around his thumb. "I haven't gone through anything like that. Nothing even close. So I got bullied a bit. So my parents split up. So I didn't get into art school. Talk about tiny violins. I feel like a fraud."

"You're not," I say. "Those things still matter. Besides, it doesnae work like that. You cannae measure everything in your life by somebody else's."

"No, but you should be grateful for what you do have. I know I've been so lucky in life, in a lot of ways. In most ways. But that doesn't change how I feel about myself."

He glides his finger through the flame again. This time, he's too slow; it burns the skin. He winces and drops the lighter, shaking off the pain. I pick it up and press it into his hand, then keep my fingers locked over his. He looks up at me, his eyes blurry and bloodshot but warm. I could swear that if I kissed him now, he'd kiss me back—but it seems wrong, to make a move when he's upset like this. So soon after Dani's left, as well.

After a second, Nico looks away. The moment's gone.

"Sorry, Brody. I'm not normally this mopey. It's just hard sometimes. It'd be even harder without that place." He presses his palms to his eyes for a moment and then looks up with his normal bright smile.

"Anyway. I'm gonna make sure you crush these exams.

Um . . . how do you calculate the volume of a pyramid? I have absolutely no idea what the answer is, so I'll give you a point either way . . ."

He keeps talking, but what he's said hangs above us like a thundercloud. He didn't really mean it, though. He wouldn't actually swap the real world for Everland. He wouldn't just leave like that.

Would he?

TWENTY-EIGHT

ALL WEEK, NICO SEEMS FAR AWAY: MY MESSAGES GO UNANSWERED, and he doesn't pick up when I try to call. Eventually, he sends me a message promising he'll see me on Thursday, but it still leaves me nervous. Like he's going to vanish at any moment. It's a relief to get back to Calton Hill and see him sitting on the steps to the monument, waiting for me with Kasia.

"Hey, Brodes." He holds his arms out to give me a hug. "Sorry for disappearing on you. I've been doing a lot of thinking."

I'm just relieved he's okay. He's hungover again—there are bags under his eyes, and his hair's a mess—but his mood isn't as dark as it was last week. He seems good. Calm.

All of Everland feels calm tonight, really. The sky is low and filled with the most amazing display of Northern Lights: Ribbons of pink and green float above us, fading into a deep velvet blue above the mountains. Kasia heads to the library, and Nico to the market (he needs some fabric for a costume he's working on for Beltane, the first he's started since he got his rejection letters), so I find Esther and the band setting up in one of the squares. Arnau is sitting on the stage tuning his bass. I wave, surprised but happy to see him after a few weeks.

"Thought you weren't coming back?"

He pulls a face. "I tried, but . . . this place, it is hard to leave."

I glance at my drum kit. Its curves glisten in the light of the lampposts. "I know what you mean."

When I get off the stage after our set, I wander down to the lake and find Nico skimming stones with Miyumi and Kasia. They're quiet—the only noise, the sound of pebbles hopping across the water, and the throb of music somewhere in the distance.

Kasia turns to me, her hands on her hips.

"So." Her voice is cold. "Has Nico told you about his plans?"

"He has." I eye him nervously. "Are you still serious about that?"

He nods. "Yep. I am."

Kasia bends down to pick up another stone. "You realize it's not like moving to France or something, right? You can't get a Ryanair flight back home whenever you feel like it. You'd be stuck in here *forever*."

"Yes, I'd worked that out, thanks." Nico smiles. "I still think you should consider doing the same, Kash. Think about how many books you'd get to read."

"What, and put up with you pissing me off for all eternity? I'll pass." She turns to him, her arms crossed. The steely look in her eye melts. "I love you, Nico, but this is such a bad idea."

"It's what I want," he says simply. "It's what's best."

He throws another stone at the water. It bounces five times before it disappears. Kasia just stares at him, her mouth twisted up with all the words he won't listen to. Then Miyumi takes a step back, her arms folded.

"I will not go back, either."

There's a stunned silence.

"What are you talking about?" Kasia says.

"I've decided." She gives a matter-of-fact nod, her eyes still on the water. "I will stay here, too."

Out of everybody I know in Everland, I never thought Miyumi would be the one to stay. Miyumi has everything waiting for her in the real world—she's only seventeen, and she already has a real career, a future, a chance to do what she's good at. But as soon as I think that, I realize I've never asked her what else she has. I don't know what her family or her friends are like. I don't know how she feels about anything.

"It's too much," she says. "It's too much pressure. Rehearsals, performances, competitions . . . It never stops. It killed music for me. When I was younger, I loved playing my violin. Later, when I looked at it, all I saw was work. All I thought about was everything I had to do, and everything that I would lose if I failed. Being in here, it's the only place I can breathe."

"What about your family?" Kasia asks. "Your friends, school . . . everything."

Miyumi doesn't answer, but her bottom lip shakes, and her eyes are welling up. Nico shoots Kasia a look, then links his arm around Miyumi's shoulders and pulls her toward him.

"Good decision, babe. We're going to have an amazing life in here. I promise." He looks at me. "What about you, Brody? Fancy joining us?"

My mouth goes dry. When he told me on Saturday he was thinking about it, I was sure he was just upset. I never thought he was serious, and I never really considered doing the same. Thinking about it, my first response is an outright no—that I couldn't do that to my family. But then another part of me looks at Nico and feels an overwhelming urge to say yes. I don't want to lose this place. I don't want to lose him, either.

Kasia answers for me.

"*No.*" Her hands are clenched, and a vein has begun to throb in her forehead. "This place isn't meant for that. It's not supposed to replace real life."

"It *is* real life, Kasia." Nico tosses his final stone at the water. It makes three high arcs before sinking beneath the surface. "It always has been."

"Thanks a lot for waiting for me, dickhead."

It's Friday. I'm sitting in the canteen, a baked potato that I barely remember buying in front of me. I can hardly remember coming here, either, or the classes I had before the bell rang:

242

Nico's question has been echoing through my head all day. But now Megan is standing by the table, her arms crossed over her school jumper.

"Did you not get my message?" she asks. "I told you to wait for me at the vending machines."

She slumps into the seat opposite; her tray hits the table with a thud, making one of the freshman kids across from us jump. Keira's at a table in the far corner of the room, talking to Amanda through a mouthful of burger.

"Sorry." I rub my eyes between my thumb and forefinger, trying to stop my head from spinning. "I was . . . I was totally starving, couldnae wait."

"What is up with you?" She leans back in her chair, ignoring the yogurt and soggy-looking salad on her tray. "You never reply to my texts anymore. You barely speak to me after school. You've been acting weird for months. What's going on?"

Snippets from last night whirl through my head. Nico saying he's going to stay. Miyumi saying she will, too. Maybe I don't need to say goodbye to them. Maybe Everland really could be forever.

I shake my head. "It's nothing."

"It's obviously not, Brody. I'm supposed to be your best friend—why can't you just tell me?"

I stab at my baked potato with my fork, but suddenly I've lost my appetite. Megan doesn't sound worried. She sounds annoyed that I'm keeping secrets from her.

"Because it's none of your business, that's why."

Megan's jaw drops. Her face starts to turn pink. "You've been unbearable since you met this Nico guy, you know that? You're so up yourself now."

"You mean I've actually started speaking," I say, my own cheeks heating up. "You mean I've stopped indulging your thousand daily monologues about yourself. Nico's got nothing to do with it."

"Yes, he does! You hardly talk to me anymore. You never listen to anything I say . . ."

One of the freshmen is holding up her phone to film us. Megan gives her the finger, and the girl hastily puts it away. She turns back to me.

"Nico has *everything* to do with this, Brody."

With brilliant timing, Leanne and Michelle appear at our table, both carrying trays of pizza and chips. Leanne leans toward me and Megan, her eyebrows raised.

"Ooh, who's *Nico*?" she asks, in this faux-scandalized voice. Then she pauses. "Oh my God, wait—is that your fairy godmother?"

She and Michelle burst out laughing. They start shouting the story about that day to some boys two tables away, only it's not how it really happened: They turn Nico into some simpering caricature screaming from his window, me into a sniveling baby clutching at my cat, and they leave out the bit where Nico stood up to them and got them to piss off.

Usually by this point, Megan would have called them bitches—or worse—and dragged me away. But today she just watches, her arms crossed, as does half the canteen. There are a dozen responses running through my head, but when I try to get them out, my mouth won't cooperate.

"Christ, Brody, you're such a loser." Leanne points to my sister, who's staring wide-eyed from a table in the corner. "This one, too, fannying about thinking she's in *Les Fucking Mis*. Mental. Runs in the family, eh?"

And I don't know why—after all the names and the jokes and the humiliation—but that's what does it. That's what makes me snap. Leanne doesn't even notice; she's moved on to taking the piss out of Anton Akande's haircut. I stand up, put my hand under her tray, and flip it into her face. Her plate flies upward and the pizza slides down her top, onto her shoes, across the floor. Leanne takes a step back and bumps against the table. I'm not going to hit her—even with all this anger pumping through me, I wouldn't hit her—but I lean in until my face is just a couple centimeters from hers.

"You keep your mouth shut about my family, you hear me? Keep your fucking mouth shut."

Every other time I've tried to stand up to her, her eyes have glinted, and her mouth has twisted into a smug smile. Like people are always telling me, that's what she wants: a reaction. But now, her face freezes. She looks . . . scared. People are turning to stare; Michelle is gawping at me, too shocked to come to her friend's defense. I hadn't realized, but I'm almost as tall as Leanne is now.

"Brody Fair!"

I let my hands drop. Mrs. Davies is storming across the

canteen, staring at us with a thunderous expression. "What is going on here?"

"He attacked me, miss!" Leanne whimpers and cowers, tucking her shoulders in to make herself look smaller. "He grabbed my arm and threw my tray at me and—"

"*What?* Is that true, Brody?"

Anton starts telling her what really happened. In the table in the corner, Keira's face is bright red, part embarrassment and part from trying not to cry. A few of her friends rush over to back up Anton's story, but the glint in Mrs. Davies's eyes hasn't disappeared. Still, she knows what Leanne's like. She's heard the stuff she says, not just about me, but about anybody she thinks she can get a rise out of. But when Mrs. Davies points down the corridor, it's me she tells to leave.

"Headmistress's office, Brody. Now."

Leanne keeps rubbing her shoulder, acting like I rugby-tackled her to the ground, but she can't hide the smile tugging at her lips. Another volt of anger surges through me. I kick the table leg, making Michelle jump.

"Fuck this. This is bullshit."

"*What* did you say?"

Mrs. Davies follows me down the hallway, shouting about detentions and suspensions and disrespecting teachers. I don't care. The words slide off me, and so do the stares of the kids lining the corridors. None of it can reach me. It's almost like I'm not there at all.

TWENTY-NINE

THEY SUSPEND ME FOR THE WHOLE OF NEXT WEEK. MAM HITS THE roof. That's putting it lightly: She practically crashes *through* the roof, past the tenth and eleventh floors, and flies into orbit, she's so mad.

"What the hell is the matter with you? You can't go around chucking pizza at people!"

"It wasnae his fault, Mam." Now she's gotten over Leanne humiliating her in front of half the school, Keira's enraged on my behalf. She hangs over the back of a kitchen chair, thumping the edges with her fists. "You know what Leanne's like—she was being a total—"

Mam cuts her off. "You have exams *next month*, Brody. Did you think about that before you started kicking off?"

"Who cares?" I toss my bag onto the floor and slump down on the sofa. "It's no' like I'm gonnae pass them anyway."

I really cannot be arsed with this. It has been a shitty, shitty day, and the last thing I need is another bollocking; I already got one of those at school. They might have let me off with a few detentions if it had just been for shoving Leanne's tray—she's not exactly popular with the staff—but that plus swearing at a teacher was enough to get me suspended. And maybe I deserve it. But I'd be lying if I said I regret it, and I'm not going to apologize. Not to Leanne, at least.

Mam picks up my bag and pushes it into my arms. "You would if you did any work! I don't want a repeat of your prelims. You need to put some effort in."

"I havnae even see you do your homework for ages," Dad chimes in, sticking his head out of the kitchen. "There's no excuse, son. Just laziness."

"Exactly." Mam nods. "How much revision have you done? Have you even started yet?"

Surprisingly, it's Jake who comes to my defense.

"Mam, will you give him a break?" He twists around from the computer, rolling his eyes. "It's just a few days. It's hardly the end of the world."

That's a bit rich coming from him, seeing as he might actually die if he had to miss a week of school before exams, but I give Mam a *See?* look. She stares at Jake for a long moment, her hands on her hips, before eventually turning back to me.

"Well, you're going to study the whole week, Brody. No going out. No seeing Megan. Nothing." She runs a hand through her hair and sighs, her shoulders sagging like deflated balloons. "Christ, this is really not what I need right now."

For the first couple of days, I actually do try. With no internet and no data left on my phone, there's not much else for me to do, anyway. I make a big show of leaving my Music notes and English textbooks lying around the flat, proving to Mam I'm trying. I even ask Jake to check my Spanish homework—he gave it up after fourth year, but annoyingly he's still better at it than I am.

By the next day, Mam's satisfied that I'm putting in some effort, at least, and has mostly forgotten about grounding me. At quarter to eleven, I slip out to Everland without anyone to stop me.

Tonight, a labyrinth has appeared not far from the library. It's enormous: dark green hedges, each three feet wide and twenty feet tall, spread out in complicated zigzags across the grass. Kasia, who loves puzzles, is really into it: She and Miyumi race along the paths, shouting instructions to each other as they try to find the center. I amble along with Nico and fill him in on what happened in the canteen last week.

"And they suspended *you*?" He clicks his tongue. "For God's sake. Those people are idiots."

"Pretty much. And now my chances of passing my exams have gone from none to, like . . . minus none."

Nico throws his arm around me. "Okay, so you might be a lost cause with Maths. But you've got Music in the bag! And I'll help you with Spanish."

"*Gracias.*" I shift slightly closer to him, my hand on his back. "*Cómo se dice*, 'I'm screwed'?"

"*Estoy jodido.* Or, *Estoy en el horno*, as Dani would say. It's literally, 'I'm in the oven.'" He lets his arm drop, but turns to me and smiles. "*Pero no lo estás.* Go to Kasia's library and do some studying if you need to. Make the most of the extra time."

Miyumi runs across the path in front of us, Kasia just behind her. We turn a corner after them. The path stretches far in front of us, with other routes sprouting off to both the left and right. The girls' voices hum behind the thick hedges. They can't have gotten far, but they sound like they're miles away.

"Alternatively . . ." Nico swings his arms as we wander along the path. "Have you thought any more about what I asked you last week?"

My stomach flips. I've thought about it *constantly*. Sometimes—like after all that drama at school and the row Mam gave me—Everland seems like the obvious choice. Other times, just the thought of disappearing on my family makes me feel sick with guilt. But then I remember how happy and content I feel in here, more so than I've felt in the real world in years, and I know I don't want to give that up, either.

Nico looks at me, biting his bottom lip. He looks nervous. Another realization hits me: He's not just asking out of interest. He wants me to stay. He wants me here, with him. Sunbursts of happiness explode in my chest.

"I'm still thinking," I say gently. "Just need some more time."

He smiles. "Okay, Brody. No rush."

But for the first time in Everland, there is a rush. Doors are closing. Time, or whatever passes for it in here, is running out.

In the end, it's not the realization that my best friend hates me, or getting suspended, or the fact that I'm probably going to fail all my exams that makes up my mind. It's not even what Nico tells me at Everland, though that's part of it. It's just something my dad says. Just a few words that wouldn't mean anything to anyone else.

It's Friday, the last day of my suspension. I'm doing my English homework while Dad mends the toaster and rewatches *Planet Earth II* for about the fiftieth time. I'm supposed to be answering questions about one of Jackie Kay's poems, but so far all I've done is type out the title and refresh my social media sites about twenty times. I texted Megan a couple of times, but she hasn't replied. I don't like that. I meant what I said, but I hate having this bad feeling hanging between us.

The episode ends, and the theme tune plays over the credits. Dad puts the toaster on the coffee table and gets up to stretch his legs. "How you getting on?" he asks me.

"Aye, fine."

Stock reply. I haven't answered a single question. When I look round, he's leaning over me, squinting at the almost-blank Word document on the computer screen.

"That doesnae look fine. That looks like six words. You needing any help?"

I pass him my printout of the poem "Gap Year." It's about the writer's son going off traveling around South America. He's grown-up, but to his mum, it seems not so long ago that he was just a baby in a Moses basket. Dad reads it silently, his lips half forming the words.

"That's bonny, that." His voice sounds different all of a sudden. Wistful. "What's the question?"

"Um." I look down at Mrs. Davies's homework sheet. *Show how the writer uses language to emphasize the rapid passing of time in the second stanza.*

Dad scans the lines again. "Well, there's the word *suddenly* here. And the last line: 'a flip and a skip ago.' Fast wee words, most only a syllable. But it's not all quick, is it? There's all this longing, too: 'four weeks after your due date,' 'home-alone mother,' 'empty bedroom' . . . It might be a flip and a skip since he was a baby, but time's dragging now he's on the other side of the world."

"Maybe I should say that, then," I say. "The question's wrong. Time doesnae pass fast or slow or whatever—it's just our perception of it."

Dad gives me a thumbs-up. "Exactly. Good lad."

It's the sort of smart-aleck answer Mrs. Davies hates, but it's something. I type out a few lines. Dad's gaze prickles at the back of my neck. After a moment, he clears his throat.

"Speaking of time," he says. "You really could have picked a better one to get suspended, what with your exams coming up and that."

I grit my teeth. This again. "Yes, Dad. I know."

He falls silent again. Dad doesn't do Serious Chats. Mam's obviously told him to try and talk some sense into me, which is pointless. It's not like I meant to get suspended. It's not like I'm trying to fail.

"Maybe you could ask your brother to give you a hand with your revision. Might as well take advantage of having a huge geek in the family, eh?"

This is clearly supposed to be some sort of jibe at Jake, but it doesn't come off that way. Dad's voice is brimming with pride, the way it always does when anyone asks how Jake's getting on at school or what uni he's planning on going to. If finding out he had an off-the-scale IQ was Jake's letter from Hogwarts, Mam and Dad are more like Hermione Granger's parents: bewildered Muggles, amazed and delighted by their kid's hidden talents.

"Jake's too busy." I type a few words. "He's barely got enough time for his own revision, let alone mine."

Dad sighs. "Well, just do your best, Brody. That's all anyone can ask."

That seems to be the end of it. Mam would probably nag at me for another ten minutes or so, but Dad throws in the towel much quicker.

On the one hand, I'm glad they don't expect the same results from me as they do from Jake. I'm never going to get straight As in my exams or a Best in School award for English; I'm not going to get into university, and to be honest, I don't even want to. But at the same time, sometimes it pisses me off that they don't expect more from me. Like maybe I could have done better if they'd pushed me harder. If they'd paid more attention.

That's probably unfair. But it's how I feel.

"She's right, you know." When I turn around, Dad's looking at the poem again. "Jackie Kay, I mean. Seems like just last week the three of you were bawling and crawling all over the place."

He smiles to himself. I can almost see the memories playing out in his head. A different time. For him, a very different life.

"Well, don't worry," I mutter. "I'll no' be jetting off to Peru any time soon."

"Not if you don't get your act together, you won't." He rolls up the poem and taps my head with it. "Keep this nonsense up, and you'll be lucky to get as far as Prestonpans, let alone Peru."

And stupid as it sounds, that's what changes my mind. Those two sentences, tossed out like pennies to a fountain, are what finally change my mind.

It's not about Peru. I've never even imagined going that far. It's the fact that Dad's right. Jake is going to go to Cambridge and then to London or New York or Hong Kong or wherever the hell he wants to go, and I'll be stuck here. Megan'll probably move away for university, and when she does, she'll forget about me—that's if we're even still friends by then. All I have is Everland and Nico. Without them . . . I don't even know what the point would be.

Dad laughs afterward. "I'm only kidding you on, Brody. You know there's other options. School and exams aren't everything.

You'll be fine." He ruffles my hair. "And listen, me and your mam—we're proud of you no matter what."

I nod, the computer screen blurring as my eyes unfocus. Those are the words I've wanted to hear for ages, but now they barely reach my ears. The decision has crystallized. Everland is my place.

Everland is what I choose.

THIRTY

I'D FORGOTTEN WHAT BELTANE WAS UNTIL NICO MENTIONED IT THE other week: a fire festival on Calton Hill, some ancient pagan thing celebrating the May Day festival. Walking along Waterloo Place, I pass people painted head to toe in red or blue, eerie figures in long white robes, a woman wearing a floral headdress that's almost as tall as she is. Nico's come dressed as some sort of deer: There's a delicate crown of twigs twisted into antlers on his head, and he's wearing strips of faux fur over his shoulders and around his wrists and ankles. Kasia's waiting beside him at the foot of the steps, wearing white face paint and a tunic decorated with flowers, while a short person covered in blue and green rags stands to Nico's right. My smile cracks even wider when I recognize her: Zahra.

"Brody!" She pushes up on her tiptoes and throws her arms around my neck. "It's so good to see you!"

"You, too. I've missed you on Thursdays."

Her face is painted turquoise, with deep indigo swirls on her cheeks. I tug on one of the green rags, laid over her hijab like strips of seaweed.

"This doesnae look like your usual kind of costume."

"I'm a water creature," she says. "Nico's earth, and Kasia's one of the White Women. It's all part of the story—you'll see when we get up on the hill."

Nico flashes me a smile. "Don't worry, I made you one, too. Probably my finest—and final—work, if I do say so myself."

He pulls a plastic bag out from under his cape and hands it to me. Inside, there's a gold mask shaped like a bird's beak, and a pile of soft material. As I hold it up to the light, my mouth falls open. It's a cape, shaped like a W to look like bird wings and covered in hundreds of tiny colored feathers: bright copper at the top, fading into a warm bronze, and ending in a soft gold fringe. Out of all of Nico's costumes, this one is the best, the most professional. It must have taken him hours—much longer than his own deer outfit.

"Here—you wear it like this."

Nico takes the cape from me, throws it around my shoulders, and fastens the tie into a knot between my collarbones. Zahra nudges Kasia, and they make their way up the steps to the hill, leaving us alone. For a minute I just stand there, lifting my wing-arms, watching the way the light from the streetlamps catches on the feathers. I feel like Harry Potter putting on his invisibility cloak. Like nothing can touch me in this.

"This is amazing," I say. "It's unbelievable."

He picks up my wrists and slips them through two fabric ties on the corners of the cape. "Figured you'd make a good air creature. And I wanted to give you your own pair of wings."

His voice sounds different. Almost shy, which is so unlike Nico. I put the mask on and run a hand over the feathers. I thank him, and then a second and a third time, but it still doesn't feel like enough.

Then I realize what I can give him in return: my decision.

Before I can tell him, he cocks his head toward the steps.

"We'd better catch up with Zahra and Kasia or we'll never find them again. It's kind of chaotic up there."

Maybe it's down to the cape, or the fact it's dark and no one will be able to see who I am in this mask, but something makes me reach out and take his hand. I sense a tiny twitch of surprise before he slides his fingers through mine. As we walk up the hill, his voice goes back to its usual upbeat tone: He tells me about the party he went to last night, and about a guy in his art class who turned in a shoebox of air for his assignment.

I am listening. But I can't stop looking at our hands.

Nico wasn't exaggerating when he used the word *chaotic*. Calton Hill is on fire. Strange pagan symbols burn between the pillars of the National Monument; a giant bonfire crackles and spits smoke into the night sky; performers carry flaming torches or swing fireballs around their heads. Nico and I squeeze through the crowd and find Kasia and Zahra watching a man in a cape chase away some birdlike characters blowing on horns and tin whistles. Over the noise, Zahra points out the main characters to me: the May Queen, wearing a white robe and a huge headpiece of flowers; and the Green Man, a tall, dreadlocked man wrapped in garlands of leaves. A band of dancers and drummers follows them in a long, colorful procession, some of them wearing nothing but loincloths. Nico fakes a gasp and puts his hands over my eyes as they pass by. I laugh and push him away.

"They must be freezing their tits off!" he shouts, shivering. He reaches into his robe and pulls out a silver hip flask. "It's almost May—how the hell is it this cold? I won't miss that when I'm living in Everland."

He unscrews the top, takes a swig of whisky, then hands the flask to me. It tastes like rotten peat and burns the back of my mouth, but it does warm me up. Kasia gives me a disapproving look—clearly she's a stickler for rules in *this* world, too, and I'm the only one of us who's under eighteen—then takes out her own bottle of vodka and glugs from it.

Zahra has been watching Nico with a panicked expression. "You're not really serious about that, are you? You're not actually going to stay in Everland?"

"It's nuts," Kasia says. "I don't know how you can do it, Nico. To your parents. To *us*."

"Guys, come on." Nico's voice goes flat. He takes another long drink of whisky, his eyes fixed on the procession. Two of the characters are now setting fire to a huge arch spanning the path, while the May Queen lifts her hands above it as if in prayer. "Did you just come here to talk about how messed up I am? Tonight wasn't supposed to be about that."

"Nobody said you were—" Zahra starts to protest, but Nico holds his hands up.

"Enough! I came here to watch the show and worship the May Queen or whatever. We can talk about this later."

We follow the procession around the hill, watching the fire-throwers and the bird people and the red-painted devils running amok. Before Everland, I probably would have thought all this was pretty ridiculous—fun, yeah, but daft and touristy and a wee bit pretentious. Now I see there's more to it than that. I mean, don't get me wrong, I have no clue what's going on. But it's obviously about preserving something, some ancient magic that's almost been lost. Maybe some people can find it in fire festivals or rituals, or maybe old songs and stories. For me, it's more literal. It's Everland.

After an hour or so, I'm too hot and a bit drunk and itching to escape from the hordes of people. Zahra and I move away from the procession and sit on a grassy bank looking toward Arthur's Seat. Behind us, Kasia is deep in drunken conversation with a tall girl from London, and Nico is dancing with two over-excited Finnish tourists.

"Weird being up here and not going through the green door," I say to Zahra. "It's no' the same without you in there, y'know."

Zahra gives a sad smile. "It was hard, but it was the right

decision. After I stopped going there every week, I realized I had to make some changes. I talked to my dad about how much pressure I was feeling between looking after Mum and school. He can't change jobs, but he talked to my sisters about visiting more, and he's asked our neighbors to check in more often. He and Mum signed me up for an illustration class, too, to make sure I get some time to myself. Things are good."

Even with her face painted bright blue, I can tell she's looking better. Her eyes seem brighter, more alert, and she smiles more readily now. I can see the difference even if I didn't notice there was anything wrong beforehand. Guilt prickles at me. I should have been paying more attention.

"I thought I'd miss Everland, but I actually don't. I miss the three of you, and Miyumi and everyone else I knew in there, but not the place. It was the right time for me to leave, even if I didn't realize it. Now I've stopped going there, the whole thing just sounds so bizarre."

Even for me, it seems unreal right now. I've kept catching myself looking toward the monument all night, waiting for the space between the pillars to morph into the green door. I know it happens, but tonight it feels as weird as expecting the sky to fall down.

"Nico told me you're thinking of staying there with him." Zahra presses her lips together. "I can't believe he asked you that. He shouldn't be putting ideas in your head."

"He never asked me. Not really." I shrug. "Anyway, it sounds all right to me. It's no' like I've got much keeping me here."

"Come on—you know that's not true. You've got family, your friends . . . your whole future."

"What future? I have no idea what I want to do. The only thing I'm good at is drumming, and there's basically no jobs going in that."

"You know it's not that simple. What if you start forgetting things from your real life, like Esther has? What if you totally forget your family?" Zahra shakes her head, the blue rags flapping from side to side. "You don't want that, Brody. Believe me. My mum's not going to be around forever. Neither are your parents. One day, memories are all we'll have left."

We're both quiet for a moment, Zahra clearly thinking about her mum—I can tell from the way her eyes mist up—and me about what it could be like to live in Everland. She's right, in a way. There's still so much I don't know about Everland.

But there are so many things I do know, too. I know that time stops in there, that there's no pressure to grow up or carve out a future in a world that's working against you. I know that there's a sort of balance that's missing from the real world. I know that you can't get hurt in there. That there's nobody making fun of you or telling you that everything about you is wrong. That feeling I get, of wishing I could crawl out of my own skin and be somebody else . . . I never get that in Everland.

Behind us, the Finnish tourists have now disappeared, and Kasia and the Londoner are kissing on a bench farther up the bank. I tell Zahra I'll be back in a minute, then jog over the grass to meet Nico, leaving my bird mask on the bench. When I reach him, I take a deep breath and gently take his hand again.

"I've made my mind up."

Behind him, the bird people give a blast of their horns. Nico cups his hand around his ear. I lean toward him: My top lip is level with his bottom one, and the tips of our noses are only millimeters apart.

"I'm going to stay!" I say louder. "I'm going to stay in Everland. I want . . . I want to stay there. With you."

Nico looks at me. There's ash on his cheeks, flames licking in his eyes. His antlers are lopsided, and his makeup is smudged, and his cheeks are a bit gaunt after all the partying he's been doing, but he still looks beautiful. If I weren't already sure that I loved him, I'd know it tonight.

For a moment, his whole face lights up. Even after knowing him all these months, that look can still make my heart do somersaults. Then he moves closer, suddenly serious.

"Brody, that's . . . It's a huge decision."

"I know. But it's what I want." I nod again. "We can go this Thursday. I'm ready if you are."

His gaze floats toward the monument. The Celtic symbols are starting to burn out, glowing a bright orange against the slate gray of the sky. Everything around us is noise and color and fire, but it almost feels like we're alone here: the eye of the storm, surrounded by chaos.

He puts his hands on my face. "You'll have to be sure.

Completely, completely sure. After the door disappears, there'll be no going back."

I look at him: at his dark brown eyes, bleary from the alcohol; at the freckles scattered across his cheeks and the hesitant smile tugging at his lips. I'm sure.

Instead of saying it, I lean in, and I finally kiss him.

There's a split second of hesitation, and then he kisses me back. I've thought about this moment a thousand, million times. It's like I imagined, and different, and better. He tastes of cigarettes and whisky and chewing gum, dirty and sweet at the same time. His bottom lip is chapped, but the top one is soft, his fingers smooth as they slide over the back of my neck and into my hair. I put my hands on his waist and pull him closer to me, amazed that this is happening, that I finally get to do this. It's almost like being in Everland: It doesn't quite feel real, and I don't know how long it's been when we eventually break apart. I just know I don't want it to end.

After a moment, Nico leans back to look at me, his arms linked around my neck. I can't stop grinning. He smiles—a different kind of smile, softer than usual.

"Well," he says lightly. "That seems pretty sure."

"I am." My whole body is sparkling with happiness. "Totally."

I lean in to kiss him again, but suddenly, a very drunk Kasia appears. Nico steps back, his hands dropping to his sides before reaching out to catch her.

"Th-think I need to go h-home," she says, hiccupping. It's

weird seeing her—serious, straight-laced Kasia—like this. "I miiight have thrown up. London girl was n-not impressed."

Nico gives her a wry smile, enjoying being the more sober one for once. "All right, babe—we'll get you back."

I don't want to go. I want to stay here, keep kissing him all night. Nico mouths *sorry* at me, then leans over and pecks me on the lips. It's not enough, but we're not in a rush. After Thursday, we'll have all the time in the world.

"Thursday," he says, echoing my thoughts.

I don't know if he's talking about Everland, or picking up where we left off, or both. But with every second that passes, I'm a little more certain that this is the right decision.

THIRTY-ONE

EVERYTHING FEELS DIFFERENT NOW THAT I KNOW I'M LEAVING.

Exams start, but I'm not as nervous as I thought I'd be. The whole thing is a bit of a blur. Music goes well (I can see from the examiner's face that he's impressed when I perform my drum piece), but in Spanish I spend so long looking in the dictionary that I run out of time to answer all the questions, and in English I zone out during the critical reading paper. To be honest, it doesn't really worry me. It's hard to care that much when I'll be disappearing into Everland soon.

There are other things I need to sort out before I go, though. How I'm going to say goodbye to my family is one. All this mess with Megan is another.

I wait for her outside her Geography exam on Wednesday.

She looks knackered: pale and tired and stressed. Her face darkens when she sees me. She shifts her backpack onto her shoulder and brushes past me. I hurry to catch up with her.

"I'm sorry," I blurt out. "For snapping at you. For ignoring you. You were right. I've been shit."

She keeps walking, her eyes fixed straight ahead. "Yep. You have been."

"I know. And I'm sorry. I really am. It was nothing personal, Meg. I've just been . . . distracted."

Megan and I have had a few spats before, but nothing like this. Usually she gets excited about something and forgets she's supposed to be in a mood with me, or I force myself not to think about it and pretend everything's fine. This time, her expression doesn't fade. She stops by the vending machines at the end of the corridor and crosses her arms.

"You don't take me seriously," she says, her eyes fixed on the chocolate and crisps behind the glass. "It's like you think that because I talk a lot, I don't have anything to say. That because I've liked a lot of guys, I don't have proper feelings. That because my parents have more money than yours, my home life is some shiny sitcom."

"I've never said any of that," I say quickly. But I have thought it. Maybe not as harshly as that, but that's more or less the gist.

She keeps staring straight ahead. "Did you know I've been seeing a counselor and a nutritionist? I collapsed after school two weeks ago, the same week you were suspended. I hadn't eaten anything in a day and a half. Harry had to take me to hospital. I was in there overnight by myself—Dad was away and my mum's car broke down, or so she says. It's been shit. And you haven't been there for any of it."

I stare at her, my mouth open. In a flash, it all comes back to me: Megan picking at pizza toppings, pulling crumbs off her sandwiches, telling me to finish her chips, her crisps, her lasagna. I remember her telling me that she wasn't hungry, that she'd already eaten, that she was going out for dinner later, that she didn't want to ruin her appetite. They weren't so much clues as huge red flags, and yet I still missed them.

"I didnae know." My face is getting red, a mixture of anger and shame. Anger because she's accusing me of being such a bad friend, and shame because there is some truth to what she's saying. "You never told me."

But I didn't ask, either. And—I remember with a kick of guilt—she did ask to speak to me. She's right. I wasn't there.

"I'm sorry," I say. "I'm really sorry."

"I'm not saying I have it harder than you," she says. "I definitely don't. I know I'm lucky. But that doesn't change how I feel about things."

There's a long pause, our silence swallowed up by the chatter and laughter of the people rushing past on their way to classes or exams. I take a deep breath. I'm leaving soon. Might as well be honest.

"Look, I know that." I swallow, trying to find the words. "It's just, the stuff that's been going on, with Nico and with my

268

family and everything . . . I thought you wouldn't understand. I guess that's why I shut you out a bit. I'm no' saying that makes it okay. I'm just explaining."

Megan's face hardens. "Maybe I couldn't. I don't know what it's like to be you. But I thought you'd at least give me a chance to try. I'm supposed to be your best friend." She shrugs. "Anyway. I kind of think it's done now."

"What is?"

"Just . . . this. You and me."

We stare at each other in the reflection of the vending machine. Megan's eyes are glossy. So that's it. Done. Seven years of secrets and in-jokes and TV marathons unraveling in my hands. I'm surprised by how much it hurts. Our friendship was going to come to an end either way, but this isn't how I wanted to leave it.

"Don't you think that's a bit extreme?" My voice comes out strangled. "This seems so sudden."

Megan finally looks directly at me. Her mouth is hanging open; her mascara has smudged beneath her eyelashes, but she doesn't go to wipe it away. "What are you talking about, Brody? You've hardly talked to me all year—we haven't properly hung out since before Christmas. It's been *months*."

She's right. She's right. It's been ages—a whole school year. I hadn't realized. With a lurch of fear, I remember Kasia's warning: that life could start to slip away from me. Maybe it already has, and I haven't even noticed.

"Right," I say. "Okay, then. If that's what you want."

I wait for her reply, but it doesn't come. For once, Megan has nothing to say to me.

I feel her eyes follow me as I turn and walk back down the corridor. *It's okay*, I tell myself. *It doesn't matter. I'm going to Everland. I have my friends there. And soon, I'll probably have forgotten Megan altogether.*

Walking home from school later, I try to fix memories in my mind. There's the smell of sweet, warm dough floating out of the bakery on the corner, the one that does the amazing macaroni pies. There's the secondhand clothes shop, which puts the most blatant lies on the posters in their windows: MITTENS KINDLY DONATED BY ZAYN MALIK—£3; BERET WORN BY GAL GADOT IN WONDER WOMAN—£5.50. There's the old soldier who sits in a wheelchair outside the pub collecting for veterans almost every afternoon, even when it's pouring.

Feels strange, getting nostalgic for a place I haven't left yet.

When I get back to Mackay House, it hits me harder. Despite the drug raids and the constantly broken lift and Mrs. McAskill always girning at us about noise, this is home. Even with Leanne and Michelle sitting on the swings, passing a cigarette between them, I feel a pang of sadness at the thought of leaving it all behind.

"Look who it is," Michelle says on cue, as I push the gate open. "Lassie-basher Brody."

Leanne takes a long draw on the cigarette. "You back for round two, Fairy? Gonnae push me off the swings now?"

Michelle starts singing her "Crater Face" song, and Leanne

joins in. My skin's actually cleared up a bit lately, but I don't think that's why it doesn't get to me so much this time. I know now that the stuff they say about me . . . it's not really about *me*. It's like they took a photo of me, defaced it, and tried to tell me that this is who I really am. It says nothing about me, but a lot about them.

Besides, there's only so much they can do to me now. After tomorrow, I won't have to deal with their bullshit ever again.

I wait until they reach the end of the chorus, my hands in my pockets. For the first time, I wonder why they're out here so much. Leanne, especially, is here all the time: I've seen her sitting on the swings in the rain, or shivering outside the front door to her block at eleven o'clock at night. Maybe there are things she's running away from, too.

When their singing tapers out, I take a step forward. I look Leanne right in the eyes. She sneers, but her hands grip the chains of the swing a little tighter.

"I'm sorry," I say. Loudly, clearly. "I shouldnae have lost the rag like that. It'll no' happen again."

There's silence. They weren't expecting that.

"Aye, whatever." Leanne clears her throat. I can see the cogs turning behind her eyes, trying to think up a good comeback. Eventually, she leans back and gives me a dirty look. "Away and piss off back to Neverland, Peter Pan."

I burst out laughing. If only she knew. Michelle's and Leanne's foreheads crinkle in confusion.

"All right, then," I say, grinning. "See you later."

Inside, Dad's doing the dishes, and Mam's reading an old

magazine. She turns around and smiles when she hears me come in; Dad leans out the door and waves a soapy hand at me. My stomach lurches. It keeps hitting me: Going to Everland means leaving all of this.

I still don't really believe I could forget it all. But just in case, I need to take something to help me remember them by.

Stuck to the fridge with a magnet, there's a photo of the five of us, taken two Christmases ago when my grandparents came to stay. I used to hate it—it was right at the start of Brody vs. Acne, and I'd have picked a ten-hour U2 concert over getting my picture taken—but it's the most recent photo we have of us all together.

When Mam's not looking, I pull it off the fridge, open my bag, and slide it into my Maths textbook so it doesn't get squashed.

Keira's out, so I slip into her room and take a stick of the strawberry bubble gum that she's always chewing and a bottle of green nail polish. I sneak one of Dad's Louis Theroux DVD cases from behind the TV, and one of Mam's nearly finished perfumes from the bathroom. I find a manky toy mouse that Tink used to play with when he was a kitten and shove that into my pocket, too. He's still part of the family, even if he does live on the other side of the city.

I even take something to remind me of Jake: a page of Latin notes that's slipped down the side of the desk. *Fugissem, fugisses, fugisset* . . . I don't understand a word of it. Kind of fitting, in a way. Jake and I never really got each other.

In my room, I pack a bag for Everland with all my mementos,

plus a Polaroid of me and Megan from one of her brother's parties and the *Drag Race* card she made for my birthday. But the nervous feeling in my stomach won't settle. I need to leave something behind for them, too.

Hidden under my bed are the presents I got at the Everland market before Christmas. I find a bit of paper, cut out tiny labels with my family's names on them, and attach them to the crafts: the purse for Keira, the typewriter paper sculpture for Jake, the pocket watch for Mam, and the village in a bottle for Dad. For Megan, I leave the copy of *Peter and Wendy* that Kasia gave me. I write her a note saying that I'm sorry again, and that I can't explain, but I just have to go, and slip it between the pages.

I don't leave any letters for my family. I don't know what I could say.

Afterward, I place all the gifts in a shoebox and hide them under my bed. Somewhere that's not too obvious, but where they'll be able to find them.

For a second, scenes flash through my mind: my parents finding my bed empty; Christmases and birthdays without me; weddings or funerals I'll never go to. The world spins. But then I close my eyes and remember why I'm leaving: Everland. And Nico. Nico. Nico.

THIRTY-TWO

THURSDAYS HAVE DRAGGED SINCE LAST SEPTEMBER, WAITING FOR ten forty-five to come around, but this one slips by far too fast. My last rushed breakfast. My last walk to school. My last lessons. My last disappointing lunch of bland sweet-and-sour chicken and a chocolate crispy cake. My last time walking through the school corridors, dodging the half-deflated basketball that some sophomores are throwing between the lockers—even that leaves me feeling almost wistful.

After school, I watch the end of a show on killer whales with Dad, help Keira out with her English homework, and suddenly we're all eating supper. Obviously, I haven't asked for a special last supper or anything, but as it happens, Mam's made one of my favorites: oven chips, fried eggs, and beans. It tastes even better than usual.

I hardly speak throughout the whole meal; I'm too busy trying to commit my family to memory. There are things I've hardly noticed before: how Mam tilts her head a tiny bit to the left when she's listening, the fact Jake's starting to get the same laughter lines around his eyes as Dad, the way Keira's eyebrows shift up and down when she's telling one of her stories . . . all the things you can't get from a photo.

Too soon, our plates are empty, and everyone's moving again. Jake goes back to the computer, Dad to the TV (there's a program on about the Russian Revolution at seven), and Keira upstairs to Amanda's. Mam disappears to her room, then comes out a few minutes later wearing her work uniform.

My stomach drops. "You've got a shift?"

"Rosie's wee boy's not well. I said I'd cover for her." She pulls her hair up into a ponytail. "It's just until two o'clock, not too long."

"Right," I croak. "Bye, then, Mam."

She kisses my forehead and tells Jake not to stay up too late. I stare at her as she puts her work shoes and her jacket on. My whole body feels numb. I thought we had more time than this. I want some more time. I want to say goodbye properly. I want to give her a hug, my last one ever. Before I can think of an excuse, she waves and leaves, closing the door behind her.

A lump swells in my throat. This is starting to feel . . . real.

The goodbyes keep slipping away from me. Keira goes straight to her room when she comes back from Amanda's, and Dad falls asleep on the sofa in front of *Newsnight*. By the time ten forty-five comes around, Jake's the only one still up. He's typing something out on the computer, his head swinging from a textbook to the screen and back again.

I pick up my bag, put on my shoes and my coat. I take one last look around the living room: the windowsill where Tink used to sit, Mam's cold cup of tea on the table, their shoes scattered by the door. I feel a sudden stab of pain, some premature homesickness. I can't just walk out of here without saying anything at all.

"Well . . . bye, then."

Jake turns around to look at me. As soon as he does, I realize I've made a mistake.

"Where are you going?" He stands up. "Are you leaving?"

"I'm—I'm just going out for a walk."

"What's with the bag, then?"

"Nothing . . . I always take my bag." The sadness turns into panic in an instant. "Leave me alone, will you?"

I turn toward the door, but Jake leaps out of his chair and grabs my arm.

"No. Not till you tell me what's going on." He reaches to take my backpack, but I knock back his hand. "I knew you were planning something. You've been in a good mood all week."

I stare at him. "So?"

"So that's a sign you've made up your mind about something. That something's about to change."

The sofa squeaks; Dad's waking up. I grab the door handle

and wrench it open, shoving Jake into the wall. Running down the corridor, I hear him swear and follow me out, then rapid footsteps chasing me down the stairs. He catches up with me, no bother—damn his rugby training—but I shake him off and push the front door open. Leanne is on the swing yet again, watching something on her phone. The bus is already waiting at the pavement. I start to run, but Jake grabs my arm again.

"Brody, will you just wait!"

Leanne stands up, the swing clattering behind her. "Whoa, what's going on? Where you off to, Fairy?"

Jake spins around. "Can you shut up for once in your life?"

While he's distracted, I slip out of his grasp and run down the path. I'm too late: The bus is already pulling away from the stop. I sprint over the bridge and down Great Junction Street, Jake right behind me. If I cross diagonally, I can probably make it to the stop at the bottom of Leith Walk before the bus gets there. I run into the road, but a loud blast of a horn stops me in my tracks—

Suddenly, I'm falling back onto the pavement. Someone shouts about watching where I'm going; people are staring down at me, Jake included. His face is white.

"What's the hell are you doing?" he shouts. "You almost got yourself killed!"

My knees shake as I stand up. "I have to go—I have to go."

My ankle starts to throb as I break into a run; I must have twisted it when I fell. Despite the late hour, there's a steady stream of traffic pouring onto Leith Walk. The number 22 glides past and around the corner, stopping outside Greggs. Ignoring the pain, I tear down the road, waving manically at the driver to wait. I leap on board and slam my money down. Upstairs, I sit on the left side, trying to find my brother on the pavement below. He's not there.

I let out a long, shaky breath. That isn't the way I wanted to leave things. This is not how I wanted my last night to be.

Traffic is slow—by the time we reach Princes Street, it's already 11:16 p.m. I hit the buzzer and hurry downstairs ready to get off. The doors open, and my heart sinks. Jake is standing there, his arms crossed, waiting for me.

"You're following me now?" I snap. "I told you, just leave it."

"No. Not until you tell me where you're going."

I push past him and head for the pedestrian crossing. Jake follows me, peppering me with questions as I wait impatiently for the light to change. It's 11:18 p.m. I've got three minutes, but my ankle is agony. I race across the road and hobble up the steps, ignoring Jake's never-ending questions. When I get to the top, I grit my teeth and start to run. The green door comes into view as I near the monument, but it's hazy, the stained-glass windows almost translucent. After another second, it disappears entirely.

I check my phone: 11:22 p.m. I've missed it.

"Shit. *Shit.*"

I throw my bag down on the ground. Jake picks it up and pushes it back into my hands.

"Is this where you come every week?" he asks, looking around. For a moment, I think he's asking about Everland, but he was too far away to see the door. "Who are you waiting for?"

I look at the Balmoral clock: 11:23 p.m. Kasia should have reappeared by now, but there's no one here but us. I ignore Jake and head back down the steps. I don't want to go back home. My ankle's hurting like hell, but I walk past the bus stop and along Princes Street, past the train station and the glowing block of the Apple store. I try calling Nico, but his phone doesn't even ring. Jake follows me the whole way, sometimes in silence, sometimes yapping at my heels like a persistent puppy. By the time I get to the front door of Jenners, my patience has run out. I spin around to face him, my cheeks hot with anger.

"All right, fine! I was leaving! I was gonnae leave—I was gonnae get the hell out of here, away from you, away from all of this."

I slump down on the steps of the department store and rub my sore ankle. It's okay. It's not over. The door was still there. It hasn't disappeared altogether—I can go next week. But it doesn't feel all right. My plan is unraveling fast, and I don't know how to stop it.

After a moment, Jake kicks an empty cigarette packet out of the way and sits down beside me. I'm surprised he's still here; this must be the longest he's gone without studying in months.

"And where were you planning on going, exactly?" he asks for the hundredth time.

I don't have the energy to lie anymore. "This guy . . . Nico." His name gets knotted in my throat. "He's leaving Edinburgh. I was going to go with him."

"So you were just going to disappear. Without saying anything." Jake nods slowly. "And when were you planning on coming back?"

I don't answer. I stare straight ahead, my eyes fixed on the glowing buses sliding down the street. Jake looks at me for a long moment. He can't possibly know how final this could have been—and still could be—but he understands enough to know I wasn't planning on coming home.

"Right," he says quietly. "Do you know what that would do to Mam and Dad?"

My phone buzzes. I snatch it up, hoping to see Nico's name on the screen, though I know that's impossible. It's Dad calling me. There are another three missed calls I hadn't noticed, all from him. I swipe them away and drop the phone back into my pocket.

"They'd be fine," I mutter.

"No, they wouldn't, you idiot. You think you could take off and—what? They'd just get on with their lives?"

The thought jabs at my conscience, just like it has every day for the past week. "You don't get it. Being there, with him . . . It's the only time I feel like myself."

For once, Jake doesn't argue. He stares at his hands, picks at a scab beneath his thumb.

"Brody, this is mad," he says. "What about school, and your friends? You can't give up your whole life for some boy."

That's not what I'm doing, I want to say. It's never been about Nico. Well, not *only* about Nico.

"Maybe you should tell Mam and Dad about him," Jake says. He cracks his knuckles, a nervous tic. "Maybe you'll feel less distant from them if you don't have to hide that part of your life anymore."

My insides flip at the thought of that. "What do you think they'd say?"

"Well, uh . . ." Jake gives an awkward laugh. "If it's anything like when I told them about me and Amir, Dad'll start rambling about these gay penguins he saw in a documentary once, and Mam'll just go on about condoms for ages."

It takes a few seconds for what he's just said to click. When it does, I spin around to face him; he's looking at me with this wobbly half smile on his face.

"Amir's your *boyfriend*?"

"Was." He tugs his sleeves over his hands. "He broke up with me in February."

Something Jett said to me when I told her Jake was my brother comes back to me: *Shame about him and Amir.* For a few seconds, I'm too shocked to do anything but gawp at him. And then a wave of anger crashes over me so fast, it leaves me dizzy.

"Are you joking?" It comes out as a shout, startling two women waiting for a bus along the road. "My whole life, you made me feel *shit* about being like this. About being different."

Jake's face falls. "What? No, I didn't—"

"Yes, you did! . . . *Those are girls' toys, Brody. Boys aren't supposed to like that, Brody. Man up, Brody. Be* normal, *Brody.*"

"That—that was ages ago. I didn't realize you remembered all that." Jake stares at me, shell-shocked. "Look, I'm sorry. I don't know why I was like that. Maybe I was jealous of you on some level. You were so . . . *yourself* when you were wee. You didn't care about being different. I was terrified of it."

His eyes well up, and that pisses me off, too—I can't even cry because he spent my whole childhood telling me not to. I stand up and start pacing, my hands clenched into fists.

"You should've said something," I tell him. "You've made me feel like an idiot. *Again.*"

Jake wipes his eyes on his sleeve. "Brody, I can hardly say or do or *be* anything without you hating me for it," he says. "Every time I try to help you with something, you act like I'm calling you thick. Whenever I stick up for you in front of those girls, you look more pissed off with me than you are with them. If I'd told you I'm gay, you'd have hated me for . . . I don't know, for stealing your thunder, probably. I can't win with you."

I open my mouth to argue, then stop. He's . . . kind of right. If he'd told me this while he and Amir were still going out, I would have been pissed off that he beat me to it. I would have been jealous that he got a boyfriend before I did. I might have worried that our parents would be fine with one gay kid, but that two would be too much for them to handle. And maybe I still will, but Jake's crying properly now. The anger still pulsing through me starts to slow. This can't have been easy for him, either. I know that much.

I sit back down and wait until he's ready. A lady walking a dalmatian comes over and offers him a tissue. He thanks her and wipes his nose.

"Why did he break up with you?" I ask quietly.

"He met somebody else," Jake says, sniffing. "Someone more fun. Someone who doesn't spend every day of their life study-ing . . . who doesn't have a panic attack every ten minutes."

"You've had more of those?"

"A ton of them." He presses the heels of his hands into his eyes. "It sucks because I keep thinking we'd probably still be to-gether if I hadn't been so obsessed with getting into Cambridge. And now I've done it, and I'm not even sure I actually want to go anymore."

His first confession was a shock. This one practically makes my jaw hit the pavement.

"What? What do you mean? Why no'?"

"Lots of reasons. The cost is one thing—it'd be so much cheaper to stay at home, instead of getting loans and credit cards to pay for dorms. And I don't know if I want to be that far away, what with everything that's going on with Mam and Dad right now. Not when I could study here and work part-time and help them out." He runs his hands through his hair. "Plus,

I like school, and I love my friends, but it's exhausting being so different from everybody else. Cambridge would be more of the same."

I shake my head. "Nah, they must have tons of people from state schools or on scholarships and that."

"Some, yeah. And I know I'm at an advantage, being white and privately educated. A massive advantage. But I still don't know if it's right for me." He shrugs his shoulders. "It's just what you do at my school: You aim for Cambridge. Maybe I was just going along with what everyone was telling me, without really thinking about what I want."

"Christ," I mutter. "You're full of revelations today."

"I know, right?" He gives a bubbly laugh and wipes his nose again. "Sorry. I'm a bit of a mess right now."

This feel so weird. All those years of thinking my brother had everything sorted, that he knew exactly who he was and what he wanted—that *I* knew exactly who he was and what he wanted.

"Look, I obviously don't hate you," I say. "It's just . . . you know those Pinterest Fail memes? Like, a photo of some amazing three-tier cake and then somebody's crappy attempt at copying it, all sad and lopsided? I feel like everyone sees me as the sad, lopsided version of you."

He snorts with laughter. "Brody. That's the stupidest thing I've ever heard."

"It's true, though." My eyes are prickling. "You're a hundred times smarter than I am. You're more confident, you're more popular, you're good at sports. You never got lumbered with the stupid Fairy nickname like I did. You even got better skin than me. I know you're not trying to make me feel like shit, but you kinda do."

Jake leans back against the shop door, shaking his head.

"That's such crap, man. I mean, for one thing, you're amazing at drumming. I could never do anything like that. I've been playing the violin for years, and I'm still terrible," he says, rubbing his eyes. "And for another, life's not all about what you're good at. It's about being a good person. And you are one. If you, me, and a packet of bubble gum were all tied to a railway track, and a train was coming, Keira would save you, then the gum, then take a few selfies, check her messages, then *consider* saving me if she had time left over."

"Hardly," I say. "It'd be phone, selfie, gum, me, you. But, aye, you'd definitely be last."

He laughs. I have to admit, it does feel good to make him laugh for a change.

"What are you gonnae do, then? Instead of Cambridge."

"I haven't made my mind up yet. I got into St. Andrews and Edinburgh, too. So maybe I'll stay closer to home."

Somewhere in the Old Town, a clock strikes midnight. Jake stands up, wipes his eyes, then holds a hand out. I take it and let him pull me to my feet.

"Come on, we'd better get back before Mam gets home," he says. "I won't tell her you were planning on eloping without saying goodbye."

"I was not *eloping*."

"You totally were. You're basically Lydia Bennett."

I actually get that reference; *Pride & Prejudice* is one of Mam's favorite films. "Aye, well, you're Mary Bennett. Slaving over your piano while everyone else is out having a laugh."

He whacks my arm, laughing. "God, I probably am and all. How depressing."

We walk back down Princes Street in an easy silence, past students on nights out and a few late-night dog walkers. I'm trying to take in everything Jake's told me. I always thought my brother didn't understand me, but clearly I don't understand him, either. Yet more things I've been oblivious to.

Neither of us has any more money on us, and Jake's bus pass is only good for one person, so we have to walk all the way home. En route, I send Nico a string of messages, but he doesn't reply. I wonder if he's pissed off at me. Or if he thinks I've changed my mind. Another missed call from Dad pops up, but I swipe it away. I'll deal with the fallout later.

It's almost one in the morning by the time we get back, and apart from a couple of drunk guys arguing in Swedish outside a pub, the streets are pretty quiet. When we reach Mackay House, the lights of our flat are still on: the one in mine and Jake's bedroom (though I'm sure I switched it off) and the living room light, too. I remember the missed calls from Dad, and a weird feeling starts to creep over me. Like that night in Everland, I can just tell—something's not right.

Ignoring my sore ankle, I start to run. Jake follows me up the stairs, asking what's the rush this time. When we reach 9B, my heart drops. The door is wide open, and Dad's not there. The TV has been left on, a show about chess still playing, and there's a dent from his head imprinted on the sofa cushion.

But my dad is gone.

THIRTY-THREE

WE CHECK HIS AND MAM'S BEDROOM, BUT IT'S EMPTY. JAKE BARGES into Keira's and turns on the light; she groans and flips onto her front, mumbling something about not wanting to get up yet, then peeks up when we ask her where Dad's gone.

"What do you mean? Is he no' watching TV?"

That nervous feeling swells into full-on fear. Jake and I look at each other, then run out the flat and back down the stairs. Suddenly, my dad's cramped little life feels enormous: He could be anywhere, and anything could have happened. Scenes from the night he was attacked flicker through my mind like strobe lighting: Dad lying in a hospital bed, machines beeping, a nurse pulling Jake and me from the room. I picture all his panic attacks, in supermarkets and on street corners. And creeping behind them, a much darker thought: Maybe he's had enough of his cramped little life altogether.

When we turn right past the co-op, a tall figure steps into the light of a street lamp. His eyes are wide and unblinking, and he's shaking. The relief snatches my breath away. For a moment, Dad just stares at us. Agoraphobia is a mental illness, but for him it has physical effects: a pounding heart, tight lungs, hands and knees that shake so hard he can barely stand up.

"Where the hell have you been?" His voice comes out as half shout, half gasp. "I've been calling you all night."

Even with Dad trembling all over and my own heart still thumping, this feels almost miraculous; it's been years since I saw him anywhere but sitting on the sofa or pottering around the kitchen. I wonder what it must look like to him, this world that he's spent so long avoiding. I wonder what it's like to feel the wind on your face for the first time in over half a decade, if the cold seems more bitter after so long inside.

"I didn't have my phone on me, Dad. We were just . . . out for a walk," Jake says. He puts his arm around Dad's back and tries to steer him toward the flat, but Dad brushes him off. Two women walk past, openly staring. "What are *you* doing?"

"I was looking for Brody." Dad looks at me and takes a long, shaky breath. "I found this."

He holds up a piece of paper, and my stomach drops. My letter to Megan. I didn't think anyone would notice it for a good few days, and only then when I never came back from Everland.

My first reaction is to ask him why the hell he's going through my stuff, but I swallow that back. It's not the time. Still, he's clearly more clued in than I gave him credit for.

"What the hell were you . . ." Dad breaks off, shaking his head. "Why would you do that, Brody?"

He looks broken. Not the way he was that time in hospital—a different type of damaged. I can't even look him in the eye. I stare at the ground, mentally tracing the lines between the constellations of dried chewing gum scattered across the pavement. After a moment, Jake clears his throat.

"Look, let's go home. We can talk about this inside."

It takes us a while to get back: Dad's legs are still unsteady, and even the slow stream of nighttime traffic is freaking him out. When we finally arrive home, Keira's up, and Mam's in the middle of dialling a number on the landline. When she sees us, she drops the handset and rushes over to Dad, bombarding him with questions about what happened and where we've been. Dad slumps down onto the cushions, still wheezing a little.

"I'm gonnae make some tea," I mutter, disappearing into the kitchen as Jake starts to explain. I don't want to see the look on Mam's face when he tells her what I was planning. As the kettle boils, I try to work out what the hell I'm going to say to them. There's no way I can pretend that letter to Megan was anything other than a goodbye note. Looking back, I don't know why I didn't just stick it in her locker at school. Stupid to think I could hide anything in a flat this size.

My hands are sweating as I carry the mugs of tea back into

the living room. Mam is reading my letter to Megan, one hand pressed to her mouth. I fight the urge to snatch it away from her and instead sink down to the carpet, pulling my knees to my chest. Dad takes a long gulp of tea, then points at me.

"You're gonnae tell us what's going on. Now."

The presents that I left in the shoebox are lined up on the coffee table like evidence in a trial. Keira picks up the tiny village in the bottle and stares at it. It looks different without the lights of Everland shining on the glass. Like somewhere small and dull . . . and impossible to escape.

"I havnae been very happy lately," I say, and the truth of that hits me like a punch to the gut. "But I've been seeing this . . . guy, and he . . . he makes me feel better, but he's leaving Edinburgh. I was gonnae go with him."

They stare at me for what feels like the longest, longest time. This is the second time tonight I've told this story, this half-truth, and it sounds even more ridiculous than the first. I almost wish I could tell them about Everland, just so they'd know it's not as nuts as it sounds—that *I'm* not as reckless as it makes me sound. But they'd think I'd actually lost it if I did.

"So you were running away." Dad swallows. "Without telling us. Without even saying goodbye."

"Well . . . you'd've stopped me if I told you."

"Bloody right we would've stopped you!" Mam snaps. "You think we'd just let you take off like that? You're sixteen, Brody!"

"Aye, but—" I grapple for a reason. "I dunno—I thought it

might be better this way. Like, I know money's tight at the moment. One less person to feed and all that."

Jake scoffs and rolls his eyes. Keira calls me a moron. Mam stands up, mumbling something under her breath, and paces around the room. If Tink was here, he might have hissed. It's a cheap trick, really, using their financial issues to try and talk my way out of this—not even I really believe my parents would ever see it that way. But to my surprise, Dad's eyes soften.

"You wouldn't believe the amount of times I've had thoughts like that." His Adam's apple bobs under his chin. "A lot of the time, I feel like a total waste of space. When your mam works all they extra shifts and I cannae even pop down the shops to help her out. Every time I miss one of Keira's shows or Jake's rugby games. It feels like I'm no' doing my job as your dad."

There's silence. This is the first time he's ever been this honest with us. The first time he's spoken about his agoraphobia at all. I can tell it's hard for him to say: He winces with each word. His eyes float over to the TV, but for once there's nothing on the screen. Just his own reflection gazing back at him.

"Honestly . . . there are days when it feels like you'd all be better off without me."

I remember the first time Leanne and Michelle took the piss out of Dad. We were eleven, and they said he was a wuss, that he was a loser who was too afraid to even go outside. When I came home and told Mam about it, she pointed out how brave he is: He was in the army, for one thing, and he almost got killed stepping into a three-against-one fight. But even if he hadn't done those things, even if his agoraphobia had just come out of nowhere . . . he'd still be brave. There's bravery in getting up every morning and battling a disease that you hardly understand. There's bravery in surviving this world when your mind can only focus on the bad in it. Not the sort of bravery that'll earn you a medal or a paragraph in the paper, but it's still bravery. He is trying.

Mam reaches for Dad's hand. Keira climbs into his lap and puts her arms around his neck. Jake leans over and pats his shoulder.

"That's ridiculous, Dad," I say, and it's my turn for my voice to choke up. "Of course we wouldnae be—how can you think that?"

"Well, how can *you*?" He shifts Keira onto one leg so he can lean toward me. "Listen. I know you think we don't see you, Brody, but we do. I know you think that you need straight As and a place at Cambridge for us to be proud of you, but that's a load of crap. The three of you are different. You're gonnae have different lives and different opportunities. I know that's unfair, but it doesn't make you any less. It's about time you realized that, son."

My eyes feel hot. I think about him finding that letter tucked inside my copy of *Peter and Wendy* and panicking—a panic that overrode his instincts and sent him running out of Mackay House trying to find me.

Jake's right. Dad and Mam, they wouldn't pick themselves up from this if I vanished. I don't know if I can risk that.

I don't know if I want to.

THIRTY-FOUR

A FEW YEARS AGO, DAD AND I WATCHED A DOCUMENTARY ABOUT astronauts coming back to Earth after years in space. I'd never thought about what that must feel like before: how weird it must seem to let go of something and see it plummet to the ground when you expect it to float away, or how messed up their brains must get having to battle gravity to stay upright. One guy said his lips and tongue even felt heavier when he got home. Like just talking was something solid and awkward, more of a chore than it had been before.

That's how waking up on Friday feels. Like I've spent a year gliding past the stars, and now I've crash-landed on Earth.

Because I can't do it.

I can't choose Everland.

Over the weekend, I try and talk myself back into it. I think about how I feel there, and all the things I'll be able to avoid there. I think about Nico a lot. Nothing works. My decision was made, but my talk with Dad last night broke it again. No putting it back together now.

Though, if I'm really honest . . . at points, I wonder if I ever really planned on leaving. Maybe part of me knew Jake would hold me back when I said goodbye to him last night. Maybe I left Megan's letter and the presents somewhere Dad could find them on purpose. It definitely didn't seem like that at the time. But maybe my subconscious has more control than I realized.

I can't do it. And if I have to give up Everland, I need to persuade Nico to do the same.

The wait for Thursday this week is torture. At first, I tried calling him and texting him, hoping that maybe he'd come back through to find me, but when it refused to connect after six or seven tries, I had to accept he'd really gone through the door and not returned.

The worst part is worrying if anyone's going to notice. I check the news on the school computers every chance I get, terrified that an article about a missing teenager in Edinburgh will pop up. There's nothing. He must have given his parents a really convincing excuse. But whatever it was, it won't work forever. I need to persuade him to come back.

Kasia's had the same idea. "I've already had to lie to the police once about Everland," she says, as we climb the steps of the monument that Thursday. "I'm not up for doing it again."

"How did Nico seem last week?" I say. Colors begin to

shimmer between the stone pillars, and the green door appears, followed by the unicorn knocker. "At Everland, I mean."

Kasia shrugs. "I don't know; I didn't make it up there." She twists the horn twice. "I was on my way, but I bumped into Magda."

"You did? Did you talk to her?"

"No. She was smoking outside a bar on Picardy Place. She never used to smoke. She'd changed her hair, too. Got an under-cut." We step through the door and into darkness. "She was with another girl. They looked pretty loved up."

Kasia's voice is flat, and it's hard to gauge her expression in the dark.

"Oh. That's . . . good—right?"

"Yeah. It is. I'm glad for her."

Slowly, the lights begin to glow between the trees. The sky above us is a delicate dusk blue, with a few stars appearing over the mountains. When the valley comes into sight at the end of the path, my heart twists. Kasia gives a long sigh.

"It *is* good," she says again. "I was really having trouble with the thought of saying goodbye to this place. But seeing Magda made me realize that maybe it's time for me to move on, too. From her, and from Everland."

I follow her footsteps down the path. "How many more visits do you think we can risk?"

"Two, maybe, or three. Depends how many more doors have disappeared. But I think next Thursday's gonna be my last time here. No point drawing it out much longer."

At the bottom of the valley, we cross the bridge and arrive in a garden I've never seen before: Two rows of neat trees border each side, and in the middle are ornate white fountains carved with all sorts of animals. There are dozens of people around us, reading or talking or just lying on the grass. I wonder how many of them are like Nico—people who have chosen to stay.

A voice calls our names from the other side of the square. Nico appears, running past the trees, dressed in the gold rose cloak that I helped him make at his house back in December. He pulls me into a hug so tight, he lifts my feet off the ground.

"Took your sweet time, mister. I thought you'd bailed on me." He puts me down and throws his arms around Kasia's neck. "Still not changed your mind about staying, Kash?"

"No, Nico, I haven't." Her usual snarky tone has gone. Her gray-blue eyes suddenly look misty. She shrugs Nico off and turns away. "I'm going to ask around about the doors. I'll see you in a while."

She nods at me before she goes. I haven't told her anything, but I get the feeling she knows what I've decided. I turn to Nico, and he smiles so wide, it makes something in my chest crunch.

"Come on—I have something to show you."

He puts his hands over my eyes and guides me from behind through the crowd. The voices quickly disappear, replaced by rustling leaves, snapping twigs, rushing water. My heart starts to sink. I know even before he takes his hands away with a loud "Ta-da!" what I'm going to see when I open my eyes.

It's the pirate ship we found back in November. Only, it's different now. The sails have been patched up and painted gold and blue, the holes in the deck and sides mended with new wood. There's a piano on deck, paper lanterns hanging from the masts, two comfy sofas covered in cushions and blankets near the helm. Colors everywhere—just as I imagine his room at art school would have been.

"What do you think?" Nico spreads his arms out and does a twirl. "Not very pirate-y, I know, but whatever."

I follow him toward the ladder. "I . . . I cannae believe you did all this."

"Well, I had a lot of help. I did the sails myself, with some canvas I got at the market, but I found this Norwegian carpenter to help me with the woodwork. You can find anything in here, honestly."

He whisks up the ladder in three swift steps and jumps onto the deck. "We're gonna need some help to actually sail it, obviously. Shouldn't be too hard—I've been asking around, and there are loads of people who want to find out what's on the other side of the water. Miyumi's up for it, too. We can leave whenever you're ready."

I climb up onto the ship after him. A gust of wind whips past, making the deck sway beneath my feet. "Nico," I start to say. "Listen—"

"I want to set up a sewing machine here, once I find one." He paces across the deck, hands spread out in front of him. "I swore I'd never make another costume as long as I lived, but screw that. I'm not gonna let some old art school tutors tell me they're not good enough."

"Nico—"

"And maybe we can take your drum kit with us! It'd fit beside the piano." He spins around to face me and smiles. "I figured you might not want to leave the band, but we'll come back here eventually. Or you and Miyumi could start a new one, or—"

"Nico!"

My voice comes out as a gasp, as if I've been punched. He turns to look at me, still beaming. It's so painful, I have to shut my eyes to say it.

"I . . . I'm not staying. I have to go back. I cannae do it to my family."

He's quiet for a long moment. His shoulders sag; the smile wilts with it. "Yeah, I thought you were going to say that."

The lump in my throat tightens, and my eyes start to tear up. I look up, my gaze fixed on the Jolly Roger rippling above us. Nico's mended it with streaks of bright blue cloth. He puts his hands on my hips and pulls me toward him.

"Brody, come on. It's better this way. I'm glad this is what you want."

"But it's *no*," I half say, half sob. "I want things to stay the same. Everything else sucks: I've failed all my exams—my best friend hates me . . . I don't know how I'm gonnae cope without this place. Without you."

"What are you talking about?" Nico puts his hands on my face, tilting it up to look at him. "You have so much going for you! You're going to have such a good life, I can tell. And you deserve it. Honestly. You deserve to be happy."

Even with the knot in my stomach, I know that's possible. Even without this place. Even without Nico. But it feels so, so far away right now. I start to shake my head, but Nico turns it back toward him.

"Yes, you do, dummy. You shouldn't throw your life away on a place like this." He caresses my cheek with a thumb. "You're not Peter Pan, you know. You're supposed to grow up."

He's right. Things have to change. I can't stay stuck the way I am forever. I *am* supposed to grow up.

So I pull him toward me, and I kiss him again. He kisses me back, fast and firm, his hands sliding into my hair. But even so, it doesn't feel like it did back on Beltane: He's too far away, and he pulls away too soon. An anxious, desperate feeling rises up in me. I grab his hands.

"Come back with me. I know things are hard right now, but it's gonnae get better. You can try again for art school; I bet you'd get in the second time. And"—my words are getting tangled in the panic—"we'll be there . . . Kasia and Zahra, and me. You'll still have . . . me."

Nico looks down at our fingers. His nails are painted again, this time a deep red. "Brody, I really do like you. I like you a lot. But we can't . . . I haven't changed my mind. I'm still going to stay. With or without you."

Dropping my hands, he goes to the other side of the ship and leans on the wooden barrier, staring out at the water. Different feelings hit me at once: confusion and sadness, fear about what could happen to him, and panic that I can't stop this.

"What about your family?" I ask him again. "What did you tell them?"

"I told my dad and Jenny I was going to Spain for a month. That should buy me some time." He shrugs. "My dad doesn't care, anyway, he just wants to put the past behind him. My mum's moved on. My sisters are so little, they won't even remember me."

But I will. And so will Zahra and Kasia and everyone else he knows. I pace past him, trying to get my head around this.

"But I don't want you to go," I stammer. "I'll never see—"

I break off. It's too hard to say.

Nico stubs the toe of his boot against the wooden floor. "I know. I know. It's hard to explain, Brody. It's just, being here . . . It feels like the only way I can keep going."

"Nico, it's mad." I'm getting panicky now, each flustered beat of my heart a reminder that time is running out. "Please. I cannae let you do this."

"It's not your choice." Then, like a puppet with cut strings, his face crumples. "I just can't anymore, Brody. I can't deal with it anymore. Any of it. I just want to stay here. I feel like a different person when I'm in here. A better person. This place lets me be who I want to be."

I stare at him. I don't want him to be a different person. He's already the best person. He's *my* person. I don't know how to say it, so I walk up to him and kiss him again. He kisses me back, but I can feel him start to drift away from me again, fading like the door. If I don't do something, he'll disappear into nothing.

There's still time. The door is still open—I can still change his mind.

THIRTY-FIVE

SEVEN DAYS LATER, I'M SITTING ON THE NUMBER 22 BUS, WATCHING raindrops race one another down the windowpane. I've made this trip so many times, on so many Thursdays, it's hard to believe that this'll be the last. My last bus to Everland.

Only this time, Jake's with me. We're sitting on the top deck, a group of drunk twentysomethings in front of us, and a guy playing bad dance music from his phone behind. Jake bites his thumbnail, fiddles with a loose thread on his jacket. Getting him away from his revision was not an easy task, but I eventually managed to coax him out of the flat by promising we'd be back before midnight.

"You really can't tell me what we're doing?" he asks for the twentieth time.

I glance up from my phone. I texted Megan earlier, asking her to meet me at Calton Hill, but she hasn't replied.

"Seriously," I tell him, "you wouldnae believe me if I did."

I change the subject to his Politics exam and the next election, something I know he'll be able to blether on about for ages, which he does. After that, he awkwardly asks what new albums I've listened to lately—something he knows I'll be able to blether on about for ages, which I do. The conversation is still a bit stilted, but given that we've barely said more than five words to each other for the past few years, it's an improvement. We're getting there.

The bus pulls up at the side of the road, and we hop off and cross over to Waterloo Place. As we reach the steps leading up to Calton Hill, a voice shouts out my name. I turn around and see Megan crossing the road toward us, her hair in a messy ponytail. She lifts her chin in a half nod of acknowledgment, her arms crossed over her chest. Jake looks from me to her, then mumbles something about meeting us up there and darts up the steps, away from all the awkward.

"Thanks for coming," I say. "I wasnae sure you would."

"Me neither. I almost deleted your number, but then I remembered you've still got that eyeliner I lent you." She shrugs. "Anyway, I'm only here because I've been curious about where you've been disappearing off to all these months. Don't think this means I forgive you."

"Right." I look down at my hands. "You think you could, though? Forgive me?"

When I look up, a wry smile is tugging at one corner of Megan's mouth. "If Coco Montrese and Alyssa Edwards can bury the hatchet, I guess we can, too. Eventually."

She's using *Drag Race* references again. We must be good. I hold my arms out, and she steps in for a hug.

"I'm really sorry, Meg."

"Whatever. Dickhead." She pushes me away, but there's a sparkle in her eyes I haven't seen for a while. "So what's going on, then? Are we going to see Nico? Am I *finally* going to get to meet him? I thought for a while you were making him up, you know. Or that he was an online boyfriend, and you were being catfished by some forty-year-old dude in, like, Slough. He does exist, doesn't he?"

"He does," I say, as we climb up the steps. "But I've told you, he's no' my boyfriend."

"You like him, though."

I swallow. "Yeah. I do."

We meet Jake at the top of the steps and head toward the monument. Kasia's already waiting there, wearing the NASA T-shirt she had on the very first night I came here. She eyes Megan and Jake a little warily, but this time she doesn't give her usual speech about how Everland isn't open by invitation. She hands me a piece of paper folded into thirds.

"I emailed Dani. He couldn't make it back home to come tonight, but he sent me this letter to give to Nico. Maybe it'll help."

"Okay, good." I carefully put it in my pocket. "I'm really worried, Kash."

"Me too." She gives me a sad smile. "It's his decision to make, though. Not ours."

Jake and Megan are looking totally lost. Jake starts to ask what's going on, but I shush him and wait for the change to begin. The clock hits 11:21 p.m., and the door starts to materialize out of the darkness. There's a kick in my stomach as I realize this might be the last time I ever see this. I watch every moment, forcing myself not to blink: the way the colors spill into the air like paint swirling in water; the strange shift as the door and the golden unicorn's head form out of nothing. When I look around, Megan and Jake are gawping at me, wide-eyed and pale-faced and stunned into silence. Kasia and I grin at each other.

"Don't ask," she tells them, as we step through the door. "Just have fun. We could be the last people in Edinburgh who'll ever get the chance."

But I know my brother: He's not going to be able to enjoy this if he doesn't understand it. As we walk down the hill, I fill them in on everything I've learned about Everland. They think it's a joke at first, but I point out what to me now seems so obvious—that there's no way of transporting all these trees to Calton Hill, let alone the waterfalls, and there's no way a village this size could fit in the city. For once, Megan is speechless. Jake shakes his head and mutters, "Unbelievable," about a hundred times.

"So this is where you've been going every Thursday," he says when we reach the steps down to the village. "I figured you were, like, meeting some boy in McDonald's or down at the park. Not . . . this."

Tonight, the bridge leads us into a huge, heaving party on the banks of the river. The atmosphere is as electric as ever. For the people who have stayed in here, nothing is going to change: This is just another night in Everland, stretching on and on and on forever. I scan the crowd and spot Nico talking to Miyumi and a man wearing a turban. He's wearing the blue wings he wore the first time we came here, the first day I met him. He sees us and rushes over, Miyumi just behind him.

"You're here!" He smacks a kiss on Kasia's cheek then pulls me into a tight hug. "It feels like . . . ages, I think. Who's this?"

I introduce them both to Megan and Jake, who are blinking from him to the crowd and back again, still shell-shocked. I edge toward Nico. My heart is already thudding in my chest. "Can we talk?"

He tugs on the straps of his wings. "You should go and find the band first, and show your brother and Megan around," he says gently. "I've got a few goodbyes to say, and then I'll come find you. I promise."

"But—" I start to say, but I stop. He's got other friends in here who need time with him, too. Maybe Kasia will be able to loosen his resolve, then I can go in for the kill. "Okay. See you later."

Reluctantly, I head through the crowd, Megan and Jake scrambling behind me. I don't think about where I'm taking them; I let Everland lead us, through the market, along the river, into celebrations and parties, into places I haven't seen before—a garden full of cat statues, a forest of red maple trees. I wonder if there's ever an end to it: if it's like a kaleidoscope pushing different parts together to make new patterns, or if it stretches on and on like space, forever creating new places to explore.

Despite the constant worry about Nico, I actually have a good time. I remember thinking that Megan would steal my thunder here in Everland, and that Jake was too serious to really get it. Turns out, I was wrong about both. I haven't seen my brother so animated in years, and Megan's too shocked to do more than listen to my attempts to explain this place. And when we come across the band, and I join them for my last set, they cheer louder than anyone else.

I'd expected Jake to run off to the library, but instead he ends up playing football with some people down by the river. Megan has her makeup bag on her, so she does my eyes while we sit watching them. I fill her in on everything that's happened since last September; she tells me all about her newfound crush on Ryan Martin, and the recovery plan her doctors have given her. It's more complicated than I would have thought: food diaries, meal plans, tracking apps, counseling . . . I'm glad I'll be around to help her through it.

She must have been really dazed when we arrived, because it's taken until now for her to comment on Nico. She gushes for ages about how hot he is, then asks the one question I still don't want to answer.

"What did he mean, 'goodbyes to say'?"

"He's . . . going away."

I can't tell her the whole story. Saying it would make it real. Megan leans in to touch up my eyeliner. "Away where?"

"Not sure," I say quietly. "But he's probably no' coming back."

The hurt must show on my face, because she puts down the pencil and gives me a hug that I don't really deserve right now. I catch the smell of her house, something floral and familiar, and realize with a pang how much I've missed this girl.

"You better go find him, then." She slides away from me and wipes a tiny smudge of black from under my right eye. "Don't worry about Jake. I'll keep an eye on him."

I head off down the river, through a quiet square and across the meadow. I find Nico among the metal animals, the place where he first told me what Everland was. I remember them looking quite eerie back then, but tonight there's something comforting about the way they tower above us. He's sitting on the elephant's foot, his legs crossed at the ankles, and his bright blue wings stretched behind him. His eyes are shiny. I go over to him.

"You all right?"

"I just got the Kasia Kowalewska treatment. Lecturing, guilt-tripping, finger wagging—the works." He laughs, but it fades out quickly. "I've never seen her cry before. Not even after Magda."

I lean against the elephant's trunk, looking down at his hair. It's covered in glitter and paint and petals, just like the first night I came here. I run the tips of my fingers over his curls. He tilts his head to look up at me and smiles. For a long moment, we just gaze at each other.

"Kash is right, Nico," I say eventually. "You have to come back."

He sighs and looks away. "There's no 'back' anymore, Brody. This is my life now. *This* is my home."

"It's not, though!" Frustration grabs me. I step back and throw up my hands. "What about your family, for one thing? What are they supposed to think?"

"I told you, they think I'm in Spain."

"And when your dad realizes you never got there?" I honestly can't believe he hasn't already. "They're gonnae think you're dead, Nico."

He falters before answering. "They'll be fine, Brody."

There's a quiver in his voice, though—a tiny chink in his armor that I might be able to work on. I sit down on the elephant's foot beside him and try everything I can think of. I talk about his family, his friends. I give him the letter that Dani sent via Kasia, but he puts it in his pocket without reading it. I even think about getting the others to help me drag him back through the door, kicking and screaming if need be, but I know he'd hate me for it, and I couldn't deal with that. Still, I keep begging. I beg him to do it for me.

"Brody, I can't. I can't." He leans forward, his head sinking into his hands. "Please don't ask me."

That's when he starts to cry. I know something then: He does love me. Maybe not the same way I love him, and maybe not in the way he loved Dani. Maybe I was never going to be his happy ending. But he does love me.

I sit back down, my knee touching his, and rub his back. After a moment, he wipes his eyes on his sleeves and takes a breath.

"We're sailing out tonight," he says. "Me and Miyumi and a bunch of others. I don't want to wait until the door disappears."

My throat is so tight I can hardly talk. "But I'll never see you again."

"You might!" He touches my cheek. "Maybe one day you'll fall down a rabbit hole or walk through a wardrobe or a door will appear out of nowhere, and I'll be right there waiting for you."

He smiles. I want to bottle that smile. I realize with a throb of grief that I've only got a handful of photos of us together, only a couple of messages to let me hear his voice. But it makes no difference: A thousand hours of footage would never be enough.

"Remember after your mum gave Tink away, when you told me about that feeling you get in here—like you belong? You can have that anywhere, Brody. There will always be people who love you and accept you. There already are."

But there are people who love him, too. I tell him that, but he's not listening. It's like he can't hear me at all.

Nico laughs and tugs on my hands. "Don't look so sad! You're gonna be fine." He kisses me lightly. "Besides, we still have tonight. There's no real time in here, not really. So in a way . . . we've still got forever."

I wish that were true. It's not. It's just a trick, a twist of words. Tonight is all we have left.

So I try to make it last. I fight the tug drawing me back to the green door and follow him all over the valley, into corners of Everland I've never seen before. I kiss him again and again, hoping that one of them will convince him that he's loved enough to come home.

Each time, he kisses me back like he means it. But all through the night, he keeps looking toward the sea, toward his pirate ship. Part of him has already left.

Then suddenly we're back in the square by the bridge, and it's all happening far too fast. The band is onstage, singing some upbeat '60s song that doesn't fit with the way I'm feeling. I say goodbye to Esther, Sandhya, and Arnau, then hurry back to Nico. Megan and Jake stand by the bridge, giving us some space. Zahra and Miyumi are crying; Kasia gives Nico a long, tight hug before turning to me.

"We'll meet you up at the door, Brody. Don't be too long."

I can't really speak, so I take Nico's hand. The lump in my throat swells. I want to thank him for all this . . . for Everland . . . for getting me through the past year. I want to tell him that I love him. But Nico got a lot of my firsts. Maybe I can save that one for somebody else.

"Are you scared?" I ask instead.

"A bit. But I'm excited, too." There's a nervous smile twitching at his lips, but his eyes are sparkling. "It'll be an adventure. An awfully big adventure."

He slides his arms out of the straps of his wings and loops the straps over mine instead. For a moment, I have a flashback to being five, wearing my green mesh Tinker Bell wings, chasing my cat around the living room. Being free.

The feeling only lasts a second, and then it's gone. Nico straightens the wings out for me, smoothing the straps down over my hoodie.

"I won't say goodbye," he says. "Just good luck. Not that you'll need it. You're magic, Fairy. Remember that."

My heart twists. I slide my hands into his hair, pull his head toward mine, and kiss him. He kisses me back, drawing me close to him. I'm trying to commit this to memory, to remember the feeling of his hands on my back, his mouth against mine, his faint layer of stubble, my fingers in his hair. I can't forget this. I won't.

Too soon, he pulls away. He smiles—a proper smile, no sign of sadness in it. The music has stopped and the band has disappeared without my noticing, but I see Miyumi waiting for Nico in the corner of the square. He goes to join her, and they both turn and wave to me. I watch as Nico slings an arm around her shoulders and they disappear between the buildings. Someone's shouting, but their voice sounds like it's coming from the other end of the galaxy. I realize I'm holding my breath—that I'm waiting for Nico to pop up around the corner, laughing about how he totally had me fooled.

I keep waiting.

He doesn't come back.

He's gone.

He's actually gone.

As always in Everland, I don't know how long I stand there. After a while, I feel a hand on my elbow and realize Kasia is standing beside me. Her eyes are blurry and bloodshot. Her lips are moving, but at first I'm too dazed to understand anything she's saying.

"It's time to go, Brody." She puts an arm around my back and steers me toward the bridge. "Come on, kiddo."

Somehow, I make it up the hill to the green door. Jake is staring at me with an alarmed look; Megan is asking what's happened and where Nico is, but her voice sounds a million miles away.

A second later, the real world hits me like a slap in the face. The night air feels cold and sharp; the traffic roars as its speeds through the Old Town. Kasia steps out behind me. The green door begins to fade; the contours of the unicorn knocker start to soften.

"Wait," I mumble. "Wait—"

I grab the horn and try to twist, but it dissolves in my hands. The windows disappear, the door vanishes. There's nothing left. I'm still wearing my makeup. I'm still wearing Nico's wings. I'm dressed for a night in Everland, but the green door is gone.

"Shit." Even if I come back next week, he'll have disappeared beyond the sea. Somewhere I'll never be able to find him. "*Shit. What have I done?*"

The pillars of the monument grow hazy. I never cry. I never cry, but I put my hands to my face, and they come back black with mascara tears. My vision blurs; the others fade into fuzzy shapes. Suddenly, I'm sobbing, actually crying for the first time in forever, and I don't even care who sees—it's too painful, too big to keep bottled up this time.

"I should have stopped him," I say, my hands pressed into my eyes. "I should've gone with him."

But then my brother pulls me into a hug, careful not to knock Nico's wings. I feel Megan slide her hand round my waist. I wonder if I knew this was going to happen . . . if I asked them here because I knew Nico would never agree to come back. Because without them there to anchor me back to the real world, I might have been tempted to stay. And even though it aches like nothing I've ever felt, some small part of me still knows this was the right decision.

That my place is here.

SUMMER

THIRTY-SIX

IT'S THE FIRST THURSDAY IN AUGUST, 11:21 P.M., AND I'M STANDING outside the National Monument on Calton Hill again. Tonight, there's no green door with a unicorn knocker appearing out of nothing; no stained-glass windows with our friends' faces emerging between the pillars. But there is a drum kit: an ancient, battered relic that Jett bought for twenty quid on Gumtree, placed just beneath the steps I used to climb up every Thursday night.

"You ready for this?"

Jett hoists her guitar onto her lap and begins to tune it. Around us, a crowd is starting to gather on the grass. I take one last look at the pillars. I've been up here a few times this summer, just in case. Nothing ever happened—and each time, I ended up walking home with itching eyes and what felt like a knife in my gut.

But tonight, I feel calm. I'm okay.

"Yep." I sit behind the kit, pick up my sticks, and give Jett a nod. "I'm ready."

I wish I could say that it always felt like the right choice. That I decided to stay, Dad made an overnight recovery, Mam got a pay raise, we moved to a flat where I could have a drum kit and a cat, I worked out what I'm going to do with my life, and we all lived happily ever after, the end.

But for the first few days after Nico left, I spent most of my time regretting my decision so hard, I could barely stand myself. When I was sitting in school or trudging up the stairs to our flat because the lift had broken again, it seemed totally ridiculous that I'd given up Everland for a life like this. I even went back the following Thursday. The door was still there, but I couldn't bring myself to go through it. The itchy desperation I used to feel . . . It had vanished. Zahra and Kasia were right. You would just *know* when it was the right time to leave, and that was mine.

When I went back the next week, the door was gone.

That's when it really sank in that I was never going back there. I missed the relief that hit me when I walked through the door, and the sense of total calm I had as I sat by the river. I missed playing with Esther and the band. I missed Nico.

More than anything, I missed Nico.

I missed him so much, it made me physically sick. It got even worse when stories about his disappearance started popping up online (along with many more about Miyumi Kobayashi, the Japanese violin prodigy who had vanished without a trace). I'd been right about Nico's family: They were frantic with worry, and absolutely devastated. Zahra, Kasia, and I talked about it, but we knew we couldn't tell them what had happened. No one who hadn't been to Everland would ever believe us—they'd think it was some horrible prank. No matter how guilty we felt, the truth would only make it worse.

It was agony. Some days, I felt so bad I couldn't get out of bed. I couldn't explain to my parents that it wasn't your regular heartbreak—that it was so much guilt and confusion and grief, too—but even so, they were surprisingly good about it all. I think Jake must have said something to them. I don't know how he explained it, or even what he remembers of the night he met Nico. But I owe him one anyway. It helped.

Other than that, the one thing that kept me going was Rusty Records. There were reminders of Nico there, too—that day he came in to apologize; every song I'd ever seen him dance to—but they weren't as sharp in the store. With a job to concentrate on and music to take my mind of things, I could almost forget.

One Saturday, while we were listening to a Shugo Tokumaru album on a quiet morning in the shop, Jett looked up from an old copy of *NME* magazine and stared at me for a moment.

"Brody," she said. "Why haven't we started our own band yet?"

Once she said it out loud, it seemed weird we hadn't thought of it earlier. Jett found the drum kit online, roped her sister

Franklin in on bass, and we started practicing in their garage three times a week. After that, getting up in the morning didn't feel quite so hard. If I got lost in my thoughts on my way to work, it might be thinking about a chorus we were writing. I found myself getting through a whole song without thinking about Nico, then two, then three. And when I did think about him, I focused on different things . . . like the adventures he must be having in Everland, and how hard he must have found this life to give it up altogether.

I didn't stop missing him or caring about him. It just got a tiny bit easier.

And slowly, everything else starting getting better, too. Leanne and Michelle have hardly bugged me all summer. They've shouted a couple of stupid comments at me as I go in or out of the building, yeah, but it doesn't get to me anymore. Money is still tight, but Mam has managed to get a few more shifts per week, and Jake got a job in Asda until he starts university in September. Mark gave me more hours in Rusty Records, too, which helps; I paid for Keira to go back to her theater classes for the holidays. (She bought me a pack of Mars bars as a thank-you—only ate three of them herself.)

I've even been to see Tink. Amir lives just a few streets away from Jett, so a couple of weeks ago, Jake came to meet me after band practice and we went over to his house together. I was worried Tink wouldn't recognize me, or that he'd remember that I dumped him there and go into one of his moods. But he wound his body around my legs and rubbed his head against my foot, purring wildly.

"All right, pal." I knelt down to pet him, not bothered that there were three people watching our reunion, and I was actually getting a bit emotional. "I've missed you."

After a while, Jake and Amir went off to talk. Mrs. Shah brought me a mango lassi, and we sat in their garden, watching Tink loll around the grass. He's gotten well fat. Mrs. Shah took my tip about him liking cheese seriously—apparently his current favorites are Comté and Manchego, and he's quite partial to a bit of Reblochon, too.

"I love having him around, but he's eating me out of house and home," she said. "Though you know, Brody, he's still yours. You can always come back for him, if circumstances change."

And for the first time in a long time, I felt like maybe they would.

"Good evening, Edinburgh!"

Jett's voice booms through the microphone, bouncing out over Calton Hill. Her sister Franklin mouths, *Thinks she's Mick Jagger*, at me. I grin, but my heart flutters nervously as I stare out at the crowd of our friends, family, and a few tourists scattered across the grass. It's hardly the Hydro, or even Leith Theatre. But when Jett suggested we try and get a slot to play our first gig during the Fringe Festival, I knew exactly where I wanted to do it.

And I knew it had to be on a Thursday.

"We are the Night Lights!" Jett announces. "And this is 'Lost Boys.'"

She counts to four and we break into our first song. Our small, loyal fan base starts singing along, Keira loud enough to wake half the city. This gig's been a bit of a group effort: Zahra designed the posters, and Jake made us a band website. Kasia's named herself our manager (though I think that's an excuse to hang out with Jett more than anything), and Megan did my makeup before I went onstage. My stomach jumped when I noticed there were people from school in the crowd: Megan's brother, Harry; her new boyfriend, Ryan; Rongrong; Anton; and a few others. But my nerves only lasted a split second. I like my makeup, and I like our music. Who cares if someone else doesn't?

We reach the end of the first song, and the crowd bursts into applause and cheers. I look across the hill, where my auntie Rhona's red Volvo is parked just off the path. Mam and Dad are sitting in the front seats, cheering us on from behind the windscreen. It's a compromise—a way of getting Dad out of the flat without being outside. Wouldn't seem like much to some people, but I'm proud of him. It's a big step.

And honestly, I'm pretty proud of myself, too. The gig goes brilliantly. We're not quite as polished as Esther and the guys were—they had a lot more practice time than we do, after all—but we're getting there. Afterward, once I've listened to Mam and Dad rave about how good we were and posed for about twenty selfies with Keira, I weave my way through the crowd back toward the monument and find Zahra and Kasia sitting on the steps. Zahra holds something up: a birthday cake, covered in bright blue icing, with wings made out of blue Smarties in the center.

"I figured an occasion like this called for a cake."

A lump forms in my throat. I sit down beside Kasia, blinking. "He would have loved that."

Zahra gives a light laugh. "Yeah, but he probably wouldn't have eaten it."

She takes out a knife and paper napkins and cuts us each a slice. It's just a vanilla sponge with raspberry jam and tons of blue icing, but it tastes amazing. For a few moments, we're all quiet, licking frosting off our fingers and thinking about Nico. I feel like I'm about to cry again. Honestly, I've done a lot of that over the past couple of months. Can't decide if I'm making up for lost time, or it's just everything that's happened since September catching up with me all at once. Zahra twists around to look at the pillars behind us and shakes her head.

"It's so weird," she says. "It all feels like a film I saw when I was little, something I can't quite remember. If it weren't for you guys, I'd probably think I'd dreamed up the whole thing."

"I'm scared I'm gonnae forget it all," I blurt out. "I don't want to forget it. I don't want to forget him."

"Me too," Zahra says quietly. "I think we might, you know. I think we might forget Everland."

"Not Nico, though," Kasia says firmly. "Pain in the neck most of the time, but an unforgettable one."

She slides an arm around my shoulders and gives me an awkward pat on the back of the head. This time, I actually do cry. Just a bit. It's been a hard year, and I kept it bottled up for so long . . . All this is long overdue. A couple of tourists give me half-concerned, half-nosy looks, then carry on taking photos of the skyline. Kasia sits up, looking down at the cake on the bottom step.

"Zahra," she says. "How many packets of Smarties did you go through to make those wings?"

"Far too many!" Zahra laughs. "I'm going to be eating them for the rest of the month."

After that, the conversation moves on: to our next gig, to Zahra's sister's upcoming wedding, Kasia and Jett's first official date next week. Jake and Megan and the others drift over to join us. Anton says he likes my makeup, and we end up talking about *Drag Race*—I've sat beside him in Spanish for two years and had no idea he was a fan. I wonder what else I've missed about him.

A couple of times, I can almost hear Nico chime in with the conversation. I can imagine the jokes he'd make, the faces he'd pull behind Kasia's back when they disagreed on something. Every so often, I find myself looking at the pillars. Maybe Nico was right. We might still meet again. Maybe one day I'll be in Perth or Paris or Peru, a door will appear out of nothing, and I'll find him waiting for me.

But even if it doesn't, it's okay. I have all of this, all of these people. I have things to look forward to. Before we leave, I take one last look at the pillars. There are no colors, just strips of night sky between the stone.

And yet the world looks a lot brighter than it used to.